PRAISE FOR **DANIEL KALLA**

THE LAST HIGH

"A thrilling, front-line drama about the opioid crisis."

Kathy Reichs

"Kalla has long had his stethoscope on the heartbeat of his times. . . . In his latest, the focus is on Vancouver's opioid crisis. . . . [A] lively story."

Toronto Star

"A riveting thriller. . . . This important, must-read book is not only well researched and entirely realistic, it gives a human face to a devastating epidemic."

Robyn Harding, internationally bestselling author
of *The Arrangement* and *The Party*

"Kalla is terrific at building suspense as the case progresses, uncovering a web of dealers, sellers, and users."

The Globe and Mail

"A sobering glimpse into the drug overdose crisis. . . . An entertaining, if slightly eerie read."

Vancouver Sun

WE ALL FALL DOWN

"A fast-paced thriller with an historical overlay and a dash of romantic tension."

Vancouver Sun

"A tightly plotted thriller, energetic and completely believable."

Booklist

RESISTANCE

"Daniel Kalla's prescription for a perfect thriller includes snappy characters, a pace that sweeps up a reader, and not too much technical jargon. . . . The kind of magnetic story you can't put down."

Vancouver Province

PANDEMIC

"Kalla expertly weaves real science and medicine into a fast-paced, nightmarish thriller—a thriller all the more frightening because it could really happen."

Tess Gerritsen, internationally bestselling author
of the Rizzoli & Isles books

"Very much in the Michael Crichton school of cutting-edge scientifically rooted thrillers. *Pandemic* is an absorbing, compulsive thriller, the sort of book you could stay up too late reading."

Vancouver Sun

ALSO BY
DANIEL KALLA

The Last High

We All Fall Down

Nightfall Over Shanghai

Rising Sun, Falling Shadow

The Far Side of the Sky

Of Flesh and Blood

Cold Plague

Blood Lies

Rage Therapy

Resistance

Pandemic

LOST IMMUNITY

A THRILLER

DANIEL KALLA

PUBLISHED BY SIMON & SCHUSTER
New York London Toronto Sydney New Delhi

SIMON &
SCHUSTER
CANADA

Simon & Schuster Canada
A Division of Simon & Schuster, Inc.
166 King Street East, Suite 300
Toronto, Ontario M5A 1J3

This Simon & Schuster Canada edition May 2021

SIMON & SCHUSTER CANADA and colophon are trademarks of Simon & Schuster, Inc.

For information about special discounts for bulk purchases, please contact Simon & Schuster Special Sales at 1-800-268-3216 or CustomerService@simonandschuster.ca.

Manufactured in the United States of America

10 9 8 7 6 5 4 3 2 1

Library and Archives Canada Cataloguing in Publication
Title: Lost immunity / Daniel Kalla.
Names: Kalla, Daniel, author.
Description: Simon & Schuster Canada edition.
Identifiers: Canadiana (print) 2020028343X | Canadiana (ebook) 20200283448 | ISBN 9781982150150 (softcover) | ISBN 9781982150167 (ebook)
Classification: LCC PS8621.A47 L67 2021 | DDC C813/.6—dc23

ISBN 978-1-9821-5015-0
ISBN 978-1-9821-5016-7 (ebook)

For my brothers, Tim and Tony

LOST
IMMUNITY

PROLOGUE

It was only a headache, Lilja Benediktsson reminds herself as she stands beside the gurney inside the chilly room. And Kristjan just couldn't miss another day of school. The principal had been clear. One more infraction and her son would be suspended from the hockey team. Neither the team nor Kristjan could afford that.

Kristjan's forehead hadn't even felt warm to the touch. Why should Lilja have believed her son this time after all the other recent excuses and illnesses he had faked to avoid getting up on school days? Lilja hadn't even bothered to call Dr. Tómasson. She could hear the old doctor's stern voice in her head. "Two ibuprofens, a glass of juice, and then off to school. Don't let the boy manipulate you, Lilja. Boundaries. You both need them."

It had been a rocky eighteen months since Kristjan's dad had walked out on them. At first, Lilja and her son had managed all right on their own. But then Kristjan's grades began to drop, and he spent more and more time alone in his room, surfing the web while listening to that god-awful death-metal music. Lilja tried to reason with him, to explain that he risked his coveted position on the senior hockey team with his lackadaisical attitude. But the more she persisted, the more he withdrew. He used to be such a perfect child. Loving, happy, and outgoing. They were so close until his father left. Kristjan would tell her everything. But Lilja couldn't reach her fifteen-year-old son anymore. In the end, she resorted to cutting off his Wi-Fi access. That didn't work, either.

And now he's gone.

It's not the lattice-like rash crisscrossing Kristjan's face or the bloody blisters scattered over his shoulders and neck that Lilja focuses on as she stares down at her son. What catches her attention is how his hands jut out from under the hem of the sheet, one on top of the other, as if clutching his chest. Kristjan would've been mortified to know how his hands were positioned.

Did I even say good-bye? Lilja wonders again as another tear falls and beads off the protective gown that hospital officials insisted she wear along with gloves and a mask.

Kristjan was too irritable to let her hug him as he stomped out the door earlier in the morning.

But I did say good-bye, didn't I? I did tell him I loved him?

That's the only thing that matters to Lilja now. Not that Kristjan passed away within two hours of reaching Reykjavík's Children's Hospital. Not that his school is closed for fear of further spread after two more classmates died. Not even the realization that she will never begin to fill the void that has been ripped through the fabric of her being.

Please God, tell me I said a proper good-bye.

CHAPTER 1

They're well dressed. Polite. Attentive. And like any good predators, they're preparing to pounce.

Lisa Dyer read the mood in the packed auditorium the moment she stepped up to the lectern. She has been Seattle's chief public health officer for only a few months, but Lisa understands these community health forums go with the territory. Usually, they're stress-free events. Fun, even, in a nerdy kind of way. Rarely are they anywhere near as well attended as this one.

Or as controversial.

The new policy she has come to present isn't even her brain-child. It came directly from the state legislature via the governor's office in Olympia. But this audience is unlikely to focus on such distinctions. Many of them appear poised to shoot the messenger.

Lisa appreciates that not all the attendees are hostile. A number have come to support, or at least to learn more about the new law that mandates immunization for all middle-school-aged girls and boys with the newest HPV vaccine. But she isn't surprised by the public outcry. Among the anti-vaxxers—or the "vaccine hesitancy" community, as most prefer to be known—the HPV vaccine might be the most outrage-inducing one of all. She has already heard an earful from her own sister yesterday about the new policy. She can't even imagine how her dad would react to it, nor does she intend to find out.

The rumblings grow throughout her talk, and even before Lisa clicks on the final slide on her presentation, hands shoot up throughout the crowd. Mentally bracing for the onslaught, she points to a willowy woman with a rainbow headband in the second row, who has already sprung to her feet.

"You used the word 'safe.' *Safe*?" The woman's voice cracks. "How can you say that when we all know what happened to Cody Benson."

The case of the Utah teenager had become a rallying point for the activists after he died a year earlier from a progressive spinal condition a few weeks after receiving the HPV vaccine.

"What happened to him is tragic," Lisa says. "But there's no definitive proof his transverse myelitis was related to his vaccination."

"How can you even *say* that?" the woman asks, visibly trembling. "He was dead within two weeks of getting that shot!"

And if he had been hit by a truck two weeks after his injection, would you still blame the vaccine? Lisa thinks. But she understands how emotional the cause is for some, having grown up with like-minded people in her own family. She views the woman solemnly. "In medicine, timing is not always evidence of causality. In other words, just because two things happen near the same time, it doesn't mean the first is responsible for the second. Millions of kids have been immunized so far. And we've only seen a handful cases of degenerative neurological disease among them."

"But you *have* seen them!"

"Yes, but the rate is no higher than among nonvaccinated children. Which tells us there is no link."

Shaking her head in what appears to be disgust, the woman drops back into her seat.

"You talk about your right to protect the community," another voice calls out from somewhere in the middle of the auditorium. "What about our right to choose? And our individual rights to protect our own children?"

Lisa scans the rows to spot the questioner, a brunette whose outstretched hand reveals a glimmering rock on her ring finger that's big enough to be seen from the podium. "All the medical evidence suggests that's just what this HPV vaccine will do," Lisa says. "Protect your children. From developing cervical cancer, of which there are forty-three thousand new cases every year in the US."

"Evidence planted by the drug companies to protect their profits!" someone else calls out from near the back of the room.

Lisa takes a breath. "No. Evidence such as the massive population study in Denmark that reviewed a million vaccinated children and found no increase in adverse outcomes compared to the general population."

"With enough money and influence, you can buy any result you want!"

And so it goes. It was as if she hadn't bothered to give her carefully crafted, data-filled presentation that reviewed the many benefits of the vaccine and debunked the myths about its risks. A few people in the audience voice their support. And there are moments of infighting among the crowd. But for the most part, Lisa faces a flurry of emotional outbursts that are as disconnected from logic or science as she could imagine. One distraught woman even raises the old myth about how a vaccine that prevents sexually transmitted cancer will lead to promiscuity. It feels like being back at her parents' dinner table.

Lisa points to the man in the front row who has been patiently holding his arm up for the past while. In a blazer and jeans with hair gelled back and wire-rimmed glasses on, he reminds Lisa of the physiology professor she had a crush on in medical school.

"Excellent presentation, Dr. Dyer." The man's self-assured grin and square jaw evoke even stronger memories of her old prof. "Thank you for taking the time to share such important information on such a vital threat."

"You're welcome," Lisa says. But his use of the word *threat* raises her guard. "Did you have a question?"

"A few, as a matter of fact," he says, rising languidly to his feet. "You covered a lot of ground in your slideshow. But there were a number of things you left out. For example, the more recent Danish study that found a link between the vaccine and neurologic complications."

"That was a study of only thirty-five participants. And the EMA—the European equivalent of the FDA—found no evidence to support its claim."

"And yet, the American College of Pediatrics claims that this vaccine is responsible for numerous bad outcomes, all confirmed through the VAERS database."

"That database—the Vaccine Adverse Event Reporting System— is only for self-reporting vaccine reactions."

"Exactly," he says. "Real reported cases, not nebulous population studies."

"We use the VAERS database to identify potential patterns of reactions." For the first time, Lisa struggles to keep the exasperation from her tone. *Breathe.* "But picking and choosing individual entries from VAERS is like substituting bad Yelp reviews for scientific evidence."

A ripple of chuckles run through the room.

The man only shrugs. "All right, then why did the Japanese government suspend the very same program that you are now proposing?"

"That was a political decision."

"And this isn't?" He frowns. "After the Japanese vaccination program was introduced, didn't they see a spike of neurologic diseases among the vaccinated? Memory loss, chronic pain, seizures? Some children lost the ability to walk."

"Again, all self-reported. Never verified in studies."

"But they did happen, Dr. Dyer."

He goes on to cite other studies, most of which Lisa recognizes as being tainted by pseudoscience, bias, or outright fraudulent data.

Five senses, she reminds herself as he speaks. The mindfulness exercise has been her latest coping skill at home as the fights had worsened.

Sight: the ring of condensation along the rim of her water glass. *Sound:* the silky cadence of the man's voice. *Feel:* the lectern against her fingertips. *Smell:* the faint scent of her own perfume—vanilla and tonka bean—*OK, I might have stolen that one right off the label. Taste:* the residual mint from her toothpaste.

Feeling calmer, Lisa waits for the man to finish. "We could argue all day over the quality and accuracy of the evidence," she says. "But the truth is that every major academic body has reviewed the data and endorsed the safety and effectiveness of the HPV vaccine. And I respect that kind of science."

"I'm extremely respectful of science, too. After all, I'm also a doctor. A naturopath." He pauses. "But academics aren't always right, are they? Science changes. Mendel's theory of genetics was dismissed as nonsense by his contemporaries. Copernicus was ridiculed for suggesting the earth revolved around the sun. The examples go on and on."

Lisa almost smiles. He's doing what they do so well. Twist real facts and examples to support their unsupportable beliefs. *Their religion.* She might as well be arguing with a flat-earther or a climate-change denier.

"Listen, Doctor . . . ?"

"Balfour. Max, please."

"Dr. Balfour, you've obviously done your research. But cervical cancer is a devastating disease that kills thousands of young women every year. And it's one of the few cancers we can actually prevent. Wouldn't you want to protect your daughter from that?"

"I don't have a daughter. But I do have a son." The smile leaves his lips, and his gaze drifts downward. "When Jack was one, I wanted to protect him from *everything*, Dr. Dyer. But right after we gave him the measles vaccine, he developed autism." His Adam's apple bobs. "And, maybe, that's what I really should have been protecting him from all along."

Several people in the audience break into spontaneous applause.

Before Lisa can respond, her phone buzzes on the lectern. She can't help but glance down at the health advisory from her office that pops up on the screen. "Four dead from meningitis. All attended the same local Bible camp."

CHAPTER 2

The sudden brilliance jerks Kayla from sleep. The violent glare is brighter than a floodlight and bores into her temples as sharply as needles. She flops over and buries her face into the mattress until the blaze subsides.

Kayla was up late texting with Connor, her first boyfriend. She had almost lost her virginity with him the previous week at camp. She was willing to, ready to, even though she understood it was a sin. It would've happened, too, if their cabin counselor, Nicola, hadn't stumbled upon them alone in the woods, tucked inside the same sleeping bag and stripped down to their underwear. Luckily, Nicola was cool about it and didn't report them to the camp director, who would've freaked.

But last night's texts with Connor had nothing to do with their sexual near miss. No. Apparently, Emma and Joseph had been taken to the hospital. The news flooded social media. It was serious, people were saying. And in Connor's last text, he mentioned that his head was beginning to throb, too. He hasn't responded to any of Kayla's messages since.

Waking more fully, Kayla gingerly rotates her head and realizes the brightness comes only from the morning sunshine that leaks through and around the drapes.

The light sensitivity and the nausea are even worse than the headache. Unless she tries to move her neck. The slightest bend jolts her like a boot to the back of the head.

Kayla trembles violently and wraps the blanket tighter to fight off the sudden cold.

Do I have it? The realization brings a chill that's unrelated to her rising temperature. *Just like Emma and Joseph?*

The panic wells along with the nausea.

Meningitis!

A rumor is circulating on social media that Joseph is already dead.

Kayla tastes the bitterness of her own vomit as it erupts up into her throat.

Oh God, am I next?

CHAPTER 3

Despite the clamoring audience at the HPV vaccine forum, as soon as she receives the health alert on her phone Lisa cuts the session short and hurries out to her car. On the way, she confirms with her office that not only have four teenagers died from meningitis, but three others are critically ill and barely hanging on in the intensive care unit.

The city basks under radiant blue skies and a benign sun, but Lisa is oblivious to the near-perfect late-summer day. As she drives southeast toward the hospital, away from the shadows of the Seattle Municipal Tower and other downtown high-rises, her mind is consumed with potential containment and communication strategies. She has no doubt Seattle is facing another public-health crisis. Meningitis outbreaks always are. The victims are inevitably young, especially teenagers, and the collective fear induced is often even more contagious than the pathogen responsible for the infection.

Her Bluetooth phone rings through the car's speaker, and expecting more news from the office, she answers before checking the name on the screen. She regrets picking up the moment she hears her husband's voice.

"Hi, Lees."

"Oh, Dom. Hi. Can I call you back? Just dealing with an emergency."

"A public-health emergency?" Dominic asks.

Maybe she only imagines condescension in his tone. Perhaps, these days, she just expects judgment even where there is none. Regardless, she can't suppress the flicker of hurt. But she keeps it from her voice. "For real. I'm almost at the hospital. Can I call you back?"

"I just wondered if you wanted to carpool to our session today," Dominic says.

Shit! She had forgotten about their appointment. Originally, she was the one who had cajoled Dominic into couples' counseling. But six months into the weekly sessions—with so little, if any, progress made—Lisa has lost faith in the counseling, their counselor, and, if she's being totally honest, their twelve-year marriage itself.

"My day's going to be crazy," she says. "I'll have to meet you there."

"See you there. Looking forward to pulling more Band-Aids off with the skin still attached," he says in what she realizes is an attempt at lightheartedness. "Love you, Lees."

"See you soon," Lisa says as she hangs up, struck by her husband's uncharacteristic words of affirmation and her struggle to reciprocate them.

She thinks again of her sister's reaction when Lisa finally confessed—after a second Moscow mule—to her growing sense of detachment and progressive loss of interest in their sex life, and how it had only made Dominic more affectionate and attentive.

"And that surprises you?" Amber asked. "People are emotional lemmings. The more you pull away, the more they throw themselves into it."

"*It* being off a cliff?" Lisa said.

"Yeah. In your case, a really rocky one, too."

Lisa brushes off those thoughts as she pulls into the on-call parking lot at Harborview Health Care Center. She spent countless hours at the hospital during her residency, but she never got accustomed to the vastness of the campus. Or to the sounds, smells, and frantic busyness of the place. As the biggest regional medical center in the Pacific Northwest, Harborview spans five city blocks and runs four separate intensive care units for trauma, cardiac, burn, and medical patients. Lisa heads straight for the East Building, which houses the medical ICU.

She weaves through the bustling corridors and rides the elevator to the sixth-floor ICU, where she identifies herself to the indifferent clerk at the front desk. She has to wait a few minutes before a chatty nurse named Mick, with colorful tattoos that encircle both biceps and resemble cuffs to his scrub tops, arrives and then leads her past individual glassed rooms—each housing a patient besieged by medical gadgetry—to the negative-pressure isolation rooms at the far end of the unit.

As a student, Lisa used to love the rush that came during rotations in critical care, but she never adjusted to the deaths and the heartbroken families that were so often the outcome of all the medical drama.

They reach the first of the isolation rooms, and Mick hands her the personal protective equipment, or PPE, kit. A folded gown supports a pair of gloves and an N95 mask, which filters out all microbial-sized particles. He departs with a quick wave.

Lisa slides the gown on top of her clothes and secures her mask snugly over her mouth and nose. The simple steps conjure grim memories of donning PPE during the dark days when COVID-19 terrorized Seattle. As she is pulling on the second glove, an African American man with contemplative brown eyes appears beside her. "You're from Public Health?" he asks as he slips into his own gown.

"Yes. Lisa Dyer."

"Edwin Davis. I'm on for ICU." He closes his eyes briefly and shakes his head. "And what a disaster of a day it's been."

"I can only imagine." In Lisa's experience, intensivists—the doctors who treat ICU patients—rarely if ever appear so fazed. Or dejected. "When did the meningitis cases show up?"

"We got the first call from the ER yesterday, late afternoon. A fifteen-year-old with suspected septic shock. By the time I got there—twenty minutes later—he was already dead. Six more kids rolled in over the course of the night and into the morning. Two others never made it out of the ER. One died up here. The other three are all on life support." Edwin sighs. "I can't say with confidence that any of them are going to survive. At least with COVID-19, most of the ones who died were much older."

His despondence is contagious. "And the lab confirmed it's meningococcus?" Lisa asks.

"The medical microbiologist ran stat gram stains on the cerebrospinal fluid as well as PCRs," he says, using the acronym for polymerase chain reaction, a rapid sequence test that allows for almost instant DNA recognition—the genetic equivalent of a reliable witness at a police lineup. "He says he still has to confirm it with further testing, but he's convinced it's meningococcus type B."

The mention of the pathogen's specific type sends a chill down Lisa's spine. *Neisseria meningitidis*, more commonly known as meningococcus, is among the deadliest of bacteria. And type B is the most feared of the four major subtypes, because of the lethal outbreaks it causes, and its notorious resistance to most vaccines.

None of that would be news to Edwin. So, instead, Lisa asks, "Do we know how many kids attended this Bible camp?"

"A ton of them. Not to mention camp counselors and other staff." He arches an eyebrow. "A lot of contacts for your team to track down."

"It's what we do." Lisa hides her doubt behind a matter-of-fact shrug. "And what about your staff? Have they been put on prophylactic antibiotics?"

He nods. "Anyone who's had direct contact with the cases has already been put on Rifampin and cipro."

"Including you?"

"I got the first dose," Edwin says as he secures his own mask. "No 'women and children first' policy around these parts."

Lisa turns her attention to the nearest room, where, behind the glass, a freckled girl with long dark hair lies motionless on the stretcher. A tube leads from her mouth to the ventilator, while other lines extend from her neck and arms and connect her to the transparent bags of fluid that dangle above her. A nurse dressed in full PPE on the near side of the bed adjusts one of those bags, while across from her, a stooped man in the same garb hovers awkwardly over the patient without touching her.

"Kayla Malloy," Edwin says. "Sixteen years old, same ballpark as the others. She's the most recent victim to reach us. Got to the ER just over two hours ago. Her kidneys have shut down, and we're struggling to keep her blood pressure up."

"What are you treating her with?"

"The kitchen sink. Three of the most potent antibiotics available for the infection. Multiple cardiac meds to support her blood pressure."

Lisa glimpses the displays above the patient's bed that list her vital signs. The dire readings validate the wariness in Edwin's tone. She nods to the man at the bedside. "The father?"

"Grandfather. Kayla's parents are dead, apparently."

Lisa motions to the window. "Can we?"

Edwin opens the door of the outer room with his shoulder and backs through the second, which seals the inner room, allowing the powerful fans and filter above to suck out any airborne germs. Lisa follows him inside. All eyes, except for those of the comatose patient, turn to the new arrivals, but no one says a word over the hum of the fan and the whir of the ventilator.

Even before Lisa reaches the bedside, her gaze is drawn to the scattered blood blisters that range in size from pinpoints to nickels and cover Kayla's exposed upper chest and arms. Lisa recognizes the skin condition as petechial purpura. The rash is a classic sign of meningococcal infection, and it also tells her that the patient is in septic shock and her blood-clotting system is in disarray.

Edwin introduces Lisa to the nurse and then Kayla's grandfather.

"Public Health?" The grandfather grimaces. "How . . . how can that help Kayla?"

"We can't. Not directly," Lisa admits. "Public Health is responsible for outbreak control, Mr. Malloy. Can you tell me when Kayla first became sick?"

"This morning, I suppose. She seemed all right yesterday when she came back from camp."

"Bible camp?" Lisa asks.

"Yeah, that's the one. Out in Delridge," he says of the suburb just south of Seattle. "Never been a churchgoer, myself. But Kay somehow stumbled onto Jesus last year or so. Fat lot of good it's done her."

"Kayla wasn't complaining of feeling unwell last night?"

"Nope. Ate a good dinner. Big plate of chops. Seconds, even. Guess they were feeding her more God than food up at that camp."

"This morning . . ." Lisa prompts.

"Kay didn't come down for breakfast. She's an early riser. So I went to check." He swallows. "She was in bed. Unconscious, or what have you. Eyes closed and groaning something awful. And the stench! Her sheets were covered in vomit. I called 911 as soon as I saw the blood in it."

Lisa feels for the older man. She can't imagine how traumatic it must have been to find his granddaughter semiconscious in a pool of her own bloody vomit. "She hasn't woken up since?"

He waves a hand over her. "She's not even moaning anymore."

"We are keeping her in a medically induced coma with powerful sedatives, Mr. Malloy," Edwin explains.

Malloy grunts, either unconvinced by or uninterested in the distinction. "This meningitis . . ." he says. "The nurse told me, but I still don't understand. What's it do exactly?"

"Meningitis is an inflammation of the membranes that surround the brain and the spinal cord. Along with the typical headache, nausea, and neck stiffness, it causes a general flu-like illness." Edwin explains patiently, waiting for the other man to digest his words before proceeding. "There are many different microscopic bugs that can cause meningitis. With viruses, the infection is usually no worse than the flu and resolves on its own. The bacterial infections are much more serious. Unfortunately, Kayla is suffering from the most aggressive form of bacterial meningitis."

Malloy reaches out and tentatively strokes the back of his granddaughter's hand, as if handling an antique vase. "Will she make it?" he asks in a small voice.

Edwin inhales before answering. "Kayla has developed what we call septic shock. Her bloodstream has been overwhelmed, and her organs have begun to shut down."

Malloy's hand freezes on top of his granddaughter's. "No, then?" he croaks.

"It's too early to know, Mr. Malloy," Edwin says. "But Kayla is in the best place she can be. And we will do everything possible to help her fight off the infection."

Malloy's shoulders slump lower. "And in the meantime?"

"All you can do is be here for her. To offer your love and your prayers." The corner of Edwin's eye twitches, and Lisa sees that he regrets the last remark.

"Prayers, huh?" Malloy snorts. "Lost my wife to an aneurysm ten years back. Then we lost Kayla's mom, dad, and her little brother to a drunk driver, not a year after. Kay's all I got left. And now I just might lose her to this meningitis. *From a Bible camp?* What kind of God would allow that?"

CHAPTER 4

Lisa is walking toward her car in the Harborview parking lot when her phone buzzes again. Since she doesn't recognize the number, she considers ignoring it, but intuition tells her to pick up.

"Lisa, it's Edwin Davis," the intensivist says. "Sorry to call so soon. But I just heard back from the microbiologist with more news."

"What is it, Edwin?"

"He ran further PCR tests on the samples. He now believes our cases are the same strain of meningococcus that hit Iceland."

Iceland. The word stops Lisa dead in her tracks. "The outbreak from last winter?"

"The very same. Thought you should know."

"Yes, absolutely, thanks," she mumbles as she disconnects.

Like most epidemiologists, Lisa closely followed developments the previous winter in Rcykjavík, where an outbreak of meningitis killed a number of people—mostly teenagers and children—in the span of weeks. Health authorities across the globe braced for a spread of the same virulent strain of the bacteria that hit Iceland, but it did not materialize.

Until now.

How the hell does a microbe travel from Reykjavík to Seattle without stopping anywhere in between?

Lisa is still mulling over the implications as she parks her car and climbs the stairs to the offices of Seattle Public Health. Inside, she weaves between cubicles, distractedly acknowledging greetings from staff members, on her way to her office in the back corner. She steps inside it to discover that her desk is already occupied.

"About time," Angela Chow says, glancing up from where she sits, typing at Lisa's computer.

"Angela!" Lisa approaches the other woman with arms extended.

Her boss—technically, former boss, since Angela left on an indefinite medical leave three months ago—waves off the approach with a flick of her bony wrist. "No hugs. I got brittle bones. Besides, this place is supposed to be all about infection control, right?"

Lisa's grin masks how alarmed she is at Angela's appearance. Along with most of her hair, Angela has lost significant weight. Weight she didn't have to lose. And the scarf tied around her scalp only accentuates the deep hollows of her sallow cheeks.

"What are you doing here?" Lisa asks.

"Taking a break from my daily poisoning session," Angela says of her chemotherapy. "Truth is, Lisa, I'm bored as fuck."

"Sounds about right," Lisa says as she sits down on the other side of the desk.

"Also, I needed to get away from Howard. He's driving me nuts with all the coddling. And I'd feel bad about putting a bullet between the eyes of a living saint."

"Poor Howard *is* a saint to put up with you." Lisa chuckles. "Seriously, Angela, how's the treatment going?"

"Treatment? Yeah. Up and down. The nausea is better for sure. Anyway, forget all that. I'm here to talk business."

"You heard?"

"Course I heard. First the new school HPV vaccine program and now this meningitis scare." She rolls her eyes. "You steal my job and in no time at all you score the public-health equivalent of the moon landing and 9/11 in the same week."

Lisa laughs. Clearly, Angela's metastatic ovarian cancer hasn't dulled her penchant for hyperbole. "All you ever dealt with was COVID."

"Yeah, that was a time to forget." Angela had led the city's public-health response to the novel coronavirus outbreak. Even after she fell ill with it herself, she worked twenty-hour days from home, videoconferencing and answering emails, brilliantly managing the response while calming the city. She never got the credit she deserved, mainly because she didn't want the recognition.

"It's been quite the morning." Lisa sighs.

"Tell me."

Lisa doesn't even bother describing the backlash she faced at the HPV vaccine forum, aware that her ailing friend has no patience for the anti-vax movement. Angela's remark to one anti-vaxxer at a public health forum—"Let's see how you feel about vaccines after you get bitten by a rabid bat"—is still legendary in the office.

Instead, Lisa updates Angela on what she knows about the meningitis outbreak, its origins in Iceland, and her initial thoughts on containment strategies.

Angela leans back, absorbing the news. "All the victims come from the same camp?" she asks.

"So far. We're heading out there this afternoon. We have to launch our contact tracing immediately if expanded antibiotic prophylaxis is going to be effective."

"And you've got no idea how our outbreak traces back to Iceland?"

Our, Lisa thinks with a smile. She'd long suspected that, regardless of her deteriorating health, Angela wouldn't be able to keep away from the job for long. "No. I only just heard. But Iceland is one of the world's most popular tourist destinations, especially in the summer. I'm assuming one of the campers' families must've visited recently."

"But Reykjavík hasn't reported any new cases of meningitis since the winter, have they?"

"Not that I am aware of. But you know how it is with meningococcus. Especially type B. You can't declare an outbreak over until you go a year without a single new case. After all, healthy people can be colonized with the bacteria growing in their noses or throats without causing any infection."

"Or them having any idea they're even carrying the murderous little bastards. Have you spoken to anyone over there?"

"I *just* found out." Lisa checks her watch. "Besides, it's got to be pretty late in Iceland right now."

Angela pushes the desk phone toward Lisa. "Trust me when I tell you, there's no time like the present."

"If you were on call, would you pick up an overseas call at almost midnight?" Lisa asks.

"Hell no! But Europeans are weird."

Lisa digs her mobile out of her purse. She Googles the number for Reykjavík's public-health officer, spots the twenty-four-hour emergency contact number, dials it on her speakerphone, and is surprised to hear a male voice answer on the second ring in a staccato of Icelandic.

Assuming that, like most Scandinavians, he must also speak English, Lisa says, "Hello, this is Dr. Lisa Dyer and Dr. Angela Chow from Seattle Public Health."

"Yes, hello, this is Dr. Haarde from Icelandic Health speaking," he says, his accent giving his words a lovely lilt. "How can I be of assistance?"

"Sorry to disturb you so late, Dr. Haarde, but we have a bit of a situation here in Seattle. A new outbreak."

"Related to our meningitis, yes?" he suggests, astutely making the connection.

"Exactly." Lisa glances over to Angela, who taps her temple, impressed. "We have a local outbreak of what appears to be the same strain of meningococcus as the one that hit Reykjavík last winter."

After Lisa summarizes the cases, Haarde says, "It does indeed sound very similar to our epidemic, yes."

His use of the term *epidemic* heightens Lisa's unease. "When was your last reported case?" she asks.

"Late February," he says. "To be accurate, the poor girl died in early March."

"Can you remind us how many victims in total you saw in Reykjavík?"

"There were seventy-six infected patients that we know of." He pauses. "And thirty-five deaths."

"So the mortality rate was almost fifty percent."

"Forty-six percent, yes."

"And the outbreak began at one of the high schools?"

"It did."

"But spread beyond the school? Into the community?"

"Yes. At its worst, we had three distinct geographical clusters of infection around the city. All of them traceable to the index cases from the high school. Most of the victims were teenagers."

"So how did you contain it, Dr. Haarde?" Angela pipes up.

"We implemented very comprehensive contact prophylaxis," he says. "We started anyone who might have had exposure—even the most casual of interactions—on antibiotics. We even closed our schools for six weeks."

"Quarantines?"

"It wasn't necessary, really. People were frightened enough. Very few people gathered in public."

"And you had no luck with vaccines?"

"None at all. We tried both commercially available products. Neither was effective." He exhales so heavily that the speaker whistles. "One boy died of meningitis only a few days after receiving his immunization."

"So antibiotics were your only real weapon?" Lisa asks.

"The truth is, we do not know how much of a difference any of our measures made. We are still unsure why the outbreak halted as abruptly as it began. Or if it has truly left us." His voice lowers, as if letting them in on a secret. "Many people here are concerned that it might be lying dormant and will return again this winter."

"Thank you, Dr. Haarde, that's very enlightening," Lisa says. "We'll probably have more questions for you once we have a more complete picture of our situation. I hope it's all right if we contact you again."

"At a more reasonable time, of course," Angela adds, as if she played no part in the late hour of the call.

"I would be pleased to share what I can from our experience," he says. "I hope Seattle is not as . . . affected as we were."

His grim tone, more than his description of the Icelandic outbreak and its frightening death toll, gnaws at Lisa. As she is just about to hang up, Haarde adds, "Incidentally, even though we have not seen a new case in over five months, we are still proceeding with our vaccination campaign."

"Vaccination?" Lisa glances at Angela. "I thought you said none of the vaccines were effective against this strain of type B meningococcus."

"That is true of the existing products on the market, yes. However, there is a new vaccine. Neissovax, produced by Delaware Pharmaceuticals."

"Neissovax . . ." Lisa vaguely remembers reading a journal article a year or so earlier about the experimental vaccine.

"The early-phase-three trial results have only recently been published, but they are promising," Haarde says, meaning that the drug has already undergone extensive testing and has been proven safe and effective among a trial group that must have included more than a thousand people to be classified as phase three. "Because of our history, we have volunteered to be the pilot site for a citywide immunization program."

"When's that supposed to begin?"

"Next month."

As soon as Lisa disconnects, she looks over to Angela again. "So Delaware has already produced enough to vaccinate a whole city?"

CHAPTER 5

Happy memories from grad school flood back to Nathan Hull as he strolls past the columns of sleek stainless-steel machinery that sprout from the polished concrete floor and spiral to the ceiling forty feet above. Visually, the state-of-the-art development facility bears no resemblance to Nathan's college lab, which was a tiny space crammed with racks of beakers, centrifuges, and other obsolete equipment. Missing, too, are the stenches of solvents, ammonia, and other chemicals. But the plant here in Littleton, Massachusetts, shares the same buzz of science, innovation, and promise that filled his lab at MIT.

Progress. Delaware Pharmaceutical's forty-five-year-old vice president and chief development officer feels it all around him. Just as the mortar and pestle gave way a hundred years before to volume-controlled recipe processes that became the backbone of pharmaceutical manufacturing, robotics and automation are now supplanting that once-core technique. Delaware has invested hundreds of millions in this new facility, borrowing expertise from the aeronautical and automobile industries to create modular continuous processing in an end-to-end integrated and totally automated system. A plant that could be picked up, shipped, and reassembled anywhere in the world in weeks, if not days. A single site where R&D of new products could seamlessly morph overnight into 24/7 manufacturing and distribution.

Still admiring the machinery, Nathan ambles over to join Dr. Fiona Swanson where she stands inspecting a stack of bins. He can tell at a glance that his team's director of product safety doesn't share his sense of awe.

"So does this mean you'll come to Reykjavík, too?" Fiona asks, in a mild Minnesotan accent that still occasionally reminds Nathan of a character in *Fargo*, one of his favorite movies among the Coen brothers' oeuvre, even of all time.

"Wish I could," Nathan says. "I can't remember a bigger trial at this stage of development than this one."

Fiona reaches into the nearest bin and extracts an individual yellow-capped vial. "Fifty thousand doses isn't a trial, Nathan. It's a full product launch."

He holds up a palm. "Agreed, Fee. Not my idea."

"But you're going to do it, anyway?"

"We didn't approach the Icelandic government. They came to us."

When Nathan first met with the country's minister of health, he told her it was premature to enroll an entire city in what effectively amounted to another phase-three trial of an unproven vaccine. And as it became clearer over the next few months of negotiations that the meningitis outbreak in Reykjavík had gone dormant or died out altogether, Nathan's reticence to release Neissovax only intensified, as he saw no upside in vaccinating for a threat that was no longer active. He stalled as long as he could. But when the internal results from Delaware's first large-scale clinical trial proved even more impressive than forecast, Nathan's colleagues grew impatient. Eventually, Peter Moore, Delaware's CEO, intervened. Nathan's boss sat him down over herbal teas—Peter had forsaken caffeine, including his six-coffee-a-day habit, ever since suffering a mild stroke—and told him: "You know as well as I do that we could wait a thousand years and never stumble onto a better opportunity to market a new product." So Nathan relented.

Fiona rolls the vial between a thumb and a finger. "And if something goes wrong in Reykjavík?"

"You saw the pooled data," Nathan says, feeling compelled to defend a decision he still doesn't fully support. "Over fourteen hundred subjects. No major reactions. And an effectiveness of well over ninety-eight percent. Better than we could have hoped for."

"All under carefully controlled trial conditions. Could be very different in the real world."

Nathan slips the vial from her hand. "You'll be there to manage things."

"Can't manage what we can't foresee."

Nathan studies the vial. He finds the block-letter font that reads NEISSOVAX across the top of the label appealing, but the yellow cap still grates. He would've gone with the green, but the marketing gurus insisted otherwise. "We got our marching orders, Fee. Neither of us likes them particularly. But our job is to ensure the rollout goes as smoothly as possible."

"Yeah, that same argument worked wonders at the Nuremberg Trials."

He can't help but laugh. "Let's get hammered on the flight home and forget it all for a few hours."

"It's a forty-minute flight to New York." Fiona shows her first real smile of the afternoon. It's slightly lopsided and brings out the luminescence in her gray eyes. As always, she wears minimal makeup, and her face is a bit long and narrow for his taste, but he still finds her attractive in a nineteenth-century, Russian-literary-heroine sort of way. He wonders if it's her lingering sadness that's so appealing.

"We'll drink triples," he says. "Then grab dinner in the city and finish the job."

"Sure. Why not? I could use a good bender."

There's no ulterior motive behind his offer. Their friendship is comfortably platonic. Nathan has hardly dated since his divorce was finalized, six months earlier. The official end of his eighteen-year marriage hit him harder than he expected and slowed his post-separation tear of casual dating, and sex, to a trickle. Besides, he would never get physically involved with a colleague or coworker. He has always considered that to be the quickest form of career suicide. And aside from his two teenage sons, career means everything to him. The last woman he dated, albeit casually and briefly, once asked Nathan if he ever got lonely, and his candid answer surprised even him: "I'm way too busy to be lonely. Or at least to notice it."

Regardless, Fiona isn't accessible in the romantic sense. She hasn't dated since she buried her husband over five years ago. It's possible she has stayed celibate the whole time. Or maybe not. Fiona is as private a person as Nathan has ever met. Despite their closeness at work, he sometimes feels he doesn't know her at all.

"Have you seen enough?" Nathan asks, handing the vial back to her.

Fiona carefully replaces it in the bin. "Here, yes. But I want at least a week of advanced reconnaissance in Reykjavík to ensure the storage and distribution facilities meet our standards."

"Of course. But you should also take a few days to drive the Ring highway. My sons and I loved it when we visited a couple summers back. Spectacular cliffs and waterfalls. And you've got to check out the hot springs at Geysir. It's where the word *geyser* literally comes from. To quote Ethan: 'Geysir blows Old Faithful out of the water!'"

"Oh, Ethan." She chuckles. "Good thing he got his mom's sense of humor."

"Thanks."

Nathan's phone rings, and he digs it out of his jacket pocket.

"Mr. Hull?" the woman calling says. "I'm Dr. Lisa Dyer with Seattle Public Health."

"Dr. Dyer, you just caught me on a site tour. I'll be back in the office tomorrow—"

"Your assistant told me. And I'm sorry to disturb you this way, but we're dealing with a time-sensitive matter here."

"In Seattle?"

"Yes," she says. "There's been an outbreak of meningitis. Four kids have died."

Nathan taps the phone's speaker icon so Fiona can listen in as Dr. Dyer fills them in on the meningococcal outbreak in the Pacific Northwest. The creases around Fiona's eyes deepen with each sentence. And her head begins to shake as soon as the woman mentions Delaware's upcoming Reykjavík vaccine trial.

"I empathize with your urgency," Nathan says. "But this isn't anything we can sort out over the phone."

"Of course not. Maybe if I email you some of our preliminary findings, we could set up a videoconference with your team—"

"It'll be easier if I just come see you, Dr. Dyer."

"In Seattle? Aren't you on the East Coast?"

Fiona taps her chest, indicating that she intends to accompany him.

"Yes," he says. "Meet at your office tomorrow morning? Say nine?"

CHAPTER 6

"**D**o you want me to get out and push?" Lisa teases as the Jeep Cherokee crawls along the gravel driveway.

Tyra Osborne chuckles. "We should be all right. This puppy has four-wheel drive."

It's a running joke between them how much Lisa's coworker obsesses over her new SUV. On the way south from downtown, Tyra drove the I-5 as aggressively as usual, weaving in and out of the carpool lane as if there were a race to get here. But once they turned off onto the gravel road leading to the main lodge at Camp Green, she slowed to the current snail's pace to prevent any pebbles from dinging her car's precious wheels or undercarriage.

"How did your HPV vaccine forum go?" Tyra asks.

"Feisty crowd," Lisa says with a small shrug.

"Anti-vaxxers?"

"Mainly." Lisa punches Tyra's shoulder playfully. "Wish you could've been there with me."

"Uh-uh. Oh, hell no. I would've absolutely lost it."

Lisa knows that's not true. Tyra is unflappable, and both Lisa and Seattle Public Health are lucky to have her as the program director, the nursing counterpart to Lisa's medical role. The fortyish, stocky African American is motivated and efficient, but perhaps most vitally from Lisa's perspective, Tyra is the consistent voice of reason and calm in the department. And she has helped Lisa avoid several missteps. But Tyra's disdain for the anti-vax movement rivals or even surpasses Angela's.

"There's going to be a ton of pushback to the new mandatory HPV vaccination policy," Lisa says.

"Even if those fools choose to ignore centuries of science, why can't they use just a pinch of common sense?"

"The place anti-vaxxers come from . . . I'm not sure we're even capable of seeing it the way they do."

"The wrong way?" Tyra says as she parks her car a careful distance from an old pickup in front of the lodge.

"It's like a faith for many of them."

"I got nothing against anyone's religion, just as long as their beliefs don't hurt others," Tyra says as she opens her door. "But in the case of anti-vaxxers, theirs really do."

Stippled sunlight peeks through the dense tree towering above, and the fresh scent of cedar hangs thick in the air as Lisa and Tyra head up the wooden steps and into the main office. The woman standing behind the registration counter appears as if she might have just checked in a ghost. Her gaunt face is drawn tighter than the bun on the back of her head.

Lisa introduces Tyra and herself to the woman, who responds with a blank nod. "I'm Maisy Campbell. The camp's director."

"Thanks for taking time to meet us, Maisy," Tyra says, sliding her and Lisa's business cards across the counter.

"I still can't believe it," Maisy says without touching them. "I'm in shock. We've never seen anything like this before."

It would be beyond bizarre if you had, Lisa thinks. But all she says is, "These outbreaks are incredibly sporadic, Ms. Campbell. Totally unpredictable."

"I just can't believe those children are gone." Maisy motions to the fireplace. "They were right here. Joseph, Emma, Grace, and Connor. Only two days ago. Laughing and singing with the rest of us. Connor played the guitar." Her voice cracks. "And Emma was so funny. She'd keep the kids in stitches with her impersonations."

"A meningitis outbreak will do that," Tyra says. "Which is why we wanted to follow up on the call you got from our office about reaching out to every single camper and staff member as soon as we can."

Maisy's eyes go wide. "Will there be others?"

"That's what we're aiming to avoid," Tyra says. "But we need to reach them right away. Start them on antibiotics. All of them. Do you have the contact information we asked for?"

"Yes, of course," Maisy says as she taps the top of the computer screen.

"And have you gotten in touch with anyone so far?" Lisa asks.

"We canceled next week's camp. And we sent a mass email this morning about the illness. I can't even keep up with all the replies . . ."

"How many people were at the camp this past week?"

"Hundred and seven campers, twelve counselors, four support staff, and me," Maisy replies without having to consider it.

A hundred twenty-four people exposed to this deadly pathogen? Christ! Lisa motions to the computer. "We'll need the whole list."

"I can email it to you." Maisy types away at the keyboard, before she stops and looks up at them. "There aren't any . . . you know . . . confidentiality issues with me sharing this?"

"You're totally protected." Tyra smiles. "Under the public-health statutes, we're legally entitled to access this information."

Maisy accepts the explanation with a nod and then copies their email addresses from the business cards. Lisa feels her phone vibrate in her pocket and assumes it must be a notification of the email Maisy just sent. Moments later, the phone buzzes again repeatedly, signaling an incoming phone call, but she ignores it. "Do you happen to know if any of the campers returned from Iceland recently?" she asks.

"Iceland?"

Lisa didn't think Maisy's eyes could go any wider, but they do. "We believe the source of the bacteria traces back there. And we wanted to know if any of the campers or staff might've visited this summer."

Maisy shakes her head. "I never heard anyone mention it. For most of the kids, our camp is as far away from home as they'll get in the summertime. If one of them had gone all the way to Iceland, you can bet he or she would have been bragging about it."

Lisa nods, feeling a bit deflated. "Do you mind giving us a quick tour of the facilities?"

Maisy hurries around from the other side of the counter. She guides them through the main lodge. With small windows, wood siding, and yellowing linoleum floors, it appeared to have been built in the fifties or sixties with minimal upgrades done to it since, except for maybe a paint job. A large cross is mounted above the fireplace, and posters of religious themes or members of Christian rock bands are scattered along the walls. They walk past the rows of long pine tables in the dining hall and through a set of doors into the kitchen. Boasting old appliances and cabinets, it's as dated as the rest of the building but smells clean and looks spotless.

Maisy leads them out the back door of the kitchen and along a dirt path that is canopied by trees. The scent of hemlock and fir meld with the cedar. Lisa picks up on the song of a robin overhead, and she feels her shoulders relax. The serene setting reminds her of her own childhood. Her early exposure to nature is one of the few things she's still grateful to her father for. Even though she chooses to live in the heart of the city, she's never happier than when she escapes it.

They stop outside the first building they reach, a basic gray square cabin with shingles that are cracked and balding. Maisy points to the door. "We have eight separate dorms on-site for the children."

"Are they separated by gender?" Tyra asks.

"Of course. By age, too. And at least one counselor sleeps in every cabin."

Lisa frowns. "So not all of the infected came from the same cabin?"

"Two cabins," Maisy says. "The Peter and the Matthew cabins. Where the oldest children are housed."

"How old?"

"Fifteen and sixteen."

Lisa thinks for a moment. "Are any of the kids dating?"

"This is a Christian camp. That's not encouraged."

"They're also teenagers," Tyra points out.

"I'm not a gossip or anything." Maisy lowers her voice conspiratorially. "But I heard the other kids teasing Emma and Joseph. And I had my suspicions about Kayla and Connor."

Lisa is slightly relieved to hear that two pairs of the known victims were connected in such a way, since the exchange of saliva through kissing is one of the more common routes to spread meningococcus. But it doesn't explain where the bug came from or how it spread among the other kids.

They tour the two cabins that housed the oldest of the campers, and two others for the younger kids. But nothing stands out in the tidy open dorms that, aside from the rows of bunk beds, are relatively austere.

Lisa's phone buzzes for a third time, and she finally pulls it out. As soon as she spots Dominic's name on the screen, she remembers their couples' counseling appointment that's supposed to be in twenty minutes. *Oh, crap! This is all I need right now.* Even though it's not intentional, Lisa still resents her husband's intrusion into her work at this critical juncture.

Lisa turns toward the main lodge. "Thank you, Maisy, you've been a big help. We'll be in touch."

"You haven't seen the rest of the facilities."

"Our team will be back soon," Tyra assures Maisy, picking up on Lisa's urgency. "We're going to need to do an environmental survey—take swabs for bacteria and such."

Lisa grabs Tyra's wrist and pulls her toward the parking area. "I've got to get back downtown. And I need your best Formula 1 driving."

CHAPTER 7

The room is cold, by preference. A steaming cup of tea sits, with the bag still steeping inside it, beside the keyboard. On the screen, the web browser is set again to incognito mode, just as it was at the eureka moment. The memory is still so fresh, as if it happened yesterday, rather than several months ago. It's not surprising. After all, that was when the whole plan gelled.

There had been nothing unusual about the day up until that point. The predictable work routine followed by the usual dogged research at night. And several more dead-end searches. Then one obscure website popped up on-screen. Nothing at first indicated that it would be a game changer. The site listed the twenty most allergy-inducing ingredients, which was neither informative nor helpful. But below those, it also divulged the agents most likely to initiate a cellular immune reaction. The kind of delayed response that would take days to manifest.

It felt as if the clouds suddenly parted, revealing not just a few stars but the entire Milky Way all at once.

Almost a year later, it still does.

CHAPTER 8

If Lisa were to ever review the seafood restaurant online, her take on it would read like most of the others, which average three and a half stars. *Spectacular views. Good service. Food left me wanting.*

But its kid-friendly environment—especially the attached playroom where her niece loves to lose herself—and the restaurant's location, at the water's edge of Belltown, is reason enough for them to come back as often as they do.

Despite—or maybe because of—her trying day, Lisa basks in the view through the floor-to-ceiling windows beside her. The sun is beginning to dip over Elliott Bay and the Olympic Mountain range beyond. A cruise ship drifts away from the neighboring pier. Sailboats and other pleasure craft dot the water as a ferry makes for the horizon with its running lights already on.

Deadly outbreaks, controversial vaccinations, and futile counseling sessions all seem more distant from where Lisa sits across from her sister, while sharing a chair with her niece, Olivia.

Drawing on the back of the kids' menu, Olivia uses a royal-blue marker to frantically color in the sky above a vessel that Lisa thinks is meant to be the cruise ship but might be the ferry. Either way, it's a pretty damned good likeness for a six-year-old.

"Is this for my office collection, Liv?" Lisa asks.

"Not sure, Tee." While *auntie* was one of the first words Olivia ever attempted, it came out more like "Tee" and the nickname stuck. "We'll just have to see."

Lisa ruffles Olivia's curly hair. "I liked you better when you didn't have such a mouth on you."

Without looking up from her drawing, Olivia says, "You're not helping your case, Tee."

Lisa laughs in surprise. "Now you're just channeling your dad."

Amber rolls her eyes. "The crap this one picks up from Allen."

Olivia drops the marker, sweeps up the drawing, and holds it out to Lisa. "You can have it, Tee." She grins. "This time."

"It's not worth anything if it isn't signed."

Olivia grabs a black marker and signs her name deliberately, in the cursive she only recently learned, in the bottom right corner. "Happy?" she asks, dropping the marker on the table.

"Ecstatic." Lisa pulls Olivia into a hug and kisses her on the forehead.

Olivia wriggles free and turns to Amber. "Mommy, can I go play?" As soon as her mother nods, she shoots out of her chair.

"What the hell? Did I miss her nineteenth birthday or something?" Lisa asks as she watches her niece race toward the playroom.

"That one came out of the womb sassy, remember?" Amber reaches for her quarter-full glass of Pinot Noir and views Lisa curiously. "So?"

"So, what?"

"You and Dominic . . . the counseling?"

Lisa looks out the window. The ferry is just a blip on the horizon now against the setting sun. "One step forward, two steps back. Sometimes three."

"The way he acted when you were named the chief public-health officer . . ." Amber shakes her head. "It takes time to repair that kind of damage."

"Sometimes you can't repair it. Dad taught us that. Remember?"

"Don't even start," her sister groans.

"Besides, the harder Dom tries, the worse it makes things. What does that say about me?"

"That you're pretty fucked up."

Lisa laughs. "Tell me something I don't know."

Amber takes a sip of her wine. "Hey, my friend Helen went to your vaccine forum today."

Lisa wondered how long it would take her sister to get around to the topic. "And she's now totally sold on the HPV vaccine, is she?"

Amber shrugs. "She told me you got into quite the debate with some cute doctor in the audience. Said he was very convincing."

"Any chance Helen might have already been on his side?" Lisa reaches for the glass of wheat ale that comes from one of the countless local craft breweries whose name she can't recall. "Like you are."

"You've got to stop taking this so personally."

"What? That I work for Public Health and my sister is an anti-vaxxer?"

"Bit dramatic, isn't that? I'm not some activist. And what's wrong with a little healthy skepticism?"

"It's not so healthy when people die." Lisa motions toward the playroom. "I still can't believe you didn't get Olivia immunized against measles."

"Here we go . . ."

"In 2000, we eradicated measles in the States. Not a single case reported that year. This year alone in Washington, we've had three deaths from it."

"And what about all the suffering and death among the healthy kids who got the vaccine?"

"Aside from a few sore arms, what suffering?" Lisa says, raising her voice in spite of herself. "Massive population studies have shown over and over again that the MMR vaccine—like all the others—is safe."

"Studies done by the same doctors who peddle the product."

"Doctors and scientists all over the world are in bed with Big Pharma, is that it?"

"You don't need to sound so condescending," Amber huffs. "It's not so simple. I'm not saying doctors are all corrupt. Just that you're biased. You're spoon-fed a pro-vaccine agenda from your first day in med school. And most of you have drunk the Kool-Aid."

"*We've* drunk the Kool-Aid?" Lisa slams her glass down on the table hard enough for the beer to slosh out. "That's rich. Show me a bigger cult than theanti-vaxxers! Besides, what the hell would you know about what is or isn't taught at medical school? You and Allen run a weed dispensary."

"Nice, Liberty!" Amber folds her arms across her chest.

Her sister's body language aside, Lisa knows she's touched a nerve. Lisa legally changed her name from "Liberty" when she was nineteen, and Amber only calls her by the childhood name when she's irate. "I'm sorry, Amber. Didn't mean that the way it sounded. It's been a long day. And maybe I get too amped up sometimes. But I'm an epidemiologist, and vaccination is a big part of my life's work."

Amber only stares at her, unappeased. "As usual, this is really about Dad, isn't it?"

"Not this old chestnut."

"It's true. Your whole life you've been rebelling against him. From your choice of names to the career you picked. Like almost every other decision you've ever made. It's all been one giant 'fuck you, Dad!'"

"Uh-uh," Lisa says. "True, I spent a bunch of my early years trying to escape his clutches. But once I did, I haven't looked back."

"You expect me to buy that?"

"Don't care. I'm just glad I'm free of it all . . . his megalomania, his conspiracy theories, his imagined slights, big and small. He's sick and you know it."

"*Was* sick," Amber stresses. "He got treatment."

"*Got* treatment? The state troopers had to drag him onto that psych ward in handcuffs." The unwelcome memory of her first day visiting her father on the locked mental-health unit floods back. His scraggly beard, wild eyes, and nonsensical ramblings. Lisa was twenty years old and hadn't seen him in two years. She felt genuine empathy then. Love, even. Suddenly all his erratic behavior and the progressive withdrawal of their family from society made sense in light of his diagnosis with bipolar disorder. She visited him regularly in the hospital, and for a few months, there was a thaw between them. Affection, even. But it fell apart soon after his discharge. Maybe his mental illness explained the extremes of his behavior, but even once he was stabilized on medication, he remained the same obstinate, self-absorbed, and closed-minded man he'd always been, characteristics that his disease accentuated rather than caused. And after Lisa enrolled in medical school, a move that her dad viewed as a betrayal of his belief system and all he had tried to teach her, they stopped talking altogether.

Dispelling those thoughts, Lisa asks, "How's Mom?"

"She's OK. Would be nice if you found out for yourself."

She chose her husband over her daughters, Lisa wants to say, but she doesn't have the appetite for any more conflict today. "Yeah, I'll call her soon."

"She'd appreciate that."

Lisa can't tell if there's sarcasm in her sister's voice, but her phone rings and, happy for the distraction, she answers.

"Hey, Lisa, sorry to bug you," Tyra says in an unusually somber tone.

Lisa already knows why her colleague must be calling, but all she says is, "What's up?"

"Three more meningitis cases were reported late this afternoon." Tyra hesitates a moment. "And another death."

CHAPTER 9

Kayla doesn't know where she is. It's been dark forever behind eyelids that refuse to open. She can hear muffled sounds, though. Electronic chirps and beeps, the reassuring words of a kind woman who hovers near her head, and, of course, her granddad's voice. She's never heard him talk so much. Or sound as concerned. Kayla can feel the pokes of needles in her arms and the roughness of something down her throat. But she's so groggy.

Have I been drugged?

The only comparable feeling in her life came right before her wisdom teeth were removed, when the doctor was counting backward from ten as the milky-white anesthetic ran into her arm. It feels the same now, except she has been stuck at *one* forever.

Her head still throbs. And her skin still burns. But the fear is totally gone, replaced by a calmness that borders on serenity. And her body is getting lighter by the moment. As if she's about to float off the bed.

Rapture.

Sirens are sounding. The wailing grows louder and softer simultaneously, as if the same fire truck is approaching and leaving at the same time.

"Don't leave us, Kay!" She hears her granddad's faint yell from what seems like miles away.

Her little brother, Thomas, somehow appears out of the darkness. He's still three years old and clutches the yellow toy bulldozer that he used to carry everywhere. When he grins at her, his front tooth is still missing.

And then Kayla sees her parents. Her dad is laughing as he sweeps Thomas up into his arms and waves to her. Despite her mother's loving smile, tears stream down her cheeks as she extends a hand to Kayla.

"Hang in there, Kay. Please. You are all . . ." But the rest of her granddad's words are swallowed up by a sudden vacuum.

It's time for Kayla to join the rest of her family.

CHAPTER 10

Lisa is hoping to slip out of bed before Dominic stirs, but just as she lifts the sheets and raises her leg, he rolls toward her. She only goes along with him to avoid another post-counseling debrief that she senses might be imminent. She can't handle another one of those this morning.

The physical release from her orgasm is unexpected and welcome, creeping up faster than usual in their frenzied tangle. But their primal connection has never been an issue. At forty-four, Dominic is in as good shape as he ever was. Though her desire has lessened and the frequency of their sex diminished—it's been weeks since the last time—Dominic can still find the right touch and pace to help bring her over the top, even when her mind and heart are elsewhere.

Sadly, the act doesn't bring her any closer to him. And as she lies in his arms, listening to his heavier breathing and feeling his bony chest press against her breasts, she plots her escape. She silently concedes to herself that their counselor's assessment at yesterday's session was accurate: she does bear more responsibility of late for the growing chasm inside their marriage. But to her, the momentum feels as unstoppable as feet slipping on a slick embankment.

Besides, Dominic's utter lack of support for her recent promotion still stings. Much of their strength as a couple came from mutual respect and admiration for each other's professional ambitions. Lisa has always championed Dominic, especially after he became his hospital's head of interventional cardiology, the specialty responsible for placing stents into all those blocked coronary arteries that genetics, diet, and lifestyle have made rampant across America. And despite his tendency toward self-absorption, Dominic used to genuinely encourage her, too. That all changed once she was named the city's new chief public-health officer. Maybe he felt irrationally threatened by her promotion—as if she had surpassed him professionally—or deprived by her longer hours away from home, but neither excused his petulance. And she can't help but resent him for it.

"I thought we got some good stuff off our chest yesterday, Lees," Dominic says, startling her.

"Yeah, me too," she answers quickly, shuffling away from him, trying to ease out of his embrace.

"It's not quantum physics, is it?" Dominic says, hanging on to her. "Nothing we didn't know. You could basically draw a line and see where our fertility issues and the problems in our marriage intersect."

Not this again. There's no way in hell. "Look, Dom, it's hard to focus right now with this meningitis scare at work."

"Of course. Work comes first nowadays. Always."

Lisa ignores the implication. *Would it kill you to ask me how I'm coping with the biggest health crisis I've ever managed?* She rises from the bed without voicing the thought. "I've got to be at the office soon. There's going to be some long hours until this mess is sorted out."

Dominic only shakes his head and rolls away.

Pushing her marital woes to the back of her mind, Lisa races to get ready, and leaves. She reaches her office by six thirty, but she's not the first one to arrive. Not even close. The place is abuzz, almost as busy as on a Monday afternoon during flu season.

As soon as Tyra spots Lisa from across the room, the program manager breaks free of her conversation with two public-health nurses and hurries over to greet her. They step into Lisa's office and sit across the desk from one another.

"Where do we stand, Ty?" Lisa asks.

"On kinda thin ice, if I'm being honest," Tyra says, but the determined glint in her eyes suggests that she's stoked by the challenge. "Eleven confirmed or, at least, highly suspected cases of meningococcus. Five deaths. All of them basically kids."

"And they're all directly linked to Camp Green?"

"Uh-huh. We haven't seen any secondary spread to relatives or household contacts."

"*Yet.*"

"True enough." Tyra sighs. "It's only been thirty-six hours since Patient Zero showed up in the ER at Harborview. And he's dead."

"Where are we on the contact tracing?"

"Felix and Yolanda worked the phones all night," Tyra says of two of her nurses. "Don't have exact numbers, but we've reached well over half the families."

"Found any links to Reykjavík?"

"Not yet. But we dispensed at least a hundred antibiotic kits so far, or got the prescriptions called in, at least. We still got a ways to go, though."

"Time is spread."

"Don't be wasting your breath preaching to the choir." Tyra motions to the window behind her, through which Lisa spots several nurses at their cubicles with phones to their ears. "The whole staff is going to spend the day chasing down any and all remaining contacts."

"Except us. We'll be bouncing from one meeting to another."

"No time for all that bureaucratic bullshit." Tyra hops to her feet. "We got an honest-to-God outbreak to contain. And we only have to look to Iceland to see how high the stakes are."

As soon as Tyra leaves, Lisa opens her email and weeds through the two-hundred-plus new ones, replying only to the few she deems most urgent. She's so lost in her work that her shy young assistant, Ingrid, has to rap on the open door to remind Lisa that her seven o'clock meeting is about to begin.

Everyone else is already seated at the long table inside the windowless conference room when Lisa takes her chair at the head of it. The first slide of her brief presentation fills the two flat screens mounted on either side of the room. Even though she didn't specifically invite Angela, Lisa isn't surprised to see her there with a bright floral scarf wrapped around her pale head. There are twelve other attendees. Five of them work for her office, including Tyra, and Lisa recognizes everyone else—an assortment of state and local officials—except for the gangly man seated to her immediate left, who reminds her of Abraham Lincoln with his Shenandoah beard.

Lisa initiates roundtable introductions and learns the man to her left is Dr. Alistair Moyes, the lead physician at the Centers for Disease Control for the western United States.

"Thanks, everyone, for coming on such short notice," Lisa says. "We are now at day three of a meningococcal eruption that has already met the CDC criteria to be classified as an organizational outbreak. Due to the lethality of the pathogen involved, we've decided to convene an Outbreak Control Team and create this subcommittee to share information and coordinate responses among all involved agencies. If it's all right with everyone, for the time being we'll aim to meet daily, if not in person then at least via videoconference."

There are nods and murmurs of agreement around the table.

Lisa taps a button on her desk and a map of greater Seattle appears on the screens along with an animated red circle made of dots that revolve around the location of Camp Green, just south of the city. She talks through a few more slides with tables and graphs that highlight a basic epidemiological survey of the outbreak—including the dates of onset for the eleven known cases and, in the case of the five fatalities, the times of death.

Next, Lisa turns to the source of the infection. An electron microscope image of the offending bacterium fills the screens. It resembles two side-by-side, fuzzy red Ping-Pong balls. "Harborview's microbiology lab has confirmed the pathogen is a particular strain of Neisseria meningitis, serotype B. The evidence suggests it's the same strain of meningococcus that was responsible for the outbreak in Reykjavík last winter. Like most type B strains, for reasons that aren't fully understood, this pathogen strongly targets teenagers and children. In Iceland, more than ninety-five percent of the victims were between the ages of five and twenty-five." She motions to the woman halfway down the table who wears gold-framed glasses and has her gray hair tied tightly on top of her head. "I will defer to our expert microbiologist, Dr. Klausner, from the state lab for further characterization."

"What's left to say?" Angela pipes up. "It's the same bug that did Iceland's kids in."

Klausner emits a quiet chortle and then clears her throat. "Well, yes, it does appear that way."

"And you've confirmed this how?" Moyes asks.

"The PCR tests are unequivocal for that specific strain," Klausner says. "The blood and spinal-fluid cultures have already grown meningococcus." She stops frequently to clear her throat in what Lisa recognizes as a vocal tic. "We hope to get the WGS—whole genome sequencing or its molecular fingerprint—results soon. Then we'll know for certain."

Angela looks over to Moyes. "The WGS isn't going to change diddly, Alistair. This is the Icelandic pathogen. There's zero doubt."

Moyes only smiles at her. "It's good to see you back, Angela. Feisty as ever." He turns to Lisa. "Does this mean you've linked one of the cases back to Reykjavík?"

"Not yet, no," Lisa says.

"They don't have any active disease in Iceland," Angela says, tugging at her scarf. "We're working under the assumption that it must've been brought back to Seattle by someone who is asymptomatic. In other words, a healthy carrier."

Moyes raises an eyebrow. "Has one of the campers recently returned from Iceland?"

"We haven't identified one so far," Lisa admits. "But we haven't reached everyone yet."

"Point is, Alistair, one way or the other, the very same killer bug has reached Seattle." Something in Angela's tone suggests that she has more than just a collegial history with the CDC doctor. "And we better stop it from detonating like it did in Reykjavík."

"You don't find it the least bit . . . odd . . . that the same deadly bacteria show up here in the Pacific Northwest without an easily traceable connection back to Iceland?" Moyes asks.

"It's an emerging pathogen, Alistair. A brand-new bug. Everything about it is odd."

"How often do emerging pathogens cross the planet without leaving a trace?"

"We're still actively looking for the link," Lisa intervenes, feeling the need to wrest control of the meeting back, although Moyes's point resonates. "Meantime, we've reached out to Public Health over there. A Dr. Haarde. He was extremely helpful. In Iceland, they ended up with three clusters of infection once it spread into the community. Thirty-five victims died, all of them young." She pauses to let the stark statistic sink in. "Reykjavík has a population of two hundred thousand, give or take. And metro Seattle is nearly twenty times that size."

One of the two state officials grimaces and pushes his chair away from the table. "So we're talking seven hundred dead, potentially?"

"Nah," Angela grunts. "Reykjavík is relatively remote. Nowhere for the bacteria to spread. If we were to be hit as hard as they were, it would be way worse than that."

The official clutches his head in his hands and turns to Moyes for reassurance. "That can't be true, can it?"

Moyes only shrugs.

"We're nowhere near that point," Lisa says. "Right now we have to focus on expanded chemoprophylaxis. Getting every potentially exposed person on antibiotic treatment. These first three days represent the prime—maybe the only—window of opportunity to catch everyone. To stop it from spreading beyond the campers themselves."

She goes on to summarize her department's round-the-clock contact-tracing strategy and distribution of antibiotics to the "usual suspects," which means people living in the same household as victims, family members, or anyone who had direct contact with the saliva of patients, including all sexual partners, along with all fellow campers, and the medical staff who treated the patients.

"What about a vaccine?" asks the other official from the state department of health, Corrine Benning, whose small features give her face a mouselike quality.

Lisa shares a quick glance with Angela, which is enough for them to wordlessly agree to not tip their hand about Neissovax. "Neither of the two available vaccines for type B meningococcus has worked against the Icelandic strain."

"Why not?" Benning asks.

"It's somewhat complicated." Klausner answers for her. "For the other serotypes of meningococcus—types A, C, W, and Y—the vaccines target the antigens—a type of protein—on their thick cell walls. But the antigens on the walls of the type B strain are too similar to human proteins for our immune systems to differentiate them as invaders."

"So our immune system won't produce antibodies against it?"

"Correct," Klausner says.

"In other words, antibiotics are all we got." Angela sums it up.

"And you know what they say? If all you got is a hammer, go find yourself a whole shitload of nails."

Much as she respects and admires her friend, Lisa is beginning to wonder if Angela's attendance is such a good idea. "The other key element we need to discuss is the communication strategy." Lisa gestures toward the goateed man at the far end of the table, who has been furiously typing at his laptop. "As our department's communications lead, Kevin will help coordinate our response."

Kevin lifts one hand from the keyboard and waves.

"Word has leaked out on social media," Lisa continues. "We're fielding calls from all kinds of media outlets. Kevin's going to release a press statement and health alert later this morning. But as always, we're walking a razor-thin line between informing and panicking the public."

"What are you going to say?" Benning asks.

"Obviously, we're going to instruct anyone who attended the Bible camp in the past few weeks to report to us right away," Kevin says. "We'll also let the public know the symptoms they should look out for. And we're going to alert health-care providers to be vigilant for possible new cases."

"In a nutshell, we're going to flood the ERs and clinics with every neurotic who feels a tinge of a headache coming on," Angela says.

"What would you have us do?" Lisa says, even though she knows Angela isn't wrong. "We already have five dead."

"Six," Tyra says, holding up her phone with a pained expression. "Just got the word from Harborview. Another sixteen-year-old died this morning."

Lisa's heart sinks. "Not Kayla?"

Tyra nods.

The unwelcome vision of Kayla's grandfather interrupts Lisa's thoughts. She can still see the heartbreak in his eyes. She can't imagine what it must feel like to lose everyone in the world who matters most to you.

CHAPTER 11

Nathan Hull has never spent much time in the Pacific Northwest—a couple of pharmaceutical conventions in the Seattle area and one corporate retreat in Portland—but every time he visits, he feels oddly at home. It's the ocean, he realizes. Having grown up in Providence, Rhode Island, he always gravitates toward the coast. And he resolves to bring his boys here soon, maybe even for next summer's annual father-sons road trip. This summer, they've already committed to driving up to Canada to tour through Quebec.

Nathan can't see the water from where he sits across from Fiona in a red vinyl booth, but he enjoys the view of the tree-lined triangular plaza in the heart of historic Pioneer Square in front of the café. He wonders what era the decorative iron pergola across the street dates to and, ever the history buff, makes a mental note to look it up.

Fiona is still working on her herbal tea, but Nathan has already finished his Americano and is considering a second. Lisa isn't late. It's still a few minutes before nine. But they weren't sure how long the cab ride might take from the hotel, and since Fiona is almost phobic about being late, they gave themselves a generous buffer and arrived fifteen minutes early.

Lisa requested they meet at this café instead of Seattle Public Health's headquarters, which is four or five blocks up the hill on Fifth Avenue. The cab ride took Nathan and Fiona right past her office building, and he couldn't help noticing the funky-looking coffee shop directly catercorner to it. Perhaps he's reading too much into Lisa's choice of locales, but in his experience, medical officials sometimes approach meetings with executives from "Big Pharma"— the cringe-worthy pejorative they often use—as something shameful to be done in the shadows, like picking up a hooker or buying street drugs.

Nathan is pulled from the demoralizing thoughts when the door opens, and a woman enters in a white blouse and light gray skirt. Spotting them, she nods and approaches them with a closed-mouth smile.

As part of his standard premeeting research, Nathan already viewed Lisa's online profile on the health department's website, but the corporate photo doesn't do her justice. In person, her oval face and high cheekbones accentuate her large almond-brown eyes. He would be at a loss to guess her dominant ethnicity—could be anywhere from Ukrainian to Spanish—*definitely a case for a mail-order DNA kit*. But it's hard not to pick up on the poise and self-assuredness she radiates with each step.

After introductions, Nathan heads up to the counter to order coffees while Lisa slides into the booth beside Fiona.

A minute or two later, Nathan lowers a cup of black coffee in front of her and sits down across from them. Lisa places her phone, screen up, beside her cup and says, "Kind of rude, I realize. But in light of the expanding crisis, I have to be connected at all times."

Nathan grins. "We're no strangers to being anchored to our phones."

"Thanks for meeting me here," Lisa says "Not just in Seattle but at this place. They serve my favorite pour-over coffee in the city. And Lord knows I'll need a few cups this morning."

"That's high praise," Nathan says. "Isn't Seattle a mecca for coffee?"

"I guess we did give the world Starbucks." Her smile is more natural than earlier. "Wonder if it can ever forgive us?"

Fiona, who's almost as averse to small talk as she is to tardiness, cuts to the chase. "Can you tell us more about the local meningitis outbreak?"

"It's bad," Lisa says bluntly. She goes on to summarize the eleven cases and six deaths that were recorded in the first day and a half, along with Public Health's preliminary efforts to contain the infection. "If we see secondary spread beyond the camp to their contacts, it could go from bad to horrendous in a big hurry."

"That sounds ominous," Nathan mutters.

"It is. Which is why I wanted to discuss your new vaccine."

"Delaware's vaccine," he says. "My role is to facilitate new product development, while Fiona's is to ensure their safety."

Lisa nods. "Word is that Neissovax has been shown to be effective against the Icelandic strain of type B meningococcus."

"In the lab, maybe," Fiona says. "It still hasn't been proven to work in the field."

"In fairness, Fiona, there hasn't been a field to prove it on," Nathan says.

"How so?" Lisa asks.

"The only known outbreak of this pathogen has been in Reykjavík—"

"Until now."

"Maybe," he says. "But by the time we had enough vaccine produced to test it in the real world, the outbreak in Iceland was over."

"Or dormant," Lisa says.

"Either way, there were no subjects actively exposed—no test kitchen, as it were—to trial the vaccine's effectiveness on."

"We had to rely on animal models and serum analyses to test for immunogenicity," Fiona says, using the elaborate term for a vaccine's ability to provoke production of specific antibodies to a pathogen in the bloodstream after immunization.

"But the lab tests have been very encouraging, haven't they?" Lisa persists. "They do strongly suggest, don't they, that Neissovax would work against the Icelandic strain?"

Fiona looks skyward. "Always a leap of faith to go from the test tube to the real world."

Lisa nods again. "How does your vaccine differ from the ones already on the market?"

"Neissovax targets entirely different proteins than the other existing vaccines," Nathan explains with unmasked pride. "Subcapsular proteins that are under the cell wall itself. Our vaccine invokes a powerful immune response after inoculation that produces high levels of circulating antibodies in subjects against multiple strains of type B meningococcus."

"Including the Icelandic strain?"

"Yes."

"Hate to sound like a broken record." Fiona sighs. "But only in the lab, so far."

"In people, too, Fee." Nathan smiles to hide his irritation. It's beyond unprofessional to bicker with a colleague in front of a client, even one as unsolicited as Lisa is. "The immunogenicity is impressive. We've seen the antibody levels go through the roof in healthy volunteers. And the animal modeling has already shown how effective it can be in protecting against this bug."

"Discovering a universally effective type B meningococcus vaccine is like finding the Holy Grail of vaccinology," Lisa says.

Nathan chuckles. "Even at Delaware, we aren't *that* grandiose."

Lisa isn't smiling. "But you must be pretty confident in your product if you're ready to immunize all of Reykjavík with it."

"Not the whole city," Fiona points out. "Fifty thousand doses."

Lisa shrugs. "I'm only requesting a few thousand doses."

That's the last thing in the world we need, Nathan thinks as he casually lowers his cup. "What would be the point of that?"

"To vaccinate the people at the highest risk. Direct contacts, health-care workers, and people living nearest to the victims."

Nathan shares a quick look with Fiona. "That would put Delaware in a no-win situation," he says.

"How is it different from the trial you're planning in Reykjavík?"

"With the relatively small sample size you're suggesting, you can't really show clinical efficacy," he explains. "And you're talking about the highest-risk group of individuals. If one of them were to still to get sick after immunization . . ."

"What if no one does?" Lisa asks. "Imagine what a powerful endorsement of your product that could be."

"No vaccine is a hundred percent effective. Besides, if no one gets infected, people would argue that it wasn't a large enough target population."

"And," Fiona stresses, "if someone does have a serious adverse reaction . . ."

"It would look even worse for Neissovax," Nathan says.

Lisa frowns. "Adverse reactions are a risk with every drug, old and new."

"But when it comes to new vaccines, those kinds of stories are magnified and distorted by the anti-vax community."

Lisa sips her coffee before replying. "What if Seattle were to take the place of Reykjavík? Let's say we dispense all fifty thousand doses here instead of over there?"

"We're all set up in Iceland," Fiona says. "We don't have any of the infrastructure in place here."

"That's true. The potential exposure for us . . ." Nathan holds up a palm. And then he delivers the message he flew across the country to give in person. "Obviously, we would love to help. But it's just too soon to release Neissovax here in the Pacific Northwest."

"You have a business to protect. I get that." Lisa's eyes bore into his. "But I was at the bedside of a young girl just hours before she died. If you could've seen her grandfather . . ."

"I can't even imagine." Nathan thinks momentarily of his own sons before focusing back on his primary goal: to minimize Delaware's exposure. "But it's our job to make sure we don't put the cart before the horse."

"And it's my job to do everything I can to prevent more deaths."

CHAPTER 12

"Hey, buddy, what's up? Your video over?" Max Balfour asks, trying to hide how startled he feels. His son has a habit of sneaking up on him, especially at times like now when Max is in his home office, totally consumed by the latest blog entry he's writing.

Without removing his bulky wireless headphones, Jack stares past his dad with a look that is simultaneously blank and intense. "I'm hungry."

Reluctantly, Max spins away from his desktop computer and rises to his feet. "Let's make you a grilled cheese."

"No crust."

"As if! What kind of amateur do you take for me?" Max squeezes his son's shoulder before Jack, as expected, jerks away.

Max can't believe how much Jack has grown. His son, who just turned thirteen, is almost as tall as him. Max is dreading the teen years—both the new challenges they will bring and the loss of childhood they mark. "Four carrots, right?"

Jack nods. "Four. Sliced in quarters."

His son is so exact about numbers. They have to be even and, ideally, divisible into one another. Max understands the obsession is a common feature of the autistic spectrum—a coping skill that helps Jack bring order to his chaotic thoughts. While deeply devoted to his son, Max finds his behavior so foreign and, sometimes, extremely frustrating. But he rarely reveals that to Jack. No, he saves his wrath for his activism. For the people responsible for his son's condition.

As they walk toward the kitchen, Max asks, "Jack, you want to tell me what happened at school today?"

Jack shakes his head. "We did a puzzle. *Water Lilies* by Claude Monet. He died when he was eighty-six years old. In France."

"That's not what I mean, Jack. What happened with you and Francis?"

"I needed that piece," Jack says. "It fit in my corner. Francis didn't have any lily pads in his."

"And so you punched him?"

"I needed that piece."

"Then you use your words and ask him for it, Jack. Now Francis has a black eye." *And I'm not even sure the Institute will take you back.* "You didn't want to hurt Francis, did you?"

Jack looks away, neither embarrassed nor engaged. "I wanted the piece."

"There are other ways, Jack. You just can't hit like that. Francis won't want to play with you anymore."

"Ms. Appleby says tomorrow we will do a Rembrandt puzzle. He lived in Holland." Jack scrunches up his nose. "He died at sixty-three," he adds with obvious disgust at the odd number.

Max's brief disappointment in his son dissipates as he's reminded again that Jack has no insight. He might as well reprimand the clouds for causing a storm. His tone softens. "OK, buddy, just no more hitting."

Jack nods blankly.

"Let's go get lunch."

Max hears the front door alarm chime and turns to see his ex-wife, Sarah, rushing in. "The Institute just called me," she says. "What's going on?"

"I spoke to them when I picked him up," Max says. "I think it's all sorted out now."

"You *think*?"

"Not now, Sarah," Max says evenly to avoid any escalation.

Their fights used to be epic. They almost all centered around how to best manage Jack's autism. Max still doesn't fully understand how their relationship fell apart. He used to love Sarah so much. And seven years after their divorce, he still misses her. His current girlfriend, Yolanda, is kind, devoted, and much more tolerant than Sarah ever was, but she will never capture his heart the way his ex-wife did.

Sarah hugs Jack and kisses the top of his head. He is motionless in her arms but, Max notes with a tinge of jealousy, he doesn't recoil from her.

"Hey, buddy, go watch another episode of your show while I make you lunch, OK?" Max tells him.

Jack turns for the other room. "No crusts," he says again as he walks out.

"What if they kick him out, Max?" Sarah asks as soon as their son is gone.

"They won't," Max replies, bending the truth. "I spoke to his teacher. They might need another aide for the class. That's all."

Her shoulders slump with obvious relief. "The Institute has been a godsend. I don't know what we would do . . ."

"It's going to be OK, Sarah."

"God, I hope so. Jack doesn't even need 'OK.' He just needs status quo for a while."

Sarah follows Max over to the counter and watches him prepare Jack's lunch. "Did you hear about the meningitis thing?" she asks.

Max shakes his head as he melts the butter in the frying pan.

"A bunch of kids at a local summer camp got sick from meningitis," Sarah says. "Five of them died. It's all over the news."

"Seriously? How?"

"They don't know, but they're advising anyone with a fever and a headache to get checked out right away."

"Maybe it's not such a bad thing that Jack got sent home today."

"Let's not overreact."

"Speaking of health threats, can you believe what's going on with this HPV vaccine?"

"What are you talking about?"

"The government, Sarah," he says. "I went to that public-health forum three days ago. They're making the vaccine mandatory for all school-age kids. So frustrating. I couldn't help but get into it with the chief public-health doctor."

She brings her fingers to her temples and begins to massage them. "This again?"

"What do you mean *this*?" he snaps. "They only announced the insane measure last week."

"Vaccines! And your quixotic quest to stop them."

"Enough with the melodrama, OK? I'm just doing my bit. I'm not alone, either. There are lots of good people who share our view."

"I don't know that it's my view. And even if you're right about the MMR shot being the cause of Jack's—"

"You know I am!"

"What good will it do, Max? You could ban every vaccine in the world, and it still won't help Jack one iota."

Max only stares at his ex-wife, suddenly remembering why he was happy the day she walked out. After all they had been through with Max, how could she be so selfish? She never did really care about helping other families avoid the kind of pain that they have to live with every day.

But I sure as hell intend to.

CHAPTER 13

It feels more like *Groundhog Day* than déjà vu to Lisa. Once again, she finds herself garbed from head to toe in infection-control gear while standing inside an isolation room at Harborview's ICU and staring down at another meningitis victim, who barely clings to life with the aid of a ventilator and an arsenal of antibiotics and other ultrapotent medications—anything and everything to improve his slim chances of survival.

But there's one key difference between Zeke Dolan and the other nineteen patients from this outbreak. And it's the primary reason for Lisa's visit. Unlike the other victims, Zeke has never stepped foot on the grounds of Camp Green.

As predictable as the spread beyond the members of the Bible camp was—community spread, as it's known in epidemiological circles—the confirmation of it slammed Lisa like a gut punch. She wasn't alone, either. The noisy Outbreak Control Team briefing for day five of the outbreak fell silent when, an hour earlier, Tyra announced the first such case. Lisa abruptly ended the meeting and headed straight for Harborview in search of answers she knows she's unlikely to find.

Zeke is twenty-eight years old but, with his smooth face and small frame, he could pass for another teenage victim. Despite all the medical interventions, his vital signs are poor, and his skin is mottled with the pinpoint red spots and larger blood blisters that are telltale signs of the petechial purpura rash. Blood trickles from his nostrils and oozes around the clear ventilator tubing that passes between his chapped lips, indicating that his blood-clotting system is failing as badly as or worse than the rest of his organs.

Dr. Edwin Davis stands close enough for Lisa to pick up on the floral scent of his shampoo. Unlike their previous encounter, the veteran intensivist no longer seems fazed. "Zeke arrived at the ER about six this morning," he says dispassionately. "He had a headache and a fever, but he was conscious and alert. Within half an hour, his blood pressure plummeted, and he went into full septic shock. He's barely hung on since."

Lisa's gaze drifts to the gobs of blood flickering inside the ventilatory tube with each forced mechanical breath in and out of Zeke's lungs. "Can he survive this?"

"Used to be, I had a sixth sense for who was likely to make it out of here. But with this meningitis?" Edwin's shoulders twitch. "We're averaging almost fifty percent mortality among the first twenty cases."

"Similar to Iceland's experience."

"Deadly similar," he says with a note of defeat.

"Does the speed of onset and/or progression of symptoms matter?"

"The quicker they go into septic shock, the worse it is. But every one of them gets so sick so fast with this infection, even that's hard to tell."

Lisa goes cold with the morbid realization that if Zeke dies, the death toll for this outbreak will reach double digits. "I understand he got antibiotics almost as soon as he got to the ER," she says. "Maybe the ultra-early administration will make a difference?"

"These patients just can't seem to survive long enough to give the antibiotics a chance to work."

"Even more reason to vaccinate."

"With what? The available ones don't work."

Lisa nods, biting back her frustration. She thinks of her meeting with the representatives from Delaware Pharmaceuticals. They might not be ready to distribute Neissovax in Seattle, but as she stares down at Zeke's ashen face, she realizes the city might be literally dying for access to it.

"You have to choke off the source, Lisa."

"We hoped we had. We've tracked down every attendee of that camp. We've started all of them on prophylactic antibiotics. And we've covered as many of their household contacts as we've been able to reach."

He motions to the patient. "Then how do you explain this?"

"Zeke is a piano teacher for the Mitchell family."

"As in Noah Mitchell?"

"Yes, the third victim," Lisa says of one of the patients who was lucky enough to survive the infection and has already been discharged from the ICU. "Zeke gave Noah a piano lesson the day he got back from camp."

"A piano lesson? That was enough for this thing to spread into the community?"

"Apparently," she mumbles, struck again by the relatively casual nature of the contact.

Edwin opens his mouth to reply, but he's cut off by the shrill wail from the overhead monitor.

Lisa's eyes dart to the chaotic squiggly line running across the screen, signaling ventricular fibrillation.

Edwin shoots a gloved hand up to Zeke's neck. "No pulse!"

Lisa reacts instinctively. She lunges forward and clamps her interlocking palms onto Zeke's breastbone. She rhythmically pumps her arms, aiming for a hundred thrusts per minute, feeling the rubbery spring of his chest with each compression.

Other staff members flood into the room. A woman nudges Lisa out of the way and assumes the role of chest compressions. Lisa steps back and presses herself against the wall to make space for the expanding team.

Edwin directs the others with concise words and gestures as each person occupies a space without being told where to go. Soon Zeke is surrounded. Defibrillator conducting pads are slapped to his chest on either side of the hands of the woman performing CPR, without her breaking her rhythm.

"Shock at two hundred joules!" Edwin orders.

As soon as the woman's hands are free of the chest, another nurse presses defibrillator paddles to the pads on Zeke's chest. "All clear!" she cries. With a quick scan to establish no one else will be in contact with the current, she depresses both red buttons on the paddles' handles.

Zeke's body jerks from the shock. But after a moment, the tracing line on the monitor reverts to its helter-skelter course. "Resume CPR!" Edwin says.

A husky man wordlessly takes over, compressing Zeke's chest even deeper than the woman had.

"One milligram of epinephrine push," Edwin orders. "And three hundred milligrams of amiodarone."

A nurse injects medications through the syringe into the intravenous line in Zeke's neck while another holds a second loaded syringe out ready for her.

Someone else calls, "Two minutes!"

The CPR is paused while Zeke is shocked again. But the jerky tracing on the monitor refuses to budge from that of ventricular fibrillation.

More shocks are applied. More meds ordered. The CPR is never stopped for more than seconds at a time.

Lisa silently admires the calm choreographed dance of the attempted resuscitation. But none of the interventions make a difference.

She feels it in her bones. Zeke is already gone.

CHAPTER 14

It's hard to remember how many times this experiment has been repeated over the past six months. But practice makes perfect, and in this case, perfect is a necessity. Especially, since the next time, it won't be a dry run.

The powder floats briefly on the surface but then begins to dissolve with a minimal shake of the vial. Soon, the clear liquid inside the vial rolls smoothly back and forth. Nothing precipitates out, no matter how hard it's shaken. It could pass for water. It looks identical to the other vials.

Perfection in a bottle.

CHAPTER 15

It's been a good streak by Pacific Northwest standards, Lisa thinks as raindrops spit across her windshield. It hasn't rained for over two weeks, which isn't that unusual for August. Unlike the rest of the year, when a week without precipitation in Seattle would be newsworthy, the summer often brings protracted dry spells. Still, Lisa's mood reflects the charcoal skies above. It's been a while since anyone died in front of her eyes, which is disturbing enough, but Zeke's case also represents the escalation of the outbreak that she had dreaded: community spread.

Lisa parks in the garage below her office and heads upstairs, hoping to reach her desk without having to speak to anyone. But Tyra stops her the moment she steps into the main office.

"We found him!" Tyra waves a piece of paper triumphantly at her.

"You found whom?" Lisa asks.

"Alex Stephanopoulos."

Lisa shrugs, unable to share in her colleague's obvious enthusiasm.

"Alex happens to be Grace Brown's boyfriend," Tyra says.

"The second victim?" Lisa says, perking up.

"I'm thinking we need to renumber the victims now. Grace was the second person to land in the ER and, sadly, the second to die. But I think she might actually be our very first victim."

"Because?"

"Her boyfriend is Patient Zero."

Lisa grabs the page from Tyra's hand. "Are you saying this Alex . . ."

"Stephanopoulos."

"Connects back to Iceland?"

Tyra points to the page. Lisa looks down at the image of five people, two adults and three kids, posing in front of a towering narrow waterfall. "That's Skógafoss—" Tyra exaggerates the *sh* sounds. "Or, however the hell you pronounce that mouthful."

"The boyfriend's family was in Iceland recently?"

"Less than two weeks ago, if you trust Instagram."

"How did you figure that out?"

"The nurses went through all of the victims' social media accounts. Stacy found a bunch of pictures of Alex on Grace's Instagram page, including a few from Iceland. The parents had no idea Grace and Alex were even dating. That's why no one made the connection sooner."

"Brilliant work, Ty. The whole staff." Lisa briefly clasps her palms together under her chin. "Is this Alex sick?"

Tyra shakes her head. "Just spoke to the mom. Alex is fine. And he never got sick over there or since he came home."

"You're convinced he's the one who brought the bacteria back from Reykjavík?"

"Yolanda is on her way to collect swabs from Alex's mouth, nose, and skin. The bacterial cultures should give us confirmation within a day." Tyra grimaces. "But, come on. Alex would've been kissing Grace just last week. What are the chances she had two separate connections to Iceland?"

"So it did start from an asymptomatic carrier, after all." Lisa sighs. "First, the spread into the community. Now this. Just when you think it couldn't get much worse."

"Lisa, haven't I taught you anything?" Angela Chow bellows from somewhere behind her. "It can *always* get worse."

"Apparently," Lisa says as she turns around. Angela's complexion is even paler this morning.

Lisa leads the two women inside her office and closes the door. She gestures to them to have a seat and then sits down across the desk from them. "I just came from Harborview," she says, and goes on to describe Zeke's cardiac arrest.

"He got antibiotics immediately?" Angela asks.

"Within minutes of reaching the ER," Lisa says. "Sounds like it was only an hour or two after he felt the first flicker of a headache."

"This little fucker is as deadly as bugs come."

"And it's spread into the community now."

"Even more reason to vaccinate."

Tyra's forehead creases. "With what? That experimental vaccine you tried to convince the drug company to release?"

Lisa sinks down into her own chair. "Neissovax."

Angela glances at Tyra. "You happen to know of any other effective vaccines?"

"Still unproven outside of the lab, though," Lisa says. "They did emphasize that."

"Those pharmaceutical types are paid to be overcautious." Angela shakes her head. "I did a little reading up on my own. Neissovax shows impressive immunogenicity."

"What does it matter?" Tyra looks from Angela to Lisa. "You told me they're not willing to release it."

"Maybe we just need to apply more pressure. What if the CDC were to weigh in?" Lisa motions to Angela. "You do seem to have a rapport with Dr. Moyes."

"Alistair and I do go back," Angela says, but there's no affection in her tone.

"Can you get him to apply some pressure for us through the CDC?"

Angela considers it for a moment. "Maybe we don't need his help."

"What are you talking about?"

"Jesus." Angela rolls her eyes. "I honestly thought I taught you better, Lisa. If people are blocking your way, and you can't get past them on either side . . ."

Lisa chuckles. "Then go over their heads."

"Yup."

"Over the executive VP's head? That would be the CEO, wouldn't it?"

"It would."

"Why not?" Lisa picks up her phone and dials her assistant's line. As soon as Ingrid answers, Lisa says, "Can you please try to track down the CEO of Delaware Pharmaceuticals for me? And tell him it's urgent."

Ten minutes later, Ingrid buzzes back announcing that the CEO, Peter Moore, is waiting on the other line. Lisa picks up on speakerphone. She introduces Tyra and Angela and then says, "Thank you so much for taking our call."

"Anytime, Dr. Dyer," Moore says. "Nathan and Fiona both spoke highly of you."

Lisa finds it telling that someone as busy as the CEO of a major pharmaceutical company recognizes her name. "I assume you're aware of the situation here in Seattle."

"Nathan briefed me," Moore says. "But even if he hadn't, I would've known. After all, your outbreak is making national news."

"And the situation has worsened since your people left."

"I'm sorry to hear that."

"Thank you, but we don't really need your sympathy," Lisa says. "What we do need is access to your company's new vaccine."

"Dr. Dyer, we took your department's request very seriously. That's why Nathan and Fiona flew out to see you."

"To let me down in person."

"To show you how much we respected your predicament and your request," Moore says. "It was a very difficult decision for Nathan."

"But the situation has changed since our conversation," Lisa argues. "We now have community spread."

There's a brief pause. "That is concerning," he says quietly.

"And, as you pointed out, the outbreak is making national headlines. If Delaware were to get involved, imagine the free publicity it would provide."

"Maybe so, but despite the old saying, not all publicity is good," Moore says. "Besides, this is about far more than just marketing. I appreciate how serious this infection is. But our company is not . . . prepared for the potential medicolegal ramifications of an American release."

"If the release were on compassionate grounds, you'd be protected, Mr. Moore. You would also be covered through NVICP." Lisa cites the initials for the National Vaccine Injury Compensation Program. The elaborate federal program was created thirty years prior as a substitute to class-action lawsuits to protect patients while limiting potential damages against manufacturers to ensure that companies continued to develop new vaccines. Even so, the adjudicated program had already cost the industry billions in payouts.

"A pharmaceutical company protected by the NVICP? That's almost an oxymoron." Moore chuckles. "Truth is: nothing could protect us from the fallout of an unexpected or untoward outcome."

"How would a massive trial in Reykjavík be any less risky?"

"To begin with, it's not on US soil. Not subject to American laws . . . or lawyers. And we'd have the control. The infrastructure. The safety valves. All in place. It's a trial that has been in development for several months. Not a kneejerk reaction to a brand-new crisis."

"That's the point. This is a crisis. And, as a colleague of mine loves to say, 'Never let a crisis go to waste,'" Lisa says with a nod to Angela.

"I like that." Moore laughs again. "However, I have to defer to Nathan's opinion. After all, he's responsible for product development and release."

Before Lisa can respond, Angela jumps in. "Mr. Moore, it's Dr. Chow here." She brings a finger to her lips, and then says, "Lisa reports to me on this. And, of course, my co-lead, Dr. Moyes, with the CDC."

"I see."

"Very soon, it will not just be Seattle Public Health making this request. It will come from the CDC, the state, and potentially even federal authorities."

"And we would entertain any and all such requests that would come through those channels," he says coolly.

"Good." Angela appears unfazed, even though Moore just called her bluff. "Also, do you happen to be familiar with MENGOC-BC?"

"Not particularly."

"It's a vaccine developed in Cuba in the late eighties," Angela explains. "It was hugely successful in fighting off a meningitis outbreak at the time in Havana."

Lisa remembers reading about the legendary vaccine, but she hasn't heard it mentioned in years. Sensing where Angela is heading, she begins to shake her head.

"Because of obvious political differences, it was only ever granted a research license in the US," Angela continues. "And it has never been trialed outside of Cuba on any large scale."

"I'm not sure—" Moore begins, but Angela cuts him off.

"The very preliminary testing on our pathogen at the CDC labs suggests that MENGOC-BC produces strong immunogenicity against the same Icelandic bug."

Lisa holds up her palms and mouths the words, "What are you doing?"

Angela waves her off.

"Does it?" Moore asks.

"It appears to," Angela says. "Of course, since it's only an experimental drug here, we would face the significant challenge of where to mass-produce the MENGOC-BC vaccine. But with the resources of the CDC, the state, and the federal government behind us, that's surmountable." She taps her temple and looks at both Lisa and Tyra. "In the past, the government has even seconded existing manufacturing plants to urgently produce vaccines. And I understand Delaware has a brand-new facility in Massachusetts."

She pauses, and when Moore doesn't comment, she continues. "I understand you already have fifty thousand doses of Neissovax ready for Iceland. Efficacy aside, that could save us vital weeks in our response versus having to produce the Cuban vaccine from scratch."

There's a long delay before Moore replies. "I'll tell you what, Dr. Chow," he says in a somber tone. "In light of the worsening outbreak in Seattle, we will revisit your department's request again with Nathan and the rest of our team."

"Thank you, Mr. Moore," Angela says. "And remember, time is spread."

As Lisa disconnects the call, she can't believe Angela's ruse might have worked. And she can't fight off her smile.

"Angela." Tyra folds her arms across her chest, her expression scolding. "Maybe you shouldn't have said all that."

"Why not?"

"Because it's not true?"

"It might be." Angela runs a finger along the bony protuberance of her cheek. "Besides, what can they do to me that cancer and fucking chemotherapy haven't done already?"

CHAPTER 16

"You don't believe that BS about Cuba, do you?" Nathan asks from where he sits across the teak desk from Peter Moore, inside the CEO's expansive thirty-ninth-floor corner office.

Nathan still hasn't adjusted to Peter's new look since his boss recovered from what he insists on describing as "only a ministroke." The new beard is foreign enough, but lately Peter has traded his Italian suits and loafers for outfits like the Indian print sweater and khakis he's wearing now. "There's a lot of mystery surrounding that Cuban vaccine," Peter says as he sips tea from an owl-shaped mug.

"They're bluffing, Peter."

"Oh, probably. But it doesn't really matter."

Nathan doubts the Peter of old—the driven, Machiavellian executive he used to be prior to his stroke—would've accepted any of this with such philosophical calm. Then again, the old Peter wouldn't have been caught dead wearing a cardigan or drinking tea from a bird-shaped mug. And especially not sporting a beard.

"How can it not matter?" Nathan struggles to keep his tone even.

"It's inevitable now," Peter says. "Particularly, if there's no there there to the Cuban story."

"How do you figure?"

"Because it would make us the only game in town when it comes to possible vaccines," Peter says. "Meningitis is spreading in Seattle, and they're desperate. What with kids dying, and all. The pressure on us to release Neissovax is only going to intensify. Even if Dr. Chow is just blowing smoke, I bet we'll soon hear from the CDC and all levels of government."

"We're not ready for this."

"Ready or not, soon we won't have a choice. They know we have a stockpile."

"Can't we stall them?" Nathan asks. "Long enough until we can dispense the vaccines in Reykjavík? After all, we do have an existing contract with the Icelandic government."

"Dumping our stockpile so they can't force our hand?" Peter grunts. "When did you become so cagey, Nathan?"

"I'm worried, Peter," he says genuinely. "It's all too rushed. Even the Reykjavík trial is premature. But this? Seattle? Dropping us into the middle of a raging epidemic without any real controls . . ."

Peter sits up straighter and lowers his mug onto a zebra-print coaster on his desk. "I've been around long enough to see that we're not going to be able to outmaneuver them. The best we can do is get out in front of this. Be proactive."

Just the thought of the logistics involved makes Nathan's heart palpitate. His gaze drifts to the floor-to-ceiling windows behind his boss. His office, though not quite as big or as strategically situated as Peter's, shares the same view. Nathan's eyes are often drawn to the United Nations' Secretariat Tower that looms at the river's edge only a few blocks away. It isn't one of his favorite buildings in Manhattan, but the simple blue-tinted glass tower has become the visual equivalent of earplugs for him when he needs to drown out the background noise and find his focus.

"Fiona is going to lose it," Nathan mutters as he turns back to Peter.

"Can't even imagine. Which is why I don't plan to be around when you break it to her." Peter's expression darkens. "You're both going to need to be on the ground in Seattle for this. Do we agree?"

Nathan thinks of Ethan and Marcus and their planned father-sons road trip to Quebec. They're supposed to leave next week. He promised Ethan, who got his learner's permit last month, that he'd let him drive some of the quieter stretches. "Wouldn't dream of being anywhere else."

"We're also going to have to delay Iceland," Peter says.

By "we," Nathan knows he means him. "I'll take care of it."

Peter reaches for his mug. "Someone told me recently that you should never let a crisis go to waste."

"Wish I believed that."

"If this goes smoothly, Nathan, it could be better for Delaware than Iceland ever would have been."

And if it doesn't, it's probably not going to be your head.

Nathan rises from the chair. "I better let them know in Seattle. We'll also need to get legal to draw up some paperwork."

As he is turning away, Peter says, "Nathan?"

"Yeah?"

"My hands are tied on this one."

"I get it, Peter."

"Good," Peter says with a small laugh. "So make damn sure nothing goes wrong in Seattle."

Nathan wishes his boss were only joking. "It's what I do."

He heads out of Peter's office and walks down the hall and around the corner to find Fiona at her desk, typing at her computer. Her office is less than a quarter the size of Peter's, and the smaller windows peer directly onto the neighboring high-rise.

Nathan raps at the open door. "A word?"

The moment Fiona looks up and makes eye contact, her face falls. She yanks off her reading glasses. "He didn't!"

Nathan shrugs. "Says he has no choice, Fiona."

"This will be a nightmare."

"It's decided."

She nods, her expression turning businesslike. "When?"

"Yesterday, ideally. Realistically, how soon could we ship?"

"The supply is already packaged and ready to go."

Nathan pulls his phone from his jacket pocket. "We might as well let them know." He taps the phone number and hits the speaker icon so Fiona can hear, too.

"Lisa Dyer," the public-health officer answers on the second ring.

"Hello, Lisa. It's Nathan Hull. From Delaware Pharmaceuticals. I'm here with Fiona Swanson."

"Oh, hi," she says without sounding the least surprised. "I wasn't expecting to hear from you so soon."

"We've been reconsidering your request, Lisa."

"That's great." Her tone warms noticeably. "What have you decided?"

"Under the right conditions, we might be willing to release our supply of vaccine to Seattle instead of Reykjavík. On compassionate grounds, of course."

"Wonderful! What conditions?"

"First, it would have to be the full distribution of the vaccine as we were planning for in Iceland. Not just targeting the highest-risk group. For the reasons we discussed in person."

"So we would have to inoculate fifty thousand people?"

"Yes."

"Hmm. And if we still need more doses after that?"

Fiona squints at him, looking as surprised as Nathan feels. "Then we'll provide it," he says.

"I think we can commit to the full round of inoculation, yes," Lisa says. "Providing, of course, we don't see any significant adverse reactions among the early vaccinated groups."

"It's a new medicine." Fiona interjects. "There will be reactions."

"And overreactions," Nathan adds. "And phantom reactions. With it being a vaccine and all, public outcry and social media fallout is inevitable."

"I realize," Lisa says. "I'm only speaking of significant and objectively verified adverse events. Not imagined or hysterical ones."

Nathan glances at Fiona, who shrugs her acceptance. "We can live with that, yes," he says. "The second condition is that Fiona and I will be present to help oversee the distribution."

"Oversee?"

"Yes," Fiona says. "We'll need full access to the storage facilities, the distribution plans, and any sites where Neissovax is to be dispensed."

"You don't trust us to run our own vaccination program?"

"This might be your program, Lisa, but it's our product and our reputation on the line," Nathan says.

"We need to be convinced of absolute quality control and compliance," Fiona adds. "It's my job. And I take it dead seriously."

After a slight pause, Lisa says, "All right, I can guarantee that."

"OK," Nathan says. "Oh, and one final condition."

"Another?" Lisa says warily.

"You need to shelter us from the anti-vaxxers."

Lisa sighs. "We'll do our best to keep Delaware out of it. We don't even have to publicize the company's name until when and if the campaign is a success."

Nathan knows it's an empty promise. Delaware's logo is stamped on every vial. But he doesn't bother to argue. He shares a despondent look with Fiona, each aware that the release of Neissovax in Seattle is inevitable. "We can be there tomorrow," he says.

"With the vaccine?" Lisa asks.

"Within a day or two, yes."

CHAPTER 17

Lisa stops at the kitchen door to view her husband and her niece as they hover over an uncooked pizza, their heads almost touching. Her mood lightens as she watches Olivia carefully distribute slices of pepperoni on top of the grated cheese.

Lisa realizes they're fortunate to have as much access to their niece as they do. Amber and her husband keep long hours running their marijuana dispensary business. Since they live in Bellevue—the affluent suburb twenty minutes outside of Seattle—they often leave Olivia for sleepovers, especially when they have evening meetings in the city.

"Dinner's not ready yet," Dominic says, looking up at Lisa with a small wink. "Your niece treats pizza toppings like they're some kind of work of art."

"I'm your niece, too," Olivia says without taking her eyes off the task.

"And my favorite one."

Olivia laughs. "I'm the only one," she says, which is true since Dominic is an only child like she is. She waves to Lisa. "Hi, Tee."

Lisa steps over and kisses Olivia on her forehead. She brushes her hand across Dominic's cheek. "Wine?" she asks him.

"OK," he says. "But only one glass for Olivia. She might have to drive home later."

Olivia giggles. "You're silly, Uncle Dom."

Lisa selects a bottle of Chilean Syrah from the rack on the counter. As she uncorks it, she contemplates again what a good father Dominic might have made. It's at these times that she appreciates her husband most, when he lets his guard down and shows his softer, playful side, one that's too often hidden behind his proud, sometimes even arrogant exterior.

Ironically, though, it was their struggle to have kids that drove the original wedge in their relationship. For the longest time, both of them assumed Lisa was the source of their infertility, because Dominic had supposedly impregnated one of his college girlfriends, who subsequently miscarried. It was only after months of invasive testing failed to find any fertility issues with Lisa that they learned Dominic's lack of viable sperm was the real problem. The sudden change in his attitude toward artificial insemination bewildered Lisa. While he had been prepared to accept a donor egg, he was unwilling to consider using anyone else's sperm to impregnate Lisa. He wasn't even open to the possibility of adoption. And the flip-flop—which Lisa still views as the ultimate hypocrisy—opened a fissure in their foundation that was only compounded by his envy over her job promotion.

Lisa whips together a salad while Olivia and Dominic finish the pizza and put it in the oven. The dinner chatter is light and frivolous, focused mainly on Olivia's excitement over the impending start of first grade at her new school—the friends she will make, the supplies she will need, and the activities she plans to master. Not dancing, though. Olivia stresses how she is "done for good" with ballet. Ever the tomboy, just like her aunt. They finish the meal with Neapolitan ice cream, Olivia's favorite. All three spoons feeding from one carton.

Once Olivia changes into pajamas and brushes her teeth—under Lisa's watchful eye because she has faked it before—they climb into bed together in the spare room that has effectively become Olivia's bedroom. They take turns reading paragraphs from one of Olivia's favorite books, featuring a wisecracking rabbit who goes to school with the rest of the kids. Olivia reads her passages so well that Lisa has a sneaking suspicion she must have memorized the words.

Olivia has always been a poor sleeper, prone to nightmares, so Lisa stays with her until she's certain her niece is asleep. She even nods off briefly herself, before she eases out of bed and joins Dominic on the sofa in the living room, where he's refilled both wineglasses.

"Thanks for doing such a good job with Olivia tonight," Lisa says.

"She's my niece, too, Lees."

"Of course, but I know you had to come home early for her."

"The cath lab wasn't too busy today," he says of the cardiac catherization unit where he works. "Speaking of work, they were talking about your meningitis thing on the news again tonight."

"It's kind of terrifying, Dom."

"A real public-health emergency, after all."

She leans in closer to him, resting her shoulder against his. "See?"

"So what's next? A vaccine?"

"Yeah, we hope so. But the only one we believe will work is basically experimental. It's a bit risky. And it's gonna be controversial."

"The anti-vaxxers?"

Lisa nods. "I had a public forum earlier in the week about the HPV vaccine. And the whole room practically piled on me—"

"I know that feeling! Just yesterday, at our staff meeting, I was trying to convince the other cardiologists to consider a new catheter that has strong evidence of better anticlotting properties. But do you think for one moment they would listen to logic or all the recent solid data behind it? No, of course not. They all know better than me."

She listens as he rails on about his colleagues' resistance to trialing the new device he covets. Much as she appreciated his flicker of interest in her world, she sees that he cannot sustain it. It always has to come back to him, usually sooner rather than later.

Lisa recognized Dominic's self-absorption before they married. She assumed it was a residual effect of being raised as an only child—something she could live with and perhaps eventually tame. But as time passed and their divide grew, she came to realize he wouldn't, or at least couldn't, change. Too often, she feels like just a passenger in their relationship.

CHAPTER 18

Six of the chairs around the conference table are empty. The attrition is natural for any committee like the Outbreak Control Team, which meets daily at the offices of Seattle Public Health. Besides, three members have logged in this morning via videoconference. The only vacant seat that catches Lisa's eye is the one usually occupied by Angela. Her friend didn't mention anything about missing today's briefing, and Lisa can't help but jump to conclusions. Angela seemed even more frail yesterday, at one point sitting down quickly in the main office as if she were suddenly light-headed.

One of the attributes Lisa has always admired most about Angela is her at times painful candor. Whether complaining about her "deadbeat" daughter—who dropped out of college to find herself and work "whenever the muse strikes her" as a Pilates instructor—or joking about her husband's clinginess, Angela used to be an open book. But that changed with her diagnosis. All Lisa knows about her friend's ovarian cancer is that it must be too far advanced for a surgical cure, since her treatment has consisted only of chemotherapy. Angela has never discussed her prognosis. When she asked Lisa to assume the role of chief public-health officer, she only said,

"Don't worry. I wouldn't come back to this dead-end job, even if I do beat this thing."

Making a mental note to call Angela after the meeting, Lisa taps the remote and launches the first slide on the screens on either side of the room. As usual, it shows the updated survey of known cases. "Today is officially the sixth day of this outbreak," she says. "And as of this morning, we have eleven deaths among the twenty-four confirmed meningococcal infections. Seven of the victims have recovered enough to be safely discharged home. In the past twenty-four hours, we've had four new cases and one more death."

"Which is better than any other day so far," Benning, the mouse-like woman from the department of health, comments.

"But this isn't like the flu or even COVID-19," Tyra points out.

"What does that mean?" Benning asks.

"With highly contagious outbreaks like those, you expect to see a steady rise in the trend of new infections," Lisa says. "The so-called epi curve, when you plot it out on a graph. In other words, each day brings more new sufferers than the previous one. When the number of new cases decreases from one day to the next—even as the absolute number of infected continues to rise—you can assume the curve is flattening and the epidemic is coming under control."

"Not true of meningococcus, though," Tyra says.

"Sadly, not," Lisa agrees. "Meningococcus tends to spread in patchy clusters. Days can pass between new cases. It's not airborne, so it's not nearly as contagious as COVID-19 or measles. But it can be carried by asymptomatic hosts: people who show no signs of illness but still act as reservoirs for the spread of new infection."

"Which is just how our outbreak started," Tyra says. "With Patient Zero, Alex Stephanopoulos. He brought it home from Iceland without ever falling ill himself."

"You've confirmed that?" Alistair Moyes strokes his Lincoln-esque beard with his thumb and forefinger.

"Yes. His nasal swabs were positive for meningococcus." Lisa wonders again how many others are unwittingly carrying the deadly pathogen. "Moreover, there is no active disease in Iceland right now. This means Alex acquired it from another asymptomatic carrier. Icelandic Public Health is trying to track down and test everyone the family was in contact with."

"It's been five months since the last infection over there." Tyra extends a hand in Benning's direction. "You see? This is exactly why you can't declare an outbreak over until a full year has passed between new cases."

The color drains from Benning's cheeks as she nods her under-standing.

Lisa advances the slide, which shows a pie chart that, unlike at the last briefing, is now uniformly red. "We've reached all the attendees and staff at Camp Green now. And we've started every one of them and their closest contacts on prophylactic antibiot-ics. Unfortunately, now that we've seen two cases of secondary spread into the community, we know this measure isn't going to be enough."

"Like closing the barn door after the horses have already left," Tyra says.

Lisa brings up the next slide, which shows an image of a syringe with a caption below from a review journal that reads: *Trial shows strong immunogenicity for new meningococcal vaccine.*

"There might be some good news on the vaccine front," Lisa announces.

"What news?" asks the usually silent, balding city hall official who is watching via videoconference.

"Delaware Pharmaceuticals has developed a vaccine." Lisa goes on to describe Neissovax, the promise it has shown against the Ice-landic strain of meningococcus, and the company's agreement to redirect the supply earmarked for Reykjavík to the Pacific North-west instead.

Moyes squints at her. "You intend to inoculate fifty thousand

Seattleites with an experimental drug? One that has never been re-leased on any scale beyond a few early-phase-three trials?"

Moyes's skepticism is annoyingly contagious. "Neissovax is the only vaccine shown to be effective for this outbreak," Lisa says with less confidence than she would've liked.

"Shown? That's debatable. But even so, why not just vaccinate the highest-risk group? Those in closest proximity—in terms of age and geography—to the known victims."

"The company wouldn't agree to that."

Moyes offers her a tight-lipped smile. "It's up to the company, is it?"

"They're doing this on a voluntary basis. On compassionate grounds." Lisa goes on to explain the concerns Nathan raised about vaccinating only the highest-risk subset. "Perhaps, Alistair, if the CDC were to get involved . . ."

"We can't force a company to release its product any more than you can," he says. "However, at the height of the Ebola crisis, the CDC and WHO both had access to an experimental vaccine. But even then, when it was raging in Africa and over eighty percent of victims were dying, including health-care workers—we still re-fused to release the vaccine because it had not undergone rigorous enough clinical testing."

Lisa meets the CDC physician's glare. "You can't compare the two situations."

"Why not?"

"Because that Ebola vaccine hadn't completed any phase-three trials. Neissovax has. And the only two Ebola deaths on US soil were both cases imported from Africa."

"You're suggesting that if Ebola was spreading among Ameri-cans, the CDC would have released the vaccine?"

"You know you would have, Alistair." Benning speaks up, sur-prising Lisa with her forcefulness. "That's how government works."

"I don't happen to agree," Moyes says, and turns back to Lisa.

"Regardless, vaccinating this many people will pose huge logistical challenges."

"Thanks for that insight." Lisa immediately regrets her sarcastic tone, but Moyes shows no obvious sign of offense. "Our team plans to set up and run vaccination clinics across the city in schools, community centers, and so on."

"Who will you target for vaccination?"

"The highest-risk demographics. Teenagers, teachers, health-care workers, and so on."

"And how do you intend to track any adverse events or unexpected dangers associated with the vaccine?"

"We'll obviously use the VAERS database so people can self-report," Lisa says. "But we're also setting up a twenty-four-hour hotline and a specific website along with an app for patients to directly report any issues with Neissovax."

"An app? That's your solution?"

"One of them."

"This is premature." Moyes shakes his head. "What does Angela think?"

Lisa takes a breath to run through her five-senses exercise—the sight of Moyes's beard, the hum of the fluorescent lights, the pressure of her heels against her shoes, the scent of an alcohol-based cleaner, and the residual taste of the mint she sucked on prior to the meeting—before responding. "Angela is a valued member of this team. But I am the city's chief public-health officer."

His stare is frosty. "And the buck stops with you, does it?"

"Yes," she says, trying to will away her creeping doubt. "In this case, it does."

CHAPTER 19

Mason can't stop shaking. Even when he bundles himself up in his favorite Mariners jacket. But nothing is going to stop him from going to the ballpark this afternoon. He has been looking forward to it for weeks. Ever since his Little League team lost their final playoff game.

Mason was the last batter in that game, and he grounded out. He hid his tears well, but he felt so responsible for the loss that he couldn't touch his pizza at the postgame meal. Coach Tony took him aside and let him in on the "surprise" that he had been saving for the team. Tony had gotten a box for Mason and all his eight-year-old teammates to attend a matinee Major League game. And the best part was the Mariners were going to play his other favorite team, the Red Sox.

Mason has been counting the days since. Even though his head aches, and he feels too queasy to even think about eating a hot dog at the game, he's more determined than ever to go. If only he could stop trembling.

Mason knows that if his mom sees him like this, she won't let him out of the house. So he digs his favorite winter sweater out of the bottom drawer and slips it on before wrapping himself back in his oversized Mariners' jacket. He can't believe he has to wear two layers in the summer just to keep warm, but he hopes it will do the trick. It will be so worth it once he's in the box with the rest of his friends, watching his two favorite teams slug it out at T-Mobile Park. With all that batting power in the lineups, there will be some homers for sure.

Mason stays in his room as he long as he can, willing away the chills and waiting for Liam's dad to pull up in front. Only when he hears the minivan roll up to the curb does he head downstairs.

His mom is waiting at the front door with a water bottle in one hand and a twenty-dollar bill in the other. "Mason, honey? You feeling all right?"

"I'm OK, Mom."

"Baby, you don't look so good." She reaches for his forehead, but he arches away from her touch.

"You'll mess my hat, Mom!"

"Mason . . ."

Grabbing the dangling bill from her hand, he squeezes past her and out the door. "There will be water and drinks at the game. Liam's waiting for me."

"Baby, I don't think you should . . ."

Before she can say another word, Mason rushes out into the bright August sunshine. He should be boiling under all the clothing, but he feels as if he's stepped into an ice rink. It's all he can do to keep moving. To not wrap his jacket tighter and drop shaking to the ground.

His head pounds more with each step.

But there's no way he's going to miss this game.

CHAPTER 20

The first thing to catch Lisa's eye is the armed security guards manning the doors. Aside from them, the open space resembles any other warehouse, down to the cement floors, bare walls, and a side-by-side set of metal roller doors for delivery access.

A forklift rumbles past her carrying a tower of boxes on its way to the pile already stacked in the center of the room. A faint whiff of lumber hangs in the air, though no wood is in sight, so Lisa assumes the previous tenants must have stored timber. The hum of fans draws her attention to the only other anomaly in the warehouse, a bank of refrigerators against the near wall. Fiona and Nathan stand beside them talking to three men in orange overalls. Nathan looks over and, recognizing Lisa, beckons her with a welcoming wave.

Lisa reciprocates the greeting, though she can't help questioning the sincerity of his smile. Wearing another slim-fit navy suit along with a brown leather belt and matching oxfords, Nathan is the epitome of a rising corporate star. Lean and fit with sandy-brown hair, he has a Roman nose, strong chin, and a youthful face. In truth, she doesn't know his actual age, but she assumes he must be well into his forties to occupy such a senior position at a major pharmaceutical company. He has been consistently respectful, professional, and, as best she can tell, forthright with her. And, yet, she doesn't trust him. She can't tell if she's responding to her intuition or her natural bias against executives, especially those who work for pharmaceutical companies—an industry that schools its members on how to charm physicians.

The men in orange have dispersed by the time Lisa joins Nathan and Fiona beside a pile of boxes stacked in front of one of the refrigerators. After quick hellos, she says, "I didn't expect you to show up with all the vaccine today."

"Technically, we flew commercial while those were shipped charter." Nathan motions to the boxes. "You did say you wanted them as soon as possible."

"Not complaining. Not at all. Just surprised. And I certainly wasn't expecting you to book the storage facilities."

Fiona squints at her. "There's no way we would entrust this to anyone else."

Lisa glances over to one of the security guards. "Apparently."

"This is Delaware's biggest product release in almost five years, Lisa. We have so much riding on it." Nathan taps his chest with two fingers. "We have to protect it with our lives."

"Your lives aren't the ones at stake. But I get it."

Nathan bends down and flips open one of the boxes near his feet. He cracks open the Styrofoam packaging, extracts a yellow-topped vial, and holds it out to Lisa. "A lot of fuss over something as simple as this, huh?"

Lisa takes the almost weightless plastic vial between a thumb and index finger and rotates it from side to side, inspecting the clear fluid as it rolls inside. "It's the standard half-a-ml dose, right?"

Fiona nods. "Already reconstituted. But it does need to be shaken well before use. And always administer in the deltoid muscle. Preferably the left arm, for consistency."

Lisa resists the urge to remind the other woman that she's not a novice when it comes to vaccinations. "And it has to be refrigerated?"

"Always. Between four and eight degrees Celsius." Fiona reaches out for the vial, and Lisa passes it back to her.

"When do you want to start?" Nathan asks.

"We had been targeting early next week," Lisa says. "But since you've already brought the supply, we could start as soon as tomorrow. We just need to finalize the locations of the vaccination clinics."

Fiona closes the box and looks up at Lisa. "We'll need to know how many sites you plan to run simultaneously."

"And why's that?"

"Because we'll need to have enough team members at each of them."

Lisa crosses her arms. "There's no way anyone aside from my nurses will be administering the vaccine."

"They can give the shots," Fiona says. "But there's no way anyone outside of *my* team will be transporting or handling the vials."

"We're all on the same team," Nathan says. "Think of us as your lackeys, Lisa. Your Amazon Prime for the new vaccine."

"Why not? Amazon basically owns Seattle, anyway." Lisa breaks off eye contact with Fiona. She doesn't resent her stance. In fact, she admires it. Fiona exudes competence. And Lisa appreciates what it means to be passionate about your job.

"So how do you plan to publicize the vaccination campaign?" Nathan asks.

"We're going to make an announcement later today."

He frowns. "A press conference?"

"A social media launch combined with a press release. No doubt the mainstream media will have plenty of questions. Might as well tackle them head-on."

He shakes his head. "Delaware won't be making any public comments on this trial."

"Launch," Fiona corrects.

Nathan and Fiona share a quick look, and Lisa wonders if there's a reprimand in his eyes, but she can't tell.

"Whatever you want to call it, we're not willing to be drawn into the media side of this," he says.

"Understood," Lisa says.

"Did your office sign off on the patient-consent forms?"

Lisa nods. The forms contain the standard legalese absolving Delaware Pharmaceuticals of any liability from complications of the vaccination. Lisa knows as well as Nathan that they wouldn't stand up in court, but it's a typical deterrent used in all drug trials. "We will get consent from all patients or, in the case of minors, their guardians, before giving the vaccine," she says.

"Good."

"And have you had a chance to review our app for reporting vaccine-related complications?"

"We have," Fiona answers for him. "It looks similar to the existing national VAERS site for reporting adverse events."

"It's meant to," Lisa says. "We plan to put our link on Seattle Public Health's home page and plaster it everywhere else we can think of. If there are any early signals of complications, we'll pick up on them right away."

Nathan sighs. "No matter how this campaign goes, you're going to pick up on a whole lot of noise, you do realize?"

"Always the way with vaccines," Lisa says sympathetically. "Hopefully, it's all just precautionary."

"It's not too late to reconsider, Lisa."

"To reconsider what?"

"All of this."

"I don't get it. The early trials have been so promising. Why can't you look at this as a huge opportunity for Neissovax?"

His shoulders sag. "There haven't been as many new cases of meningitis in the past few days, have there?"

"Another seventeen-year-old died last night," Lisa says. "You know how it is with meningococcus. It waxes and wanes. It doesn't behave anything like the flu."

"But what if this outbreak is naturally resolving? What if it's about to disappear just like it did in Iceland?"

"It's way too early to contemplate that."

"But if it is, and you subject the whole city to an immunization campaign with an experimental vaccine . . ."

Lisa doesn't blame him for his reticence. The same concern has already crossed her mind. As her gaze drifts to one of the rigid security guards and comes to rest on the holster on his belt, she feels the sudden weight of responsibility pressing heavily on her shoulders. The buck does stop with her. As does the potential liability of exposing an entire city to an unproven vaccine.

A phone rings, and Nathan reaches into his pocket and pulls his out. Lisa sees the name *Peter* on the flashing screen.

"Excuse me," he says. "I have to get this. I'll just be a minute."

"Can't be easy, huh?" Fiona says to Lisa, once Nathan has stepped out of earshot.

"What can't?"

Fiona's gaze softens. "Being responsible for controlling an outbreak like this."

"It's not like I'm doing it alone. I've got a terrific team," Lisa says, downplaying the accuracy of the observation.

"I suppose, but I can still empathize. My role is all about managing risk and exposure."

"Yeah, but you seem so . . . certain to me. Like you never doubt."

"And you do?" Fiona raises an eyebrow. "You strike me as supremely confident. Fully in charge. How you persuaded Peter Moore, of all people, to change his mind about releasing Neissovax is nothing short of a miracle. He's a stubborn as they come."

"I've had a lifetime of experience with pigheaded men, but to be honest, I'm not the one who convinced him." Lisa feels herself relaxing, enjoying the moment of candor. "Besides, the deeper I get, the harder it is not to second-guess myself."

Fiona smiles. "Maybe we're both just good actors, huh?"

"Maybe. But acting only gets you so far."

CHAPTER 21

Yolanda Stern sits at the back of the conference room, listening to the announcement. Unlike the other public-health nurses, she never speaks up at meetings. If she has questions, she saves them for later and emails her boss, Tyra, who's always so conscientious about answering in a nonjudgmental way.

Her whole life, Yolanda has been a wallflower. By choice. She avoids public attention at all costs. Her therapist blames Yolanda's mother for being overbearing and overprotective. But Yolanda knows better. She doesn't like the sound of her own voice. And she's never been comfortable in her own skin. If she could only shed those stubborn twenty extra pounds, she's convinced she would feel more confident in group situations. The exercise and diets never seem to work out for her as billed, but that doesn't stop her from endlessly trying.

Yolanda does have questions for Tyra, though. This new vaccine rollout has come out of nowhere and seems insanely ambitious, targeting fifty thousand people over the next three to four weeks. *How can we possibly achieve that?*

Yolanda already knows what her boyfriend, Max, will make of the vaccination campaign. She wants to tell him, but Tyra has sworn the staff to secrecy until the announcement is made public later today. Besides, Yolanda vividly remembers how much the news of the mandatory HPV vaccine enraged Max. She doesn't want to add to his burden. The poor man suffers enough.

Yolanda was thrilled when she matched with Max online, six months earlier. She fell in love with the handsome doctor by the end of their first date. He listened to her in a way no man—especially anyone from a dating app—had ever done. And he was so interested in her career. Most of the other dates didn't even seem to notice or care that she worked as a public-health nurse. But Max brought it up within minutes of their first meeting.

Yolanda had never met a naturopath before, but she was wowed by the breadth and depth of Max's knowledge and the way he made her feel so at ease from the outset. She did have some serious reservations when she first learned about his fierce anti-vax beliefs. Vaccinations are an essential part of her job. And before meeting Max, she had never once questioned their necessity. But he was so persuasive. So dogged. He sent her scientific article after article, filled with data, to back up his passionate views. It was enough to make Yolanda question the value of some vaccines, like the one against HPV. It definitely gave her more sympathy for the anti-vax side, especially once she learned how much his poor son struggled with what Max blamed on a vaccine injury. Besides, she was already so smitten that Max could've probably told her the moon landing was faked and 9/11 was an inside job, and she still would've stuck with him.

"So tomorrow morning at nine a.m., we'll open the first clinic," Tyra announces, drawing Yolanda back to the moment. "It's going to be all hands on deck. We're hoping to get at least five hundred clients through. And there's bound to be lots of kinks to iron out. After the first clinic, we'll divide up and run multiple sites across the city." Her gaze circles the room. "Tomorrow is our dress rehearsal, people. Let's get it right."

"Hey, Tyra," calls Felix. He lifts a copy of the generic consent form that Tyra handed out before the meeting. "You expect us to go through this whole form with each client and/or parent before *every* single vaccination?"

"No vaccine without a signature." Tyra wags her finger. "But that's why there'll be two of you at each station. One nurse reviews the consent form while the other labels a syringe and draws up a fresh vial of the vaccine."

"Fun," Felix grumbles.

"You get to swap halfway," Tyra says. "And word around the office is that you love to swap, Felix."

Even Yolanda laughs. Felix and his wife are devout Catholics, but the joke has followed him ever since they showed up at last year's Halloween party—the theme of which was "come as you aren't"—dressed as swingers.

"And while the vaccine is a huge priority for us, so is the continued contact tracing," Tyra says. "We still need to follow up with every single new meningitis victim and ensure all their close contacts are started on appropriate antibiotics."

A collective moan rises in the room.

Tyra blows them an exaggerated kiss. "This is why I love you folks so much! There's nothing this team can't do when we set our mind to it."

But fifty thousand vaccinations in two weeks? Yolanda thinks. *Oh my God, Max is going to lose his mind.*

CHAPTER 22

"**H**ave you called Mom yet??" Amber's text reads.

Lisa can practically hear the accusation in her sister's written words. The guilt creeps up again.

She peeks at the time. The communications team sent out a press release and launched the supporting social media campaign earlier in the afternoon, but the response from the media was so overwhelming they decided to hold a formal press conference. Lisa still has forty-five minutes before she has to face the reporters.

No time like the present.

Lisa picks up her phone and calls her mom's number. It's the landline for both of her parents, since neither of them carries a mobile. Something about cell towers and electromagnetic fields. She can't even keep up with all her dad's conspiracy theories.

Her parents still live on the same farm in eastern Washington, about forty miles outside of Spokane, where Lisa and her sister grew up. It began as a decentralized farming commune that was intended to be a self-sufficient nirvana for the enlightened and the disenfranchised. It bore all the stereotypical attributes of such a commune—or a cult, as she sometimes thought of it in her teen years: group parenting, potluck meals, homeschooling, "gentle forestry," beekeeping, natural building, varied crafts, and live arts. In retrospect, Lisa suspects that free love and open marriages could have been part of the post-hippie lifestyle there, too, but she never confirmed the hunch.

As a young child, Lisa loved the vibrant environment. The thriving grounds were filled with families and other kids to play with. She remembers music constantly playing, with live performances almost every evening. But petty squabbles—many of which her father instigated—and natural attrition eventually set in. By the time Lisa and Amber were teenagers, most of the other families had departed and there was only a skeleton crew left to manage the farm. It felt like a dying community, and Lisa couldn't wait to escape it and her father's domineering presence.

"Hello?" Her mother's voice pulls Lisa from the memories.

"Hey, Mom."

"Lisa!" says Elizabeth Dyer, whom most people know as Beth. "How are you?"

"I'm good. Fine. Very busy at work right now."

"I can only imagine."

For a moment, Lisa considers telling her mom about the meningitis outbreak. But she realizes it will mean little to her and probably only lead to an argument. Her mother has never been as vehemently opposed to Western medicine as her father is, but she would never defy his opinion, either. Beth doesn't so much share her husband's views as she absorbs them for her own. Lisa has come to see her mother as more of a disciple than a wife. As a teenager, Lisa vowed to never let a man dominate her in the same way, but sometimes she wonders if she hasn't ended up with a partner who's just as obstinate as her father.

"How's Dom?" Beth asks, as if reading her daughter's mind.

"He's all right," Lisa says. "You know how it is, Mom. There are ups and downs in every marriage."

"I suppose," Beth says, sounding unconvinced. "But you two are hanging in there? Working things out, I hope."

"We'll be fine," Lisa says, opting to bend the truth. "How are things on the farm?"

"Busy. We're still selling corn, literally by the bushel."

Lisa clears her throat. "And Dad?"

"Your father goes nonstop. Almost seventy, and he hasn't slowed one iota." She hesitates. "He would love to hear from you sometime, darling."

"OK. I'll call him soon," Lisa lies again. "I've only got time to catch up with you today."

"You're not calling with . . . news, are you?"

"What news?" Lisa asks, fully aware that her mother is hoping for word of a positive pregnancy test.

"Any kind, darling. After all, you don't call very often."

"Maybe I inherited that trait from you, Mom?"

"Amber and Allen brought Olivia over last weekend," Beth says, ignoring the barb. "That little one is growing up so quickly. She talks about you nonstop. It's kind of adorable."

"Liv's so headstrong," Lisa says, happy for the change in subject. "Were Amber or I like that at her age?"

"Both of you, in a way," Beth says. "Mainly you, though. You always needed a concrete explanation for everything. The sun, the moon, the seasons. So scientific. So skeptical of anything spiritual or faith-based. I'm not surprised you ended up as a doctor."

There's no judgment in her mother's tone, but no praise, either. Lisa doesn't understand why she still seeks her mom's approval, but she does. "This is the right life for me, Mom."

"I'm sure it is. Just as this farm is the right life for us."

"And Dad really is doing OK? He's still taking his medication?"

"Yes, darling. Every day. I promise."

"OK," Lisa says. "Well, it's good to hear your voice."

"Likewise. It would be even nicer to see your gorgeous face . . ."

"I'm only a couple hours' drive away, Mom."

"As are we, darling."

Lisa looks up to see Tyra standing expectantly at her door.

"I love you, Mom," Lisa says as she hangs up with the glum realization that there's considerably more than a hundred miles of highway keeping her and her parents apart.

Lisa and Tyra ride the elevator down to the conference room on the main floor in silence. Lisa wishes Angela was with them. Her friend would know how to handle the press. But she hasn't had any updates from Angela, who hasn't replied to the text or voice mail she sent this morning.

The room is as noisy and full as Lisa expected. Each of the forty or so chairs is occupied. A few reporters are forced to stand alongside the cameramen and photographers in the aisles. Along with a whiff of body odor, Lisa picks up on an unsettled vibe. She senses the room could turn on her quickly.

The noise only dims when she steps up to the lectern. She introduces Tyra and herself and then reads verbatim the brief press release, which officially announces the launch of the vaccination campaign. Looking up from her notes, she says, "The first vaccine clinics will open tomorrow morning at nine o'clock. We will publish the list of other sites and schedules on our web page and other social media sites. To reiterate, we are offering the vaccine to anyone between the ages of ten and twenty-five. We'll take a few questions now."

Arms shoot up across the room while some reporters just shout their questions. Ignoring them, Lisa holds up a hand and waits for the room to quiet. Finally, she points to a young woman in the first row whose arm is extended as straight as a flagpole. "Yes?"

"Is it true there have only been four new cases in the past two days?" the reporter asks.

"In the past thirty-six hours, yes."

"Isn't that a very good sign? That the outbreak is slowing down?"

"We are always pleased when the rate of infection falls," Lisa says, measuring her words carefully. "Unfortunately, two of those new cases actually represent spread of this infection into the community. In other words, beyond the camp where all the other victims came from. Moreover, we know from the Icelandic outbreak that there are carriers of this disease who show no symptoms but can still spread it to others."

"Does that guarantee it will continue to spread?" the stocky man beside the first reporter asks without being called upon.

"We don't know for certain," Lisa says. "But it is likely."

"And that's why you're launching this vaccination campaign?" the same man demands.

"One of the reasons, yes."

"Isn't it premature, Dr. Dyer?" a woman with short-cropped hair and square-framed, red glasses asks from the back row. "To expose so many people—mainly kids—to a new vaccine based on little more than handful of cases?"

"Twenty-four is more than a handful," Lisa says. "And each one of the eleven deaths is a tragedy. Seattle Public Health is committed to doing everything to prevent more loss of life. It is standard public-health practice to vaccinate the highest-risk groups—in this case, high school and college-age youths—during a meningococcal outbreak once it has spread into the community."

"But isn't this particular vaccine untested and unproven?" the woman persists.

"It's not untested," Lisa says, feeling doubt worm its way back into her consciousness. "In fact, it has been proven safe and effective in three significant clinical trials. This is our best option since the only commercially available vaccines do not prevent infections with this particular strain of bacteria."

"So you're going to use thousands of kids as guinea pigs?" another male reporter blurts from the middle of the audience.

"Not at all. We plan to monitor the response to the vaccination vigilantly. We've set up a hotline and a website for reporting unexpected reactions." Lisa begins to sweat under the glare of the camera lights and the demanding stares from the faces in the audience. She tries to clear her throat, which suddenly feels full. "The idea is to give maximum protection to the at-risk groups. And ideally to create herd immunity to this new infection. We can only accomplish that with a widespread campaign."

"What if it doesn't work?" asks another reporter whose face is hidden by the balding head of the man in front of her. "What if you're acting prematurely?"

"The only other known outbreak of this particular strain of meningitis happened in Reykjavík," Lisa says. "It's all we have for comparison. Thirty-five people died there in a matter of weeks last winter. Seattle has a population twenty times the number of Reykjavík's. If we do nothing different—in other words, if we don't try this new vaccine—then we predict our death toll could rise into the hundreds. Or more."

"You just told us you can't assume anything . . ." another reporter begins to say, but Lisa's attention is drawn by Tyra, who tugs gently at her sleeve.

Tyra leans in close enough for Lisa to feel her breath on her ear. "Just got a report of a kid on a ventilator at Children's Hospital. Meningitis and sepsis," she whispers. "Youngest case yet."

"How old?" Lisa murmurs.

"Eight. Had a full-blown seizure at a baseball game. He's from Bellevue," Tyra says of the suburb to the east of Seattle where Amber's family also lives. "Never been near Camp Green. No obvious connection to other victims."

Lisa nods, instinctively thinking of Olivia. With that, her resolve cements again as she turns back to the reporters. "As I said, the vaccine clinics will open tomorrow morning. We urge everyone in the Seattle area to bring in their children. This is the best way—maybe the only way—to prevent this outbreak from spreading."

CHAPTER 23

Max has been so absorbed in the op-ed he's been writing for the community newspaper on the mandatory HPV vaccination policy that he has been ignoring his phone for the past hour. The paper is offering him a chance to make his case with a broad readership against the ill-conceived policy. And he takes the opportunity seriously.

Max is all too aware of the stigma associated with the vaccine hesitancy movement. Many people—if not most—view them as wing nuts, zealots, or uneducated hysterics. And, in truth, Max has met a number of people in the community who do fit the bill. But most of the ones he associates with are like him, concerned people—usually parents—who are driven to effect social change. Many have suffered the devastation of a vaccine injury to themselves or a loved one. And, also like Max, many are motivated to protect others, since it's too late for their own families.

His phone buzzes again. Max turned the ringer off, but it's been vibrating steadily on his desktop, alerting him of new texts, tweets, and emails. He wonders what's causing the literal buzz, but he's on too much of a roll to stop to find out.

His concentration is finally broken when a Facebook message from Cole, his best online friend, pops up on the corner of his computer screen. "Dude, where the hell have you been? Everyone's going crazy over the news of this vaccine!" The message is punctuated with a series of emojis of exploding heads.

Max immediately saves his document and logs onto the group chat page. He scans the rolling list of messages until he reaches the top of the thread. He clicks on the link in the first message that takes him to an article describing how Seattle Public Health is launching a campaign to inoculate the youth of the city with a new meningitis vaccine.

"Not another one," he mutters to himself as he returns to the conversation thread and sees a similar response echoed in multiple messages.

Fighting back his simmering anger, Max reads every comment on the thread before posting one of his own. Some people are saying that they need more information to evaluate the dangers of this new vaccine. Others are advocating active resistance right away through social media and public protests. A march is being planned. One person, Daryl, who often goes too far in these chats, suggests that they find out where the supply is being kept and sabotage the site. "Burn it to the ground!" as Daryl puts it.

"Big Pharma always finds a way to flog their next drug," Max types. "Isn't it convenient that this 'epidemic' hits just as they're ready to market a new poison? Is it possible this is all just one ugly marketing ploy?"

The group chat lights up with responses to his comment, almost all in agreement. The like-minded people on the site see the emergence of this outbreak as more than just coincidence.

A private message from Cole pops up on his screen. "Well said, dude! Eventually they're going to figure out what dangers this new toxin poses."

"Agree," Max replies.

"Like always, though, it'll take months or years to find out what exactly that is."

"I hear you."

"If only we could tip the scales now somehow. Before it's too fucking late."

Max stares at the screen. Cole is right. All the social media posts and marches in the world won't accomplish anything.

Maybe words aren't enough this time?

He grabs his phone and calls Yolanda. "Why didn't you tell me about this new vaccine?" he asks as soon as she picks up.

"That's why I've been texting and calling you!" she replies in a slight whine. "You wouldn't answer."

As doting and sweet as Yolanda is, especially toward Jack, her neediness still grates. "Work's been crazy. And I've had Jack all week."

"I get it," she says, acquiescing too easily, as usual.

"Yolanda, I need to know everything about this new vaccine and your office's vaccination campaign."

"Why?"

"Come on. Right after the HPV debacle? They're going to force *another* vaccine on the public? This one totally unproven. You know how I feel about this."

"This meningitis is awful. It's killing kids, Max. Sometimes in just a few hours."

"How do you know this vaccine will do anything to prevent that?"

"I . . . I don't."

"And how do you know it won't end up hurting or killing even more children?"

"They wouldn't release it if it wasn't safe."

"Really?" Max scoffs. "I thought I'd already proven to you that just hasn't been the case in the past."

"Maybe. I guess."

"Listen, beautiful, I need one more favor."

"What's that?"

"Do you think you could get your hands on a few vials for me?"

"Steal the vaccine?" Yolanda's voice cracks.

"No, no," he says soothingly. "I just need the empty vials."

CHAPTER 24

The gymnasium is absolutely packed, and Nathan assumes the lineup out front—which had already formed by the time he arrived two hours before the clinic opened—must still snake around the block.

People in Seattle are scared. The news of the latest meningitis death, the boy from the ball game, has hit the city hard, especially in the emotional aftermath of the damage left by COVID-19. Someone posted a video online of him collapsing with convulsions at the Mariners game the previous afternoon, and it instantly went viral. The social media site has since pulled the clip down, but the damage was done. Nathan couldn't resist viewing it. Even beyond the voyeur's guilt, it was hard to watch. But he can't help picturing it again now.

The video was shot on a cell phone at the ballpark, under cloudless blue skies. The camera panned back and forth across the packed seats and private boxes from the perspective of somewhere in the bleachers above. Suddenly, in the left corner of the frame, there was a frenzy of movement in one of the boxes. A tinny scream followed, and a man shouted, "Call 911!" The camera zoomed in on the box. The people inside encircled a boy who lay on his back. His arms and legs twitched and jerked wildly, and his head flopped side to side as he thrashed on the ground. The video ended seconds after someone dropped down to his knees and hovered over the boy, obscuring him.

Nathan shakes off the disturbing memory, focusing instead on the activity around him. He wouldn't have missed this inaugural Neissovax immunization clinic for anything, but he's aware he's only in the way of the people doing the actual work. He stands as unobtrusively as he can behind the desks and watches with a mix of admiration, pride, and worry.

The front of the line spits a steady stream of people to the first of the five desks to free up for the next inoculation. Each desk is crewed by two public-health nurses. The first one explains the impending vaccination to the next person in line, and then gets each patient, or the guardian, to sign a consent form. Meanwhile, the second nurse draws up the vaccine under the watchful eye of a Delaware staff member, labels the syringe with a sticker, and then injects it into the exposed left upper shoulder of the recipient. Every tenth patient also has blood drawn—Nathan understands it will be used later in a comparison of the pre- and postvaccination antibody levels.

Aside from a few tears, one panic attack, and two teenagers who fainted immediately after the blood draw, the clinic seems to be proceeding smoothly. Nathan has noticed that most of the clients make it through the process from consent to vaccination in under ten minutes, usually closer to five.

And yet, the line keeps growing.

As Nathan scans the room, he can't help wondering which of the recipients will later log Seattle Public Health's website to report adverse events. Last night in his hotel room, he spent ages on the web page reviewing the self-reporting form set up specifically for Neissovax. The local form is even more nebulous than the national VAERS one. Anyone can log on and claim any possible reaction, without proof or validation. Nathan regards the whole thing as a beacon for loonies, hypochondriacs, and, especially, scammers. He believes it inevitable that people will try to milk the system for money, attention, or both. He understands that Delaware would have faced scrutiny no matter when or where Neissovax was eventually released, but with all the media attention on the vaccine and the focus this website will generate, he's fearful of the negative impact it might have on Neissovax's natural trajectory.

"Bet you wouldn't have pictured yourself standing here a few days ago," someone says.

Nathan turns to see Lisa at his side, looking very much in charge, and, he notes, attractive in a navy pantsuit. "Actually, I was kind of picturing myself in Quebec," he says.

"Quebec?"

"Family road trip."

"Oh." Lisa looks around the room. "You had to cancel because of this?"

"Postpone, hopefully."

"That sucks, Nathan."

He shrugs. "The boys took it pretty well, all things considered."

"You have sons?"

"Two. Sixteen and fourteen. The older one just got his learner's permit, and you can't keep him off the road." He grins. "Even though it would probably be best for everyone if we did."

"Two teenage boys, huh? That must be a handful for you and your wife."

"We don't handle them at the same time. We're divorced." He clears his throat and decides to ask, "How about you? Kids?"

"Nope. Got a little sparkplug of a niece—a twenty-year-old trapped in a six-year-old's body. But my husband is a workaholic. And I'm almost as bad. We're just a couple of dinks."

Nathan wonders if he misheard. "Dinks?"

She laughs self-consciously. "As in dual-income-no-kids. Guess no one uses that term anymore?"

"Thou seldom doth hear it, m'lady."

"Yeah, yeah, cute. I'm out of touch, I know." She nods to the table in front of them where a boy is squeezing his eyes shut and scrunching his neck as the nurse plunges the needle into his upper arm. "This seems to be going all right."

"So far, so good. I can't believe the demand."

"We expected it. Once we've ironed out the kinks, we'll run three or four clinics simultaneously across the city. That'll take some of the pressure off."

"Should help," he says as he watches the boy breathe a sigh of relief after the needle slides out of his arm. "I keep thinking about the poor kid from the ballpark."

"Only eight years old." Lisa shakes her head. "Even worse, it's already spreading. Three of his friends have been admitted to Children's Hospital. One of them is in the pediatric ICU. She's only seven."

"And you still haven't found the connection to the camp or other campers?"

"No," she says. "But these cases represent a distinct second cluster of the outbreak."

"That's a problem, isn't it?"

"A big problem. Bellevue is fifteen miles from Delridge."

"This pathogen is covering a lot of ground on its own."

She tilts her head. "Are you suggesting the spread might not be natural?"

"No. Not at all. Just that it's spreading far and wide."

She studies him for a long moment and then nods. "Not only that, but it's infecting a whole new age demographic."

Nathan spots the intent in her eyes. "Lisa, you're not thinking . . ."

"What choice do we have? Four cases in less than twenty-four hours. All in kids under ten. We've got to lower the age requirement to cover those kids, as well."

"Neissovax isn't approved for children under ten." Nathan

shakes his head adamantly. "It's never even been properly tested in that demographic."

"How else are we going to protect the younger kids?"

"I don't mean to sound harsh, but that's not our problem, Lisa. We've stretched our risk and exposure as far as we can on. We can't do this."

Lisa meets his stare with a look of absolute conviction. "We have to, Nathan."

CHAPTER 25

Lisa steps into her office to find Angela again seated behind her desk, with another colorful scarf tied around her head, this one in a tie-dye design. While she's still pale and gaunt, she doesn't look any worse than the last time Lisa saw her.

"Hi, stranger," Lisa says, masking her relief. "Where have you been?"

"Remind me again which one of us is paid to be here," Angela says, without taking her eyes off the computer screen.

"Good point. But everything is OK with you?"

"Depends what you mean by 'OK.' I still got a drama queen for a husband. And a daughter who thinks that you can opt out of society and still live like a top one-percenter."

Lisa sits down across from her. "You know what I mean, Angela."

"It's a process, my oncologist keeps reminding me." She shrugs. "What a miserable job she has. Makes working in public health seem like a traipse through the meadow."

"What process?"

"Well, maybe, not so much of a meadow these days, huh? What

with young kids dropping left, right, and center from meningitis. In Bellevue, right?"

Lisa realizes her friend doesn't want to talk about her own health issues, and she knows better than to pry. "Yeah, four kids now. A new cluster in Bellevue, all from around the same neighborhood. But we have no idea how the index case—the boy from the ball game—connects back to the camp." She swallows. "Only eight years old. He died in the middle of the night."

Angela closes her eyes for a moment. "What do the parents say?"

"I'm going out to see them this morning."

"Want some company?"

"No. Thanks, though." Lisa also declined Tyra's offer to accompany her, sensing that another person—even one as sympathetic as Tyra or Angela—would only make it more uncomfortable for the parents. "I think this is a one-person job."

"Maybe oncology isn't looking like such a miserable career after all." Angela sighs. "How did the first clinic go yesterday?"

"Surprisingly well. No medical disasters. No protests. No huge meltdowns."

"Excellent. How many people were vaccinated?"

"Eight hundred," Lisa says. "Double what we planned for on the first day. They were still lined up for blocks when we closed the clinic. The biggest complaints were from those who didn't get inoculated."

"And what about the website? Anything untoward?"

"There are fourteen reactions listed so far." The data is fresh in her mind, as Lisa spent the last hour before coming to work reviewing the first reactions to be logged onto the website. "Most were redness or sore arms near the site of injection. Very typical for any vaccination. Two unusual ones, and I tracked down both of their parents. One mom said her daughter had a high fever. But I soon learned that she considers ninety-nine point two degrees to be a critically elevated temp. And that was before taking Tylenol."

Angela rolls her eyes. "And the other one?"

"A kid with a diffuse rash. Her mom texted me a couple of photos." Lisa grabs her phone, finds the photos, and turns the screen around for Angela to see the images of the girl's exposed thighs, which bear scattered red wheel-like welts the size of nickels. "They're definitely hives. But the kid has a long history of allergies. And the rash disappeared with a couple of antihistamine tablets."

Angela nods, satisfied. "All in all, a good day, then."

"Yeah. But in light of the new meningitis cases among younger kids, I think we have to lower the minimum age of immunization to at least six." She exhales heavily. "Nathan is pushing back hard. He says Neissovax has never been tested in kids under ten."

Angela rubs her chin, considering it. "The other commercially available meningitis vaccines have been approved for kids as young as two months."

"Exactly."

"You're driving this bus, so follow your gut. Either way, it will be key to get all teens and middle-schoolers immunized. That should create enough herd immunity to prevent the spread to the younger kids or anyone else, eventually."

Eventually. Lisa suppresses a sigh. "I've got to head out to Bellevue now. Are you going to stick around here today?"

"Nah. I've got my own shit to do." Angela taps her head scarf. "Thankfully, at least I don't have to worry about keeping the hair colored and as damn stylish as it used to be. I'd never find the time."

Lisa grins as she stands up, resisting the urge to ask Angela what medical interventions she is facing today. "I'll see you later, then?"

"Better than a fifty percent chance of that, according to Vegas odds."

Lisa heads down to the garage and climbs into her car. She drives a few blocks east until she turns on the ramp that merges south onto the I-5. At rush hour, the freeways can slow to a snarl, but Lisa marvels at how well the traffic is flowing through the city's major arteries now. In no time at all, she's heading across the Lacey V. Murrow Bridge over spectacular Lake Washington, which forms the eastern border of Seattle and turns the city into the isthmus it is. She's almost disappointed when she reaches the quiet tree-lined neighborhood in Bellevue in under twenty minutes, uncertain whether she's been enjoying the drive or just dreading the destination. She considers dropping in on her niece while she's in the vicinity but remembers that Olivia is enrolled in a sports camp all week.

Lisa parks in front of a big Craftsman-style house on Hilltop Road and trudges up the driveway to the entrance. A fortyish man in sweatpants and a black T-shirt with a few days' worth of scruff on his cheeks and chin meets her at the door. The devastation on his grim face pales in comparison to that of his wife, who's already sobbing as she joins them in the foyer.

Lisa introduces herself to Mason's parents, Sam and Kimberly Pickering. They lead her into the living room, and she sits down across from them as Sam wraps an arm around his wife's shoulders.

"I let him go," Kimberly blurts between sobs.

Lisa tilts her head. "Go?"

"To the game. Mason looked awful that morning. So pale. I knew he wasn't right."

"Nothing would've stopped Mason from going, Kimmy," Sam says as he squeezes her arm. But her chin drops, and her head bobs up and down.

"It wouldn't have mattered if he didn't go," Lisa says. "We're seeing kids die within hours of getting this meningitis."

Kimberly looks up, rubbing her puffy eyes. "Really?"

"Really. It's such an aggressive infection. Half the time, we can't stop it at all. Mason going to the game had nothing to do with his . . . outcome."

Sam looks at his wife. "See, Kimmy?"

"Yeah," she mumbles as fresh tears drip down her cheek.

Her anguish is so palpable that Lisa feels a ball form in her throat. "Mason has a sister, right?"

"Two," Sam says. "We've got twin girls. They're five."

"And everyone in the family has taken their prophylactic antibiotics?"

"Of course," Sam says.

Lisa is tempted to offer Neissovax for the twins, but she knows she doesn't have authority to do so yet. "Did Mason go to Delridge in the past week or so?"

"Delridge?" Sam frowns. "Don't know if he's ever been there. We don't get into the city that much, except downtown."

"So neither of you has been there recently, either?"

"No."

"Camp Green in Delridge. Where this outbreak began. Are you familiar with it?"

Sam shakes his head. "Only from the news."

"It isn't a Bible camp, is it?" Kimberly murmurs.

"It is," Lisa says, straightening.

Kimberly turns to her husband. "Isn't Nicola a camp counselor at some Bible camp?"

"Yeah," Sam says. "My older sister's kid. They're kind of a religious family. We're not super close."

Lisa leans forward. "Did Mason see Nicola in the past week at all?"

Kimberly and Sam share a look of sudden recognition. "Grammie's birthday," he mutters.

"Mason and Nicola were at the same party?"

"Yeah, last Sunday. My grandmother turned ninety. My uncle threw a big party at his place out on Mercer Island."

Lisa's heart beats faster. "How old is Nicola?"

Sam shrugs. "Eighteen? Nineteen?"

"Do you have her phone number?"

Sam shakes his head, but Kimberly lifts her phone. "I think I do. She babysat a couple times for us a few years ago."

Lisa jots down the number and thanks the Pickerings for their time. Relieved to escape the pervasive despair that feels as thick as smoke, she hurries out of the house to her car. Once inside, she tries the number Kimberly gave her and is comforted to hear Nicola answer. After confirming she works at Camp Green, Nicola agrees to meet Lisa in person.

Lisa races back across town, too preoccupied to appreciate the sumptuous Puget Sound scenery that is bathed in bright sunlight. She drives through the streets of Greenwood in northwest Seattle until she finds the address Nicola gave her, which turns out to be a modest bungalow.

Nicola and her mother, Heather, are waiting for Lisa at their open front door. They bear a strong resemblance to one another, down to their matching short haircuts. They even wear similar loose-fitting jeans and baggy T-shirts.

After introductions, Heather guides Lisa into the modest kitchen. Lisa declines her offer of tea but joins mother and daughter at the table.

"It's so tragic about poor little Mason," Heather says, shaking her head. "I only just heard this morning. He was such a sweet boy."

"That's why I've come," Lisa says, turning to the daughter. "So far, the only connection we can find back to Camp Green is through you, Nicola."

"What does that mean?" Nicola asks in a voice that's eerily similar to her mother's.

"You were at a party with Mason, last Sunday? Your grandmother's ninetieth?"

"Great-grandmother," Nicola corrects. "Yes."

"Did you spend any time with Mason?"

"A little, I guess. I felt bad for him. There were no kids his age at the party. So I pitched a few balls for him out back of the house. Not for too long, though. It was really hot."

"Hot?" Lisa echoes, considering the implications. "You didn't share a drink with him, did you?"

She shrugs. "He might've had a few sips from my water bottle."

Lisa feels a chill run down her neck.

Heather's forehead creases. "You don't think that has anything to do with Mason's illness?"

"Yeah," Nicola says. "It's not like I was sick or anything."

Lisa shakes her head. "You don't have to show symptoms to be contagious."

"Contagious? Nicola?" Heather gasps. "How is that possible?"

Lisa ignores the question. "You were seen by one of the public-health nurses last week, right, Nicola?"

Nicola glances at her mom. "Yeah."

"When?"

"Saturday, I think."

"So the day before you saw Mason?"

Nicola nods.

"And our nurse gave all of you doses of prophylactic antibiotics?"

"Yes," Heather interjects. "We took them right away."

Nicola says nothing, but Lisa notices the guilty look that flits across her face. "Nicola? You did take the medicine?"

The teen looks helplessly over to her mom. "Remember when I was in seventh grade, and I took that penicillin for my tonsillitis? How you had to rush me to the ER when my throat closed over?"

"It was terrifying," Heather says.

Lisa bites back her frustration. "The drugs we gave you weren't related to penicillin, Nicola."

"That's what the nurse told us," Nicola says in a sheepish voice. "But I almost died that time with the penicillin. And I was feeling fine. I was sure I didn't have meningitis."

Lisa rubs her forehead. "So you didn't the take the antibiotics the nurse gave you?"

Nicola looks down at the table. "I was too scared."

Everything suddenly makes sense. Nicola must be an asymptomatic carrier of meningococcus. She had to have spread the infection to Mason—and with him, all of Bellevue—through the shared water bottle. Maybe it was also a shared drink or two that spread meningitis through Camp Green originally.

Lisa knows she should be relieved. But as reaches for the bacterial swabs and extra kit of prophylactic ciprofloxacin she's carrying inside her bag, she feels anything but. How many other people could Nicola have already infected? And even worse, how many other asymptomatic carriers might have felt too scared or too complacent to take the antibiotics they were given?

CHAPTER 26

The yellow cap flicks off easily enough. Some specks of adhesive adhere to the underside. But they're only noticeable if one looks for them.

It seems so easy now, but it has taken ages to perfect the technique.

All innovators face roadblocks. And for months this one step threatened to be the most insurmountable, like the Hillary Step for summiting Mount Everest. The challenge was to secure the cap seamlessly in place. It took countless hours of experimentation to find the right medium. Numerous attempts with almost every imaginable adhesive failed to meet the standard. Then, about three months ago, one type of glue emerged as a genuine contender. It left hardly any residue. It took only two drops, and once hardened, it became impossible to distinguish a difference with the naked eye between the resealed and the unopened vials. The caps even pop back off with exact same click and feel.

The vials debuted brilliantly at the first vaccine clinic. No one seemed to notice.

CHAPTER 27

Perched high above the iconic Pike Place Market, Nathan and Fiona sit at a high-top table beside one of the windows encircling their hotel's rooftop bar, where they're treated to a panoramic view of Elliott Bay and the Olympic Mountain range beyond. Puget Sound in all its glory. There's a door nearby that leads to an outdoor patio with overhead heat lamps, but Nathan prefers the view from inside.

I'm definitely coming back with Ethan and Marcus, he vows again. It will be the trip to follow Quebec. *If we make it to Canada.* The window for squeezing in a northern road trip before the start of the school year is closing rapidly. And the guilt gnaws. He's determined not to become one of those divorced parents who are full of promises but weak on the follow-through.

Lisa suggested the three of them meet in her offices at Seattle Public Health, but this time Nathan was the one who wanted a more neutral venue. He has learned that business conflicts are best settled over food and wine. Not that there is much to settle. *Surrender* might be a better choice of term.

Nathan looks over to Fiona, who wears a simple blue dress with her hair tied back. There's a serene quality to her as she sips her

Chardonnay and studies the harbor below. He expected her stress levels to peak once the vaccination campaign launched, but paradoxically, the go-live seems to have had the opposite effect on her.

"You seem . . . satisfied?" Nathan ventures.

"It's way too early for satisfaction," Fiona says, before turning to look at him. "Sometimes, though, the anticipation is the worst part."

He lifts his bottle of hazy IPA in a small toast. "Waiting sucks."

She raises her own glass. "Plus, I'd rather not be stuck in Seattle for too long."

"Your mom?" Nathan asks.

Fiona's mother suffers from debilitating rheumatoid arthritis and lives, wheelchair-bound, in a private-care home in Connecticut. Fiona visits her several times a week, even though it's a one-hour train ride each way from Manhattan.

"It stresses Mom when I'm away too long." Fiona takes another sip of wine. "Your boys must be bummed about potentially having to miss this summer's road trip, huh?"

"They're OK," he says, downplaying his sense of shame. "Spoke to Annie this morning. They've moved on for now. Apparently, their older cousins are taking them ATV-ing this weekend, and now they're like 'Quebec who?'"

She laughs. "It's good you and Annie can still be friends. Especially for the boys."

Fiona has always shown a deep interest in Ethan and Marcus. She doesn't have kids of her own. And while Nathan never met her husband, he knows Walt was fifteen years older than her, and she was only in her midthirties when he died. What Nathan doesn't know is whether they chose not to have kids, were still planning to, or simply couldn't. With most friends, he would feel comfortable asking. Not Fiona. It would be too much of an invasion of her well-guarded privacy. So instead he asks, "Did you and Walt travel much?"

"When we could," she says. "Walt was so busy between his teaching and his research. Most of our vacations had to be built around his academic conferences. And sadly, math profs don't tend to meet in the most exotic locales."

"How did you end up with a math prof?"

"In the most clichéd way imaginable." Her cheeks flush. "I had to take a master's-level statistics course as part of my doctor-of-pharmacy program. Walt was my prof. You know what's funny?"

"What?"

"I found him so arrogant at first. He used to wear bow ties or, sometimes, even scarves. Those goofy ascots. I couldn't stand him."

"Couldn't stand whom?" Lisa asks as she appears beside the table.

"Walt," Fiona says, reddening further. "My husband."

Lisa sits down beside her. "Isn't that normal? To not be able to stand your spouse sometimes?"

"The only time for me, ever, was before I got to know him."

"You're a lot more tolerant than I am, then. How long have you been married?"

Fiona takes a sip of her wine. "Walt died a while ago."

Lisa touches the back of the other woman's wrist. "Oh, Fiona."

"It was a long time ago, to be honest." Fiona moves her hand away to grab the bar menu and pass it to Lisa. "Will you have a drink?"

"Sure, why not?" Lisa says.

But Nathan sees through Fiona's feigned dismissiveness. The grief is as fresh in her eyes as it was the first time they discussed her husband, almost five years earlier.

The server, a muscular young man who doubles as the bartender, sidles up to the table. Lisa orders a glass of Merlot, while Nathan opts for a different IPA, and Fiona a refill of her Chardonnay.

"How about you, Lisa?" Fiona asks. "Are you married?"

"Yeah. Twelve years. No kids, though."

Nathan throws Lisa a conspiratorial look. "They're dinks."

"Oh," Fiona says.

"An inside joke," Lisa says with an amused glance at him. "And not a particularly good one, either."

Nathan appreciates her sardonic smile. Despite her senior position, Lisa doesn't come across as the kind of physician—of which he has met several—who takes herself too seriously. It only makes her more appealing.

The server returns and distributes a drink to each of them.

"How do you think it's going so far, Lisa?" Nathan asks as soon as the bartender is gone.

"Depends what you mean. The outbreak or the vaccination clinic?"

"Both, I suppose."

"On the outbreak front, we tracked down the source of the Bellevue cases. But it's not very reassuring." Lisa goes on to explain about Nicola, the asymptomatic carrier who was too frightened to take her post-exposure antibiotics. "There could be several others like her out there, noncompliant with the treatment."

Nathan groans. "Carrying that bug around like a time bomb, huh?"

"Yeah," Lisa says. "As far as Neissovax, I think the campaign has gone as well as can be expected. With today's clinics, we've vaccinated almost fifteen hundred people."

Fiona tilts her head. "But twenty-four adverse events have already been reported on your website. That's substantial."

"Nothing we didn't expect. I've gone through them all. Most are just pain and swelling at the injection sites. A couple of them seem like kooks, frankly. Only one genuine allergic reaction, and it was minor."

Nathan takes a long swig of beer, which tastes particularly satisfying. He's aware that his fear of the reporting site has begun to verge on paranoid; he spent hours in bed last night with his laptop, carefully reviewing each reported reaction, looking for any hint of possible trouble. So, while they're nowhere near out of the woods, the relief is profound.

"We just heard this afternoon about another infection in Belle-vue." Lisa's expression darkens. "This girl is only six."

"How's she doing?" Fiona asks.

Lisa just shakes her head.

With a quick glance to Fiona, Nathan says, "We've been discussing your request with the head office, Lisa."

"And?" she asks.

"Delaware is prepared to lower the minimum age of eligibility to six years old."

"That's great news. Thank you."

"Don't thank me." Nathan nods to Fiona. "This one convinced us."

Earlier that afternoon, Nathan was shocked to hear Fiona suggest they go along with the proposal. He had expected her to be even more opposed to it than he was. Instead, she argued that aside from live virus vaccines, such as the one against measles and mumps, most other vaccines like Neissovax contain only partial proteins and are safe for children as young as infants. She reasoned that including younger kids would be unlikely to increase Delaware's risk or exposure any more than where it already was.

Nathan didn't require much persuading. He'd already come to realize how poor the optics of Delaware blocking access to its prod-uct while younger children were dying would look under growing media scrutiny.

Lisa turns to Fiona. "Thank you. I really appreciate your support on this."

Fiona raises her glass in another toast. "In for penny, in for a pound. Right?"

"What's in that Chardonnay?" Nathan motions to her glass with a chuckle. "I don't even recognize you today, Fee."

Fiona's features harden. "Don't get me wrong, I still think this launch—while maybe well intentioned—is premature. But that bridge is burning way behind us now. And statistically speaking, younger children are less likely to have adverse reactions, such as severe allergies, than older kids or adults."

"Agreed," Lisa says.

Fiona points her finger at her. "But what happens when a baby comes down with this meningitis? Are you going to expect us to vaccinate infants, too?"

Lisa turns her head and gazes out the window. "I hope we don't ever have to find out."

CHAPTER 28

Darius Washington had assumed he was just getting a cold. The pain from the open sores inside his mouth woke him a few times through the night. He thought about getting up to swallow a couple of ibuprofen tablets but didn't want to disturb his roommate, Jayden, a notoriously light sleeper. They're both in the summer engineering co-op program and have to sit the same term-ending physics exam this afternoon.

Shit! I don't have time for this today, he thinks in the morning, regretting ever going to the vaccination clinic. *Always happens. Just like with the flu shot. You get a vaccine, and a couple days later you get sick.*

As he struggles to even sit up, Darius realizes he's not going to be writing any exam. His mouth feels as raw as if it had been scalded by boiling soup. And his throat stings like there are razor blades wedged inside. But his lips bother him most of all. They feel like two sausages stuck on his face, worse than any dental freezing. And he can't control the drool that streams down onto his neck and chest.

Darius instinctively reaches up to touch his face. His fingers meet the taut, tender blisters that run all the way along his swollen lips. Fear grips him as he realizes the fluid pouring down his chin isn't saliva but liquid leaking from those blisters.

He opens his mouth to call for help, but all that emerges is one long, barely audible croak.

CHAPTER 29

It's a factory. Even though the gymnasium is clean, and the process runs in an orderly manner, the whole setup still reminds Max of some kind of sweatshop. Probably because he finds it all so toxic.

Max didn't plan to stay as long as he has at this vaccination clinic. It looks no different than the other two he already visited. And they all function just as Yolanda described.

I've got to be careful with her, he reminds himself. Despite her gullibility and eagerness to please, even Yolanda is beginning to tire of his constant questions and requests. She doesn't understand why he cares so much. *She couldn't, though, could she?*

Max is discouraged to see the line for today's clinic is even longer than the previous ones. But it only hardens his resolve. On the pretense of searching for someone, he moves forward relatively unnoticed until he's standing beside a family at the front of the line. He watches intently as the nurse at the nearest desk raises a yellow-topped vial in her hand. She pops off the cap, flips it upside down, and pokes the syringe's needle in it, withdrawing the clear liquid.

He is so focused on the procedure that he doesn't even notice the woman beside him until she says, "Hello."

He looks over to see Seattle's chief public-health officer at his side. "Oh, hi."

"You're a naturopath, right?" she says. "You questioned me at the public-health forum. I'm sorry, I can't recall your name."

"Max Balfour."

"Lisa Dyer," she says. "Based on our last conversation, Dr. Balfour, I wouldn't have expected to see you at one of these clinics."

"I have a teenage son." He shrugs. "I'm worried about this meningitis, just like any other parent."

Her expression is skeptical. "And you're planning to get him vaccinated?"

"I'm considering it. I wanted to understand the process for myself. To wrap my head around it."

"Would be a big step for you and your son, wouldn't it?"

"It would."

"So you're not opposed to all vaccines?"

"Not all. Vaccines have their place. Smallpox was a good example. Although the disease was naturally waning anyway."

"It only waned because of the vaccine." She frowns. "Smallpox used to kill one out of every seven children in the world. When we developed enough herd immunity through global immunization, the virus died out. That's how vaccines work."

"That's how they're supposed to work," Max counters. "But they don't always, do they? Take the tuberculin vaccine. It was meant to cure tuberculosis. But it only ended up killing more people than it helped."

"That was a hundred years ago."

"There are more recent examples." He speaks louder, aware that the people nearest them have begun to listen in. "Like the Cutter incident in the 1960s, when forty thousand people were infected with polio through the vaccine that was meant to protect them from the same virus. Or the swine flu vaccine in the late seventies that caused hundreds of people to be incapacitated by that neurologic disease, Guillain-Barré syndrome, after being vaccinated against a nonexistent threat. It led to the biggest class-action lawsuit settlement in the history of medicine."

"You can't compare historical incidents to today's standards. Quality control is far more rigorous now. By law, every single batch of vaccine is individually tested for purity and compliance."

Max motions to the chair where a young girl is being jabbed in the shoulder. "So tell me. What's your standard for this vaccine?"

"To begin with, it has already undergone vigorous phase-three clinical trials involving well over a thousand recipients without any concerning outcomes."

"Phase-three trials don't always replicate results in the real world, do they? That's why there's a phase four. Postmarketing surveillance. To study the real-world clinical outcomes."

"I understand how trials work, Dr. Balfour."

"Then you must remember the first rotavirus vaccine that came out not twenty years ago?"

She sighs heavily. "Yes."

"It sailed through phase-three trials, didn't it, Dr. Dyer? It was only after they started to broadly distribute it that they discovered that it caused kids' intestines to twist until the blood supply was cut off."

"It's called 'intussusception.' And that's an exaggeration. It was only slightly more common among the vaccinated kids but still rare."

You people! Max struggles to hide his disgust. "I'm guessing you would view it differently if it had happened to your child?"

"And that's why we have also set up such a rigorous surveillance system. To monitor for any unexpected outcome. Have you seen the website?"

"Yeah, I've seen it. Even if it does alert you to dangerous complications, it won't help the initial victims of any serious vaccine injuries, will it?"

"That's a big if, Dr. Balfour."

He shrugs. "It's a bit of a coincidence, isn't it?"

"What is?"

"This new strain of bacteria. It's never been seen before. Until Iceland. And now here in Seattle."

"That's what pathogens—especially bacteria—do. They mutate. New strains appear all the time."

"Oh, I understand that," Max says. "But isn't it coincidental that it happened to mutate exactly at the same time that Delaware Pharmaceuticals was ready to market the perfect vaccine against it?"

CHAPTER 30

Lisa had to postpone the Outbreak Control Team meeting until the morning Neissovax clinics were complete. She walks into the conference room at two in the afternoon to find it fuller than any previous daily meeting since the first one. There's a buzz of anticipation around the table that is, at least in part, fueled by the intense media coverage of the pediatric cases in Bellevue.

"Dead children," Angela said matter-of-factly just before she and Lisa walked in together. "They tug at the heartstrings even more than dead teenagers. Great for hits and engagements online. 'Earned media value,' as the publicists call it."

Despite Angela's cynicism, Lisa is glad to have her back in her usual seat.

Lisa calls the meeting to order and advances to the second slide of her presentation. A map of Seattle appears, highlighting the city's two geographical hot spots. "It's day nine of the outbreak. As of this afternoon, we've had twelve deaths among twenty-eight confirmed cases in the Delridge area—home of the original Camp Green cluster. Meaning there've been only four new cases there in the past three days. But the news isn't nearly as hopeful in Bellevue, the second cluster. We've had eight cases there in the past three days with two deaths, and two critically patients still in the ICU. All these victims between six and eight years old."

Tyra motions to one of the screens. "We're aggressively tracking and treating all contacts within both clusters with antibiotic prophylaxis." Her professional façade momentarily gives way to a pained expression. "The girl who died this morning was only six."

Lisa can't help but think of Olivia. She has already studied the map and discovered that the nearest victim lived less than a mile away from Amber.

"Have we figured out how it spread from Delridge to Bellevue?" asks Benning, the insightful woman from the department of health.

Tyra nods. "The culture swabs from Nicola Ford's nose grew meningococcus, confirming she was the one who carried it from the first cluster to the second."

"The *asymptomatic* carrier," Angela emphasizes. "Just like the boy who brought this disease back from Iceland. God knows how many other Typhoid Marys we've got running around this town."

"Even more reason to accelerate the vaccination program," Tyra says.

"And on that front, we do have some good news." Lisa looks over to the medical microbiologist. "Dr. Klausner . . ."

Klausner clears her throat noisily. "We have analyzed the early post-immunization blood samples from the first group to be vaccinated with Neissovax." She stops to clear her throat again. "We have seen strong immunogenicity within forty-eight hours of inoculation. The levels of the antibody titers against this specific Icelandic strain appear to be high."

"That quickly?" Angela's nose wrinkles. "Holy crap!"

"It *is* somewhat unusual," Klausner concedes. "Normally, it would take weeks to generate this kind of immune response. But that does bode well for the effectiveness of the vaccine."

"Does this mean the vaccinated kids will be immune to this meningitis?" Benning asks.

Klausner pushes her glasses back up the bridge of her nose. "We never draw clinical conclusions from lab results . . ."

"What a classic pathologist's disclaimer." Angela laughs, and then turns to Benning. "The answer is yes. Or more accurately, *Hell, yes!* Those who got Neissovax are now immune."

Lisa nods. "And in light of the Bellevue outbreak, Delaware Pharmaceuticals has approved lowering the minimum age of vaccination to six."

"I'm delighted the drug company is behind an expanded market for their product." Moyes speaks up for the first time. "What about this committee? Do *we* approve it?"

"What choice do we have, Alistair?" Angela asks. "This thing is starting to ravage young'uns."

Moyes strokes his beard with the back of his hand. "This vaccine has never been given to children under the age of ten. Not even in any of the trials."

"Six? Ten? What difference does it really make?"

"Well, we don't know, do we, Angela?"

Her eyes lock on to his with uncharacteristic ferocity. "We do know that kids of that age are dying. How many vaccines are you aware of that are tolerated by ten-year-olds but not six-year-olds? Are we going to let a theoretical risk stop us from protecting the group that is currently the most vulnerable?"

Ignoring Angela, Moyes turns to Lisa. "What do we know of the adverse reactions to Neissovax so far?"

Lisa advances a few slides until she reaches the one with a summary of all reported side effects. "With over two thousand doses administered, we have received forty-six reports of adverse events through our website and the hotline. None required hospitalization. None met the criteria to qualify as serious. And almost all have subsequently resolved."

"The vaccine is safe, Alistair," Angela says.

"So far," Moyes says. "Two days' worth of data isn't enough to draw conclusions. Are you forgetting what happened with the rotavirus vaccine?"

"I don't forget anything," Angela snaps.

"You thought it was safe, too, though, didn't you?"

Angela only glares back in response.

Lisa is struck again by the tension between Angela and Moyes. She wishes she understood their background better. But at this moment, she's more concerned about focusing everyone's attention on the necessary next steps. "We need to revise our publicity campaign to include the lower age group," she says, nodding to the goateed publicist, who's typing madly on his laptop. "Kevin?"

"I've drafted a new press release, encouraging parents to bring younger children to the vaccine clinics," says Kevin. "We'll be circulating it through the usual media and social media channels."

"The press is going to lap that up," the balding rep from city hall grumbles. "Seattle's outbreak is already regularly headlining CNN."

"Not just cable news," Kevin says, as if almost proud of the coverage. "The big networks all covered the story last night. In prime time, too. Since COVID, this kind of story is a huge deal."

"Do we even have the capacity to expand the program to younger kids?" Benning asks.

"The manpower, yes," Lisa says. "In terms of supply, we calculated that the initial fifty thousand doses would be enough to cover the original demographic target of youths and young adults. But with the younger kids included, Delaware will have to ship us more vaccine."

"This product launch just keeps growing bigger and bigger," Moyes says.

Something in his tone and his earlier comment about rotavirus reminds Lisa of her conversation with Max. She wrote off the naturopath's insinuations about the pathogen emerging contemporaneously with the new vaccine as little more than the musings of a conspiracy theorist. But the coincidence is undeniable. *And besides, what the hell was Max really doing at that clinic?* He clearly had no intention of getting his son vaccinated.

Lisa ends the meeting with the slide that lists the schedule of the upcoming vaccination clinics, and then opens the floor to a roundtable discussion. People have little more to add and quickly file out of the conference room.

Lisa's assistant, Ingrid, is waiting for her at the door. "Your sister's in your office," she tells her.

"Amber?" Lisa frowns. Her sister has never visited her at work before.

Inside the office, Amber greets her with a tight hug, and Lisa picks up on a whiff of marijuana. She understands that her sister works in the industry and is a relatively regular user of weed, particularly for insomnia or stress, but she's never smelled it on her before.

Lisa slips out of the embrace. "What's up, Amber? Everyone OK?"

Amber nods. "I was just in the neighborhood."

"Nope."

"What does that mean?"

"I don't buy it. You basically work in the neighborhood. Not once have you ever thought of dropping by my office before today."

"OK, OK. I'm worried about Olivia."

"Why? What happened?"

"No. Nothing," Amber assures Lisa. "She's fine. But the girl who died this morning. Rebecca Cohen—"

"How do you know her name? We never released it."

"She was in Liv's kindergarten class. The posts are flying around the parents' social media pages."

Lisa grabs her sister's arm. "Has Olivia been around Rebecca this summer?"

"No. Not since school ended in June."

Lisa releases her grip. "Thank God."

"But it's too close a connection. And all these sick kids in Bellevue . . ." Amber looks at her plaintively. "Just how bad is it, Lisa?"

"It's bad, Amber. Very bad."

"So what do we do?"

"It hasn't been announced yet, but we're about to lower the age of eligibility on the new vaccine."

"And Olivia would . . . qualify?"

"Yes."

Amber slumps down into the chair beside her. "A vaccine? That's all you can offer? You know how I feel about those."

"Listen to me. This isn't tetanus or measles. Some theoretical infectious risk, where Olivia already benefits from all the immunity around her."

"Nice, sis," Amber snaps.

"You know what I mean." Lisa kneels beside the chair. "This outbreak is deadly, Amber. And you live in the heart of the hottest zone. There is no herd immunity. We don't even know exactly who's contagious and who's not. If Olivia were to be exposed . . ."

"But a vaccine . . ." Amber drops her chin in silence for a few moments. "Can't imagine what Allen would say, let alone Dad."

Fuck Dad! Lisa has to bite her tongue. "Fine. Skip all the others—polio, tetanus, measles, HPV . . . Who cares? But this meningitis vaccine? Oliva can't skip this one, Amber. She just can't."

CHAPTER 31

Susan Meyer's hand brushes up against something firm, but she's not awake enough to recognize it as someone's back until the person stirs. For a disoriented moment, Susan wonders if there's a man in her bed. No. No one has slept over since it ended with Owen, that hopeless man-child of a broke guitarist.

Waking more fully, Susan realizes her daughter Mia has crawled into bed with her. Susan is touched. Her fiercely independent fifteen-year-old usually keeps her bedroom door locked at night and hasn't climbed into her mom's bed in years.

"My mouth hurts, Mom," Mia says without rolling over toward her.

It's not Mia's words but rather her extreme hoarseness that jolts Susan to full alertness. "You mean your throat?"

"That, too," Mia croaks. "My mouth feels like I burned it. And my lips are all weird."

"Weird?"

"I dunno. Swollen."

Susan switches on the bedside lamp. "Let me see."

Mia turns over to face her.

It's all Susan can do not to cry out. She can't even discern where her daughter lips end and the blisters begin. "Oh my God, sweetheart! Your mouth."

CHAPTER 32

The usual chaos reigns inside Harborview's emergency room. Lisa has to flash her ID badge and ask three separate staff members before she's finally directed to the correct room within the department's resuscitation zone.

"Never seen one like this," says the harried ER doctor, Sofia Cortez, as she stands with Lisa outside a door with the curtain drawn across it.

Lisa wonders what possible experience Cortez could already have. To her eyes, she looks barely old enough to have graduated college, let alone work as an attending physician at a major teaching hospital. "How so?"

"The swelling spread in front of my eyes," Cortez says. "Mia was talking—I mean barely, but she was—when she showed up. Her throat closed over as I had my stethoscope to her chest. We had no choice but to intubate her. There was so much swelling and debris in her airway that I could barely pass the tube through the vocal cords. She got lucky. Five minutes longer at home and she probably would've suffocated."

Lisa has yet to see Mia, but the description is enough to send a chill through her. "And you're sure it's Stevens-Johnson syndrome?" she asks, referring to the potentially life-threatening reaction that causes severe swelling and blistering, especially of the skin around the lips and inside the lining of the mouth.

"Yes. The dermatologist already saw her. He agrees. We started her on high-dose steroids, but it's progressed so rapidly. Even he was shocked."

"And has she been on any new medications lately? Antibiotics? Anticonvulsants? Or any other drug associated with Stevens-Johnson syndrome?" Lisa asks.

"No medications. Only the meningitis vaccine."

Lisa's heart sinks. "When did she get that?"

"Two days ago, apparently."

"And she didn't develop the reaction until this morning?"

Cortez makes a gesture toward the curtain in front of the door. "According to the parents."

"Can I see her?"

"Sure."

Lisa pushes the curtain aside and steps into the room. Despite the beeping equipment and hive of activity around the bed, her gaze is immediately drawn to the patient, who lies with the head of the bed elevated to almost the sitting position. Mia's eyes are glassy but open, meaning that, while sedated, she's still conscious. A ventilator tube passes into her mouth, but Lisa can't identify her lips through all the blistering and swelling.

"Who are you?" demands the wide-eyed man at the foot of the bed, who looks as if he could be a biker with his cropped hair, bulging shoulders, and sleeves of tattoos.

"I'm Dr. Dyer. With Public Health."

The woman standing closer to the head of the bed grimaces. "Public Health?"

The man's eyes narrow. "Does this have something to do with that vaccine Mia got?"

"That's what we are trying to figure out," Lisa says. "You're the father?"

"Yeah, Jim Meyer." He nods toward the woman. "My ex-wife, Susan. The mom."

Lisa offers them a sympathetic smile. "When did Mia first complain or show any signs of this reaction?"

"Mia seemed OK at bedtime," Susan says. "She crawled into my bed early this morning complaining of a sore mouth." She stares helplessly at Lisa. "She never comes into my room at night."

Lisa views Mia, whose head is still, but her eyes appear to follow them as they discuss her. She can't imagine how terrifying it must be for the girl or her parents. "I know Dr. Cortez already asked you, but has Mia taken any medication in the past few days? Even over-the-counter pills."

"Nothing," Jim answers for his ex-wife. "Just that vaccine."

Lisa turns to the patient. "Hi, Mia."

The girl stares back groggily.

"Is it true, Mia?" Lisa asks. "You've taken no other medications? Not even ibuprofen or acetaminophen?"

After a slight delay, Mia shakes her head.

"So it's got to be that fucking vaccine, doesn't it?" her father barks.

"Please, Jim," Susan says, exasperated. "The doctor is here to help."

"It could be," Lisa admits. "But we've inoculated over two thousand people, and we haven't seen anyone react this way so far."

His lips curls into a sneer. "And now you have."

"We'll see," Lisa says. "Meantime, Mia is in good hands. Now that her airway is protected and she's on the steroids, her doctors expect her to improve."

"She just about died!"

"Jim!" Susan snaps.

"I understand," Lisa says.

Susan turns away from her daughter and runs a finger in a circular motion around her own lips. "Will it scar?" she whispers.

"I don't think so," Lisa says, realizing that she's not entirely certain of what the long-term complications from Stevens-Johnson syndrome are.

Jim spins away with a disgusted snort, but Susan's eyes remain fixed on hers. "That vaccine was supposed to protect her, wasn't it, Dr. Dyer?"

Lisa doesn't try to argue. Instead, she simply nods.

Even after Lisa says her good-byes and drives back to the office, she has trouble shaking the memory of the mother's betrayed eyes. She's still thinking about it as she steps into her office. She has barely sat down behind the desk when Tyra walks in.

"Well?" the program director asks as she drops into the chair across from her.

"It's not good, Tyra." Lisa summarizes Mia's condition.

Tyra shakes her head. "But this Stevens-Johnson syndrome can happen spontaneously, right? You don't need to have been exposed to any medications?"

"The timing seems just too coincidental for that. Even the dermatologist has never seen the syndrome progress this rapidly."

"But it's not an allergy, right?"

"No. Technically not. It's classified as a type-four immune hypersensitivity, because it's mediated by T-lymphocyte cells. It's more of a severe idiosyncratic reaction than a true allergy."

"Exactly." Tyra holds up her palms. "It could have happened after almost any medication, not just the Neissovax immunization."

"But it *did* happen after Neissovax."

"OK, OK. Let's say Mia had a bladder infection and was started on a sulfa drug for treatment? And then she broke out in the exact same severe rash."

Lisa rubs her eyes. "What's your point, Tyra?"

"My point is: you wouldn't stop giving out sulfa drugs to everyone else with a bladder infection because one person reacted as badly as Mia did."

"You'd make a good lawyer, Tyra." Lisa chuckles. "This is different, though. The amount of scrutiny this vaccine faces. Once word of this gets out . . ."

Tyra's face scrunches up. "We can't let those damn anti-vaxxers and their hysteria dictate how we manage a public-health crisis. Not after a single adverse reaction."

"Even if it's a near-fatal drug rash?" a voice asks from her doorway.

Lisa looks over to see Alistair Moyes. "Bad news travels fast," she says.

"It does." He steps into the room. "How is the patient doing?"

"Stable. Now."

Moyes raises an eyebrow. "Stable on a life-support system?"

"Only to protect her airway until the swelling settles down," Lisa says. "Besides, isn't it a bit early to say 'I told you so'?"

"That's not why I'm here."

"Why then?"

"I came to discuss the lab results we just received at the CDC."

"Which results?" Lisa asks warily.

"The post-exposure antibody titers."

"And?"

"They're through the roof. Even more impressive than Dr. Klausner suggested."

"So Neissovax confers full immunity against the Icelandic meningococcus?"

He nods. "In a hundred percent of the samples we've tested so far."

"And what about this girl with Stevens-Johnson syndrome?" Lisa asks, bracing for the worst. "Is that enough to derail our vaccination campaign?"

Moyes studies her for a long moment. "As nasty as it sounds, it's still only one reaction among thousands of inoculated."

"It is," Lisa agrees, surprised.

Moyes turns to Tyra. "And fifteen children have died from this meningitis so far."

"Sixteen, as of this morning," Tyra corrects.

"So, in my opinion, no, it's not," Moyes says. "It's enough to raise a red flag. Maybe a bloodred one. But it's too early to halt the campaign."

CHAPTER 33

"There's been a serious reaction." Lisa's five-word text pops up in top right corner of the laptop's screen and stops Nathan cold in mid-sentence as he's addressing Delaware's senior executive committee via videoconference from his hotel room.

"Nathan?" Peter Moore prompts on the screen. "You still with us?"

"Oh yeah," Nathan mutters as his stomach knots. "Excuse me, everyone. I have to run."

"We've only got two more items on the—"

But Nathan slams his laptop shut before the CEO can even finish his sentence. He grabs for his phone and taps Lisa's number. "Your text?" he demands as soon as she picks up.

"There's a girl at Harborview who's in critical condition," Lisa says. "She got Neissovax two days ago."

"A girl?" he blurts.

"Yeah. She has Stevens-Johnson syndrome."

"What the hell is that?"

"A type of immune reaction that causes a potentially life-threatening rash—terrible blistering like severe burns, especially around the mouth."

"You're certain it's from the Neissovax?"

"There's no other explanation."

He listens, numb, as she describes the girl's condition. He takes little solace in the fact that the victim has stabilized on the ventilator, or that Lisa's team has decided not to suspend the vaccination campaign.

Lisa's tone softens. "We'll figure this out, Nathan."

"No doubt," he says, his mind already gearing up into damage-control mode. "Thanks for the heads-up."

As soon as he hangs up, he dials Fiona, but her phone goes straight to voice mail. "Need to talk!" he texts her.

As he waits for her to call back, Nathan opens his laptop and searches for photos of victims of Stevens-Johnson syndrome. The online images of faces disfigured by blisters, open sores, and puffiness pain him to view. He knows this case can't be a coincidence, but he refuses to consider the full implications.

Fiona calls about ten minutes later. "I just spoke to Lisa," are the first words out of her mouth.

Nathan hears a lot of background noise. "Where are you?"

"At the vaccine clinic downtown," she says.

"Let's meet."

Nathan heads down to the lobby and grabs a waiting cab that drops him off at their arranged spot in front of the Seattle Center, one of the city's busiest cultural and tourist hubs. The iconic, six-hundred-foot-tall Space Needle looms overhead, but Nathan barely notices it as he hurries across the lawn toward the fountain where Fiona is waiting.

Her face is calm, but as he nears, he sees the worry dancing in her eyes. "I tracked down the clinic the girl attended," Fiona says in a low voice even though no one else is within earshot. "I ran the serial number of the vial she received. That batch was tested back at the plant in Littleton last week. Twice. Zero imperfections."

"Of course," Nathan says. "They've all been perfect. No one's doubting the quality control here."

"But Stevens-Johnson syndrome? We never saw anything like that in our trials."

"It's idiosyncratic, right? As I understand it, it can happen with almost any drug."

Fiona only nods. "Maybe we should pause the campaign until we can investigate further."

"No one in Lisa's office is suggesting that."

"But isn't it what we should do?"

Only if we want to initiate the single biggest publicity disaster in Delaware's history. The repercussions of halting the Neissovax campaign would be catastrophic. Even if the reaction was subsequently found to be entirely unrelated, the fallout would likely doom the vaccine's commercial release. But all Nathan says is, "We should probably follow their lead, Fiona, and not overreact."

"I'm the one responsible for product safety."

"And you report to me. Look, this a big setback, Fee. I get it. But this syndrome is a rare reaction. It can happen with multiple medications. It's probably a one-off."

"So we do nothing?"

"There's nothing we can do right now but look into it. Even then, we're unlikely to find a connection." He exhales. "This girl didn't die of her reaction. She's going to get better. Meantime, there are kids dying of meningitis every day in this city. And Neissovax can help prevent that."

Fiona stares at him. If possible, her eyes look even sadder than usual. But when she speaks, her tone is calmer. "Maybe you're right. Maybe it's not the time to stop. But I'm going to go back and turn over every stone. Run the testing one more time. See if there's anything at all different about the batch that girl's vaccine came from."

Nathan forces a smile. "That's why we pay you the big bucks, Fee."

"Big bucks? Yeah, I suppose. Relatively speaking." She sighs. "But a lower-paying academic career is looking pretty damned attractive right now."

"As if. I wouldn't we be able to do this without you."

Fiona breaks off her eye contact. "I'm not sure I want to be part of this anymore," she murmurs, and he doesn't even try to argue.

She sets off down the trail, and he catches up to her. They walk in silence for a few hundred yards down a path that heads toward the Seattle Children's Museum. The irony of their randomly chosen destination isn't lost on Nathan in light of the expanding crisis.

The complex is full of museums, green spaces, and playgrounds. He knows the Museum of Pop Culture with its funky architecture and high-tech interactive displays is somewhere nearby. His sons would love it. But the thought of bringing them back to Seattle suddenly holds little appeal. To him, the city is now tainted.

"Have you seen the media coverage around lowering the age of vaccination?" Fiona asks. "It was all over the news this morning."

"A feeding frenzy, huh?"

"The clinics are going to be even more swamped. We're probably going to need more supply."

"Shouldn't be a problem. I'll let them know at Littleton," he says distractedly. The idea of surpassing fifty thousand vaccinations is both alarming and reassuring to him. The higher the denominator, the easier it will be to dilute the impact of any other serious vaccine-related complications.

Fiona stops in the middle of the trail and turns to him. "What if the media finds out about this victim?"

"They're bound to, Fee. Eventually."

"Then what?"

"I'm on it. We'll work with Lisa's team to manage the fallout. But we'll also get our internal comms people to spin the message as needed."

"Spin, Nathan? We're talking about a girl's life."

"I know. And I feel awful for her." He shakes his head. "But we're also talking about saving other lives. Not to mention a billion-dollar investment that's being threatened by something we wanted no part of in the first place."

CHAPTER 34

"**Y**ou had to go all gaga over the vaccine, didn't you?" Angela says from her seat on the other side of the desk. She's so poker-faced that it takes Lisa a moment to be certain she's joking.

"If all you have is a hammer . . ." Lisa says, citing one of Angela's favorite expressions. "Anyway, how can we abandon the campaign after one reaction? Even one as serious as Mia's."

"Agreed. Only a jackass would pull the plug now."

"Even if that jackass has to justify a critical, potentially disfiguring reaction to the parents of an otherwise healthy kid."

"It's a clusterfuck. I'll give you that."

"No kidding."

"Actually, it's more of a FUBAR."

"Which means?"

"Fucked up beyond all repair," Angela says with a satisfied nod. "They're all military terms. Clusterfuck, FUBAR, and even snafu, which stands for 'situation normal, all fucked up.' Those soldiers, they do like to cuss."

"As opposed to you?"

"I never really fucking noticed," Angela deadpans. "Regardless, Lisa, it's lonely at the top."

"I had no idea how tough your job was. I used to think you just sat in this big office and surfed the net."

"Netflix isn't going to watch itself, is it?" Angela shows a hint of a grin and then motions to the other side of the desk. "This is a lot for you to be handling this early in the role."

"Or potentially *mis*handling." Lisa sighs. "I never expected my decisions to have such huge repercussions."

"I think you're doing all right. Well, for a placeholder appointee, anyway." The grin leaves Angela's lips. "How are you feeling? Are you coping?"

"I think so. Thank you." Lisa feels as if her eyes might mist over. For Angela, of all people, to worry over her welfare. Despite her friend's baggy sweater, Lisa noticed the bulge of Angela's lower abdomen when she first sat down. It can only mean that her belly is full of fluid, caused by the ovarian cancer. But Lisa resists the urge to question her health status.

"I've been meaning to ask you about Alistair," Lisa says.

"Moyes? What about him?"

"I have this nagging sense that you two have a lot more history than I'm aware of."

"It's true." Angela's eyes dart in either direction, and then she says in a hush, "Alistair and I were lovers back in the day. We had a child out of wedlock."

It takes Lisa a moment to confirm her friend is joking again. "What is it? Really."

"We worked at the CDC together for a while. In Spokane, of all places. We never saw eye to eye." Angela shrugs. "He was already old when I met him, and he was only in his thirties back then. But behind that stodgy exterior and war crime of a beard, he's actually a very officious man."

Lisa laughs. "That's all, huh?"

"Annoying as he is, Alistair is very smart, and his judgment is good. Too good, maybe. The rotavirus vaccine was a particular bone of contention between us back then. Still is, if our last meeting is anything to go by. He loves to rub it in that he was right."

"What if Neissovax turns out to be another rotavirus fiasco?"

"There's no comparison. Rotavirus was never going to save the lives that Neissovax will."

"Not sure it will matter once word gets out about Mia and what's happened to her."

Angela frowns. "You're going to announce it?"

"I haven't decided," Lisa says. "What do you think?"

"I'd wait. The anti-vaxxers are going to soil themselves when they get wind of it."

"It's going to spook people, no question. But it's bound to get out sooner or later."

"From our point of view, later is preferable."

Tyra appears at the open door. "You two got a sec?"

Lisa recognizes the purposeful look on her colleague's face. "What's up, Ty?"

She steps inside and closes the door behind her. "We had three new meningitis cases reported this afternoon. One's already dead."

It never ends. Lisa sighs. "All from Bellevue?"

"Two."

"And the third?"

"A fifteen-year-old boy who lives in Magnolia," Tyra says of the upper-middle-class neighborhood in northwest Seattle. "Logan Hinds. He's in rough shape in the ICU."

Angela grimaces. "A third cluster?"

Tyra shrugs. "Not sure you can classify it as that."

"Why not?"

"Because Logan attended Camp Green with the original victims."

Tyra's eyes convey the same level of alarm that Lisa feels. "I thought we tracked down all contacts connected to that camp," she says.

"We did," Tyra says.

"Including Logan?"

Tyra nods.

"So why wasn't he started on prophylactic antibiotics?"

"He was. Logan had the full dose. Rifampin and cipro. It didn't protect him."

Lisa's heart sinks as she digests the implications. "So not only do we have a new geographical cluster, we've now got antibiotic failure, too."

"It never was going to be a hundred percent effective," Angela says. "As long the vaccine doesn't fail us . . ."

A new worry forms in Lisa's head. "Logan wasn't vaccinated already, was he?"

"No," Tyra said. "He wasn't."

"Thank God," Lisa mumbles. "Didn't we prioritize the Camp Green contacts to the top of the vaccination list?"

"Course we did, but it's like herding cats. We haven't been able to get all of them to the vaccine clinics yet."

"Ty . . ."

"We'll get them there, Lisa. Or we'll bring the vaccine to them. All of them. Promise." Tyra turns for the door. "Meantime, I got to track down the new contacts Logan might've exposed in the Magnolia region."

"Hey, can you fire me a list of those new victims and how best to reach the families?" Lisa calls after her, and Tyra waves her acknowledgment without turning back.

"I have to run, too." Angela starts to rise, but she gets less than halfway up before her legs buckle and she falls back into the chair. Lisa hops up and hurries around the desk to help her. By the time she reaches the other side, Angela has managed to push herself up with both hands planted on the desk. "I'm good," she says, leaning away from Lisa's outstretched arm.

Lisa's heart breaks watching Angela hobble out of the office with such obvious effort, but then her phone buzzes, and she looks down and sees the reminder on the screen for a marital counseling appointment in thirty minutes that had totally slipped her mind. *It will never work*, she thinks, struck by her own inadvertent double entendre. Taking a breath, she calls Dominic.

"Hey. I hate to do this to you—to us—but I don't think I can make our session."

There's a pause. "You can't?"

"We've got a new cluster of infections. And a bad vaccine reaction. I'm being pulled in every direction."

"I'll let Beverly know we're canceling."

The quiet in his voice tells her how upset he is. "I'm sorry, Dom. Even if I did go, I couldn't give this the attention it deserves." What she doesn't say is that she couldn't handle the added stress from another postcounseling debrief on top of all she's facing at work.

"I get it, Lees. It's just that I thought we agreed to make us a top priority."

"We did."

"Ever since you got this new job, it seems like you only have one priority."

Is it too much to ask for one iota of support or understanding? But Lisa bites her tongue. "It's chaos here, Dom."

"Are you sure you even want to give this—us—'the attention it deserves'?"

Lisa doesn't mean to hesitate, but she wasn't prepared for the question.

"Got it," he says, without giving her another moment.

"Don't read too much into this, Dom. Please. I'm in the eye of an ever-growing shit storm right now. I can't think about anything else."

"I know the feeling," he says. "We'll talk later."

"OK. Thanks, Dom. I really am sorry—" But she hears dead air before she can get the words out. "FUBAR," she mutters to herself.

The phone buzzes again. She glances down to read the text from Nathan. "Got time to talk?" it reads.

Aside from notifying Nathan of Mia's vaccine-related reaction, Lisa hasn't had a chance to discuss the potential impact with him. "Call me?" she types.

"Need coffee. How about we meet at our usual spot?"

Lisa smiles to herself before answering his text. "Sure."

She heads out of the office on foot down the hill toward the coffee shop. Halfway there, the gray skies begin to drizzle, and she regrets not grabbing an umbrella as the rain steadily intensifies. Her hair is soaked by the time she walks through the door to the café and spots Nathan sitting at the same orange booth where they first met. There's a steaming cup of coffee on the other side of the table.

He motions to it as she sits across from him. "Pour over. Black. Right?"

"Nailed it." She shows him a grateful smile as she wipes away the drops running down her forehead. "Can't believe I forgot my umbrella. Lived here way too long to make that rookie mistake."

"Give yourself a break. You've had a pretty eventful day."

"You don't know the half of it." She tells him about the latest victims, including the antibiotic failure.

He shakes his head. "Beautiful as this city is, I'm glad my sons don't live here."

"Right now I kind of wish my niece didn't, either."

"And the girl with the rash? How is she?"

"Mia was stable an hour ago on the ventilator. But her skin's in rough shape. It'll be a long road to recovery."

Nathan looks down at his own cup. "Nothing in the trials suggested this could happen."

Lisa resists the urge to reach out and give his arm a reassuring squeeze. "Of course not."

"You haven't heard of any other concerning reactions?"

"Nothing substantial, no. I just checked the website before I came."

"That's a relief," he says. "Does this change anything with respect to the vaccination campaign?"

"From my perspective, no," she says. "In fact, it's becoming more and more clear that we need to get the most vulnerable population vaccinated. Could be the only way to halt the spread."

"And your whole team is on board?"

"More or less," she says, thinking of Moyes. "Obviously, there will be even more scrutiny over any further side effects."

"Understandable."

"On a separate note, Nathan . . ."

"Yes?"

"Now that we've lowered the age of kids eligible for the vaccine, there's going to be even more demand for it."

"We're shipping out more product. Will be here in a few days. Fiona tells me we should be OK with our current supply until then."

Lisa sips her coffee, realizing that Nathan hasn't touched his cup since she sat down.

"It's really coming down now, huh?" He motions to the window, where, beyond the streaks and drips pooling on the glass, the rain is falling in sheets. "Sorry to drag you out in such a deluge."

"Beats marriage counseling," she murmurs.

"Oh?"

"It's no big deal." Lisa clears her throat, wondering why she mentioned it. "My husband and I were supposed to have gone to an appointment this afternoon. I couldn't fit it in today."

"Been there, done that." Nathan nods. "Kind of like undergoing an amputation. Except without all the anesthetic."

"It does leave you pretty raw sometimes, huh?"

"Like road rash."

"You didn't find it helpful?" she asks, surprised she's discussing any of this with a man she hardly knows.

"Helped me get divorced. Wait. That's not really fair. We had a good counselor. I learned a lot about my marriage. And myself."

"Such as?"

"Annie and I . . ."

Lisa leans forward. "Yes?"

"Guess we eventually figured out that just because you still love each other, that doesn't always mean you're meant to stay together."

And what if you've fallen out of love? Lisa keeps the thought to herself.

"How about you?" His eyes penetrate. "Are you finding it useful?"

"I think so. Maybe. I don't know." She runs her hand through her still-damp hair. "Probably would've helped more if we'd started five years sooner . . ."

"You'll know when you know, right?"

"Our counselor likes to tell us that it takes longer to undo the damage in a relationship than it does to cause it in the first place." Feeling her face heating, she forces a laugh. "Then again, she bills by the hour."

"Makes sense, though."

"How did you know, Nathan?"

"To be honest, it wasn't my decision. Annie moved out."

"Ah."

"Said she couldn't compete anymore with my true love."

"Oh."

He grins. "She meant my job. In hindsight, she was right."

"But if you still love her . . ."

"She's got a new partner now." He shrugs. "It's fine. We're all friends. He's good to her and the boys. Sometimes, though . . ."

"What?"

"I worry I'm doing the same thing to Ethan and Marcus. Putting my career way ahead of them."

"I'm the one who dragged you out here and away from your Quebec trip."

"And I'm the one who came."

"You mention your kids a lot. You sound like a very involved dad to me. When I was their age, I would've killed to have a father who treated me with that kind of concern."

He tilts his head expectantly. "Care to elaborate?"

"No. Not going there." She laughs, waving a hand in front of her. "We've dug up enough of my skeletons for one coffee."

"Fair." His phone dings three times, and he reaches inside his jacket to extract it. "Sorry. Just got to check."

"Please."

The color drains from his cheeks as he reads the texts. When he looks back up at her, his jaw is clenched and his eyes distressed. He slowly rotates the phone until she can see the headline of the online article. It reads: "Teen Fights for Life After Vaccination."

CHAPTER 35

Jack sits in the middle of the hardwood floor and rocks rhythmically on the spot without uttering a sound. Max finds it painful to watch. He knows his son is this silent only when he's most distraught. "Jack, it's just a new class," he said reassuringly. "You'll still be in the same school."

But Jack's stare remains blank, and he continues to sway like a human seesaw.

Earlier in the afternoon, Jack punched a second classmate. The poor girl required two stitches to close the inside of her lip where her own tooth had cut her. Fearing expulsion, Max and Sarah were incredibly relieved when the principal informed them that he was only reassigning their son to a different classroom with fewer students and more aides. What the principal didn't say, but they both understood, was that this class was designated for the most aggressive children at the Institute. On hearing the news, Jack was inconsolable. Not only does he abhor change, but he's also incredibly attached to his current teacher. She's one of the few people who can reach him.

Max sits down beside his son. "It's not so bad, Jack. You'll still have all your old friends at school. And you'll still get to see Ms. Appleby."

Jack stares past him without acknowledging the comment.

Max gently lowers his arm over his son's shoulders. At first Jack doesn't respond, but then he begins to rock faster. Max jerks his arm away, recognizing the warning sign, shamefully aware that he's afraid of his own son's unpredictable response.

For a minute or two, Max just sits in silence beside his son. Then his phone buzzes, and he pulls it out of his pocket.

"Have you seen it yet?!?" the text from Cole reads. Below it, his friend has attached a hyperlink to the *Seattle Times* website.

The headline launches his pulse racing. His excitement only grows as he reads the specifics in the article about a fifteen-year-old girl who suffered a life-threatening reaction to the meningitis vaccine. Max responds viscerally to the accompanying photos. He wonders why the paper even bothered to add the anonymizing black bar across the girl's eyes, since her face is barely recognizable through all the blistering and puffiness.

None of the details described surprise Max. A small part of him even feels guilty, especially for the satisfaction he takes in the graphic photos. He understands that the girl is suffering and that her parents must be beyond worry. But he also sees them as incredibly fortunate. The doctor quoted in the article predicted the girl would make a full recovery, which is more than most vaccine victims can expect.

The news is better than what Max could have hoped for. It's exactly what the cause needs. Not another cautionary tale told from the fringes. Not another voice in an echo chamber. No. This is irrefutable, visual proof of the dangers of vaccines, coming from the kind of mainstream media that usually marginalizes anti-vaxxers.

It is the smoking gun he has dreamed of.

Maybe now people will listen.

CHAPTER 36

Lisa is running on sheer adrenaline, having hardly slept overnight. The tension she came home to the previous evening was even worse than anticipated. Despite her preoccupation with the crisis at work, she tried to engage Dominic. But he wanted no part of her explanation or her apology for canceling their counseling session. He spoke few words, and he physically shrugged off her attempt to lay a hand on his arm. The rare times he did meet her gaze, his eyes burned with wounded contempt. He ended all further discussion by grabbing a bottle of red, stomping off to the guest room, and slamming the door behind him. She hasn't seen him since.

Ingrid is waiting for Lisa at the door to her office when she arrives at seven fifteen. Her eyes are puffy and red, and her lip trembles.

"What's wrong, Ingrid?"

"They won't stop."

"Who won't?"

"Reporters. Worried parents. Everyone. The phone won't stop ringing. I have over forty voice mails and twice as many emails. They all want an explanation . . . About that girl the vaccine made so sick."

Lisa shudders inwardly at the phrasing but smiles reassuringly. "It's OK, Ingrid. Just tell them that we'll be releasing a statement later this morning."

Ingrid nods, still visibly fighting back tears.

"Is Kevin in yet?" Lisa asks about the department's publicist.

"Haven't seen him."

"Tell him to drop by as soon as he gets in."

"OK." Ingrid begins to turn away, but then stops. "Oh, there's a Dr. Miriam Khan looking for you. From Children's Hospital. She left a message. I'll forward you her contact info."

"Thanks, but I've got her number," Lisa says, wondering why her old friend from medical school didn't call her directly.

Lisa sits at her desk, pulls her phone out, and locates Miriam's cell number. The pediatric infectious-disease specialist answers on the third ring. "Miriam, hi. It's Lisa Dyer."

"Oh, Lisa! It's been too too long. I miss you, honey." Miriam's voice is as perky as ever and still holds a trace of her Farsi accent.

"Likewise, honey. But why did you go through my assistant to reach me?"

"Your assistant?" Miriam says.

"You left a message for me in my office at Public Health."

"Oh no. I was looking for Angela Chow."

"You haven't heard? Angela's on medical leave. I'm the public-health officer now."

"You are? Oh, wonderful! Obviously, I hope Angela gets well, but you understand. I'm so proud of you."

"It's not exactly a dream job right now. Trust me. Not with this meningitis outbreak."

"This is exactly why I was calling, Lisa," Miriam says. "The situation is a disaster here at Children's Hospital."

"I've been following. Those kids from Bellevue, right?"

"You heard about the new family, then?"

"Family? No."

"Three siblings. They came in last night. All have meningococcus." Miriam's voice quiets. "The youngest one—only five years old—she died just a few minutes ago."

An entire family with meningitis? "They're from Bellevue? Part of that cluster?"

"Very much so. The middle boy played on the same baseball team as one of the previous victims who died here."

"Mason Pickering?"

"Precisely."

"If he was a contact of Mason's, then surely the boy would've been given prophylactic antibiotics?"

"He was! It didn't prevent the infection. This is why I called your office."

Not another one. "I'll come to you!" Lisa is already on her way out the door as she ends the call. She gets in her car and races over to Children's Hospital.

Miriam is waiting for her just inside the PICU, Children's Hospital's state-of-the-art pediatric intensive care unit, which is bathed in natural light from window wells and skylights. Miriam wears a white lab coat that is, just as it was in medical school, too long for her petite frame. Her deep brown eyes light at the sight of Lisa, and she wraps her in a tight hug, enveloping her in a rose scent.

Miriam pulls Lisa by the hand past four adjoining glass-walled rooms. Inside each, a child lies on a stretcher connected to a ventilator and multiple intravenous drips, while everyone else in the room wears a mask, a face shield, and a protective gown. The parents are easy to distinguish from the staff through their anguished body language alone.

"Meningococcus," Miriam says, shaking her head. "Every one of them."

She stops in front of the fifth room, where the curtains are drawn inside the glass. Lisa doesn't even need to ask. Miriam grabs two folded yellow gowns off the shelf and hands one of them to Lisa.

Once they're both gowned, masked, and gloved, Lisa follows Miriam into the room. It's empty aside from the little girl with a round, cherubic face who lies lifeless on the stretcher, covered up to her neck by a sheet. A disconnected ventilator tube pokes out between her pale lips as a reminder of the failed resuscitation.

A year younger than Olivia.

"Nora, the youngest of the three Hawthorn children," Miriam explains as she steps up to the head of the bed. "She wasn't even showing symptoms when the parents brought the two older brothers into the ER last night, both with fevers. Mom and Dad are next door with Stefan, the older brother, who's fighting so hard to hang on."

"The speed this bug strikes with . . ."

"Awful. None of these children should've been infected, Lisa. Stefan was treated with a full course of antibiotic prophylaxis after his exposure."

Lisa appreciates that there's nothing accusatory in her friend's tone, but she can't help feeling somehow responsible. "This is the second failed contact prophylaxis, Miriam."

"The second?"

"There's another case. A fifteen-year-old who's at Harborview now."

"Maybe we need to change the protocol? Add a third antibiotic to the regime?"

"Maybe. But there will still be failures. No matter what antibiotics we give them." Lisa's thoughts turn to Nicola Ford, the asymptomatic carrier who ended up spreading the infection to Bellevue. "Besides, there will be other contacts who are too scared, too lazy, or too ignorant to even take the prophylactic antibiotics."

"What about this new vaccine?"

"So far, it's been universally effective in raising the recipients' antibody titers to what we believe are protective levels."

"Then we need to vaccinate every child in this city! We have to create herd immunity."

"Agreed."

Miriam clears her throat, and when she speaks again, her voice is resigned. "I've managed children suffering from COVID, cholera, malaria, flesh-eating disease . . . you name it, Lisa. But I have never seen anything as aggressive as this strain of meningococcus."

Lisa and Miriam leave Nora's room, strip out of their PPE, and walk out of the PICU together. Promising to see each other soon, and realizing they probably won't, they part ways after hugging again beside the elevators.

As Lisa is pulling out of the hospital's parking lot, she calls her sister on her car's hands-free phone.

"Funny," Amber says. "I was just about to call you."

"What's up? Olivia OK?"

"She's fine. But I was just reading about the girl with the vaccine injury."

"It wasn't an injury," Lisa snaps. "The shot didn't break her arm."

"Reaction. Whatever. It sounds awful."

"It is," Lisa admits. "But it's also the only major adverse effect we've seen among thousands of inoculations."

Amber is quiet for a moment. "And you still think I should get Olivia vaccinated?"

"I do."

"You're not worried about the risk?"

Lisa thinks of Nora's round, lifeless face. "I'm way more concerned about the risk of not getting Liv vaccinated."

Amber silently digests the comment for a short while. "Another girl from Olivia's school is already in the hospital," she says.

"You'll do it, then?"

"I think so." Amber hesitates. "But can I ask a favor?"

"Name it."

"Will you give her the shot yourself, Lisa?"

CHAPTER 37

Accessing the vials has proven to be much simpler than replacing them. They're distributed in scaled packs, so the only opportunity arises when a pack is already open, during a vaccination clinic. Even then, there are so many eyes on the supply. Getting in and out without being noticed, therein lies the real challenge.

CHAPTER 38

If it weren't for the armed security guard at the door, Lisa would've thought she had wandered into the wrong warehouse. Gone are the boxes, pallets, forklifts, and even the lingering scent of lumber. Individual offices are now walled off by temporary partitions and are filled with desks, chairs, and other furniture. Laptop computers are everywhere. There are even a few rugs scattered across the floor.

Lisa is directed by a young man wearing a tight royal-blue suit and no socks to a makeshift office in the far corner of the warehouse where she finds Fiona sitting at her desk, working on her laptop. The only other object on the desk is an analog clock made of walnut, carved in a sleek conical, art deco design.

At the sight of Lisa, Fiona shuts her laptop and rises from her desk. "Hello."

"Hi." Lisa swirls a finger in front of her. "Your portable head-quarters are impressive."

"Don't know about impressive. But certainly necessary, if we want to safely distribute fifty-thousand-plus doses of Neissovax."

"Looks like a seamless operation to me. No wonder Nathan has so much faith in you."

"Nathan is generally too trusting," Fiona says with a small grin as she walks past Lisa and into the abutting cubicle. She returns moments later wheeling in another chair. "Please, sit."

"Thanks," Lisa says as she takes a seat.

"Coffee? Tea?"

After Lisa shakes her head, Fiona eases back into her own chair. "What can I do for you, Lisa?"

"You've seen the news coverage on Mia's skin eruption?"

"Impossible to miss."

"The media is having a field day. We're issuing a statement this morning to reassure the public. But so far, it hasn't dulled the appetite for the vaccine. This morning's clinics are swamped."

"I triple-checked the batch where her vial came from. Every sample sailed through the quality-control standards." Fiona sighs. "We never saw anything equivalent to this in the trials."

"It's damn rare, is why."

"This is what Nathan and I worried about when you first approached us. We wanted more time. More trials. As you know, sometimes it takes tens of thousands of inoculations to uncover rarer associations."

Lisa thinks of the rotavirus vaccine, but she doesn't say anything. "And sometimes, isolated reactions are just random. And have nothing to do with the vaccine in question."

"Lisa, I live and breathe Neissovax." Fiona folds her arms across her chest. "But it's impossible not to associate this girl's skin eruption with the vaccine."

"What I mean is that Stevens-Johnson syndrome can be associated with any number of common drugs. And we wouldn't be doing such soul-searching if one of them had caused the rash, instead of Neissovax."

Fiona considers that for a moment while the clock ticks steadily in the background. "I'm not responsible for any other drugs."

"You're not responsible for Mia, either."

"I am responsible for product safety, though." She views Lisa with somber eyes. "What if there are other Mias?"

"We'll cross that bridge, when and if we come to it," Lisa reassures her, relating to the weight of responsibility Fiona must be carrying. "Right now we have a lethal bacterium attacking the vulnerable children in this city. I just saw the latest victim. Postmortem. A little waif of a girl. The antibiotics her older brother got didn't protect her family. Neissovax might be all we have."

"I suppose," Fiona says, lapsing into another silence that is filled only by the ticking of the clock.

Lisa nods to the timepiece. "I don't know squat about clocks, but I love the design. Reminds me of the dome of the Chrysler Building."

"Same vintage, too."

"Are you a collector?"

"Walt always had a passion for clocks, especially the early and midcentury ones. I wouldn't call him a collector, but he definitely had an eye." She shows a sad smile. "He gave me that for our fifth anniversary."

"How sweet."

"I'll never forget what he wrote in the card. 'The wood symbolizes the five years we've already had. The clock, all the time left ahead of us.'" Fiona looks away. "At least he was right about the wood. It's the traditional five-year anniversary gift."

Thinking of her own marriage, Lisa feels a pang of envy that she realizes is completely irrational considering how Fiona's ended. "Sounds like you two had something incredible."

Fiona shrugs slightly. "I thought so."

"Do you mind if I ask . . ."

"Guillain-Barré syndrome," Fiona says of the disorder in which the body's immune system attacks its own nervous system, causing debilitating weakness.

"But most people survive that, don't they?"

"His hit so quickly. Just ate his nerves up. He went from jogging one morning to not being able to stand by dinnertime. The next day he couldn't breathe on his own. He ended up on a ventilator, and then developed pneumonia. Everything went wrong from there. So many complications. His body just shut down. He was dead in seventy-two hours."

"God, that must've been so hard for you."

"A lot harder for Walt," Fiona murmurs.

"Do they know what caused it?" Lisa asks, aware that most cases of Guillain-Barré syndrome are caused by a haywire immune response to an infection or, though far less frequent, even to a vaccine.

"It was flu season," Fiona says as she reaches over and adjusts the position of the clock. "It's ancient history now, anyway."

"Some things last forever."

Fiona's cheeks and forehead flush slightly. "You didn't come here to talk about clocks. Or Walt."

"No. But thank you for sharing," Lisa says, nodding solemnly. "Actually, Fiona, I was hoping to ask you a favor."

"What kind of favor?"

"I have a niece. Olivia. She's six. Sassy as anything. Would mouth off to a cop." Lisa laughs. "Anyway, my sister's family lives in Bellevue. And two of Olivia's classmates have already developed this meningitis."

Fiona frowns. "I'm sorry, Lisa."

"Maybe I'm just being an overprotective aunt. But Olivia is probably the closest thing I will ever have to a kid of my own . . ."

"You want to get her vaccinated?"

"Yeah. My sister is skeptical of vaccines, though. To put it mildly. But I think I've managed to convince her."

"Good."

"Look, I know we agreed that all vaccinations would be

supervised by a Delaware rep. And I can definitely bring Olivia into one of the clinics. But my sister asked me if I would give Olivia the—"

Fiona stops her with a raised hand. Her lips curve into an understanding smile. "Let me go get you a vial, Lisa."

CHAPTER 39

Nathan sits in his hotel room in front of his laptop, once again logged into the administrator's portal on Seattle Public Health's website for reporting Neissovax complications. He rereads each one of the seventy-nine reported entries, eyes peeled for any sign or symptom remotely consistent with a skin reaction similar to Mia's. The more he snoops, the guiltier he feels.

A pop-up appears at a corner of his screen, announcing a video call from Peter Moore. He clicks open the video chat window, and his boss's face fills the screen.

"Enjoying your vacation?" Peter asks with a smile that appears less than sincere.

"About as much as a getaway to the Congo at the height of Ebola season."

"You work best under pressure, Nathan."

"Not this kind, Peter."

The grin vacates Peter's lips. "This girl with the skin condition? She's doing better?"

"She's still in the ICU, but I understand she's stable and improving."

"That's good. Also, it guarantees a bigger financial payout for her and the family if she survives."

"That's a bit cavalier."

"There's more money in disability than in death," Peter says matter-of-factly. "And there will be a lawsuit."

"How do you know?"

"My spies tell me the father is out for blood. He was the one who leaked the story and the photos to the media."

Nathan's eyes narrow. "Your spies, Peter?"

"Does it surprise you that I'm keeping close tabs on this?"

"No," Nathan says. "But it does surprise me that you're keeping me out of the loop."

"It's no big deal, Nathan. We hired a local investigator to poke around. Didn't think it was significant enough to even tell you."

"Everything related to Neissovax is significant."

"So we're on the same page, then," Peter says unapologetically. "No other adverse reactions that we need to be concerned about?"

"I've been monitoring the website. Nothing, so far."

"It's a one-off, then."

"Only time will tell."

Peter's gaze ices over. "That won't fly."

"What does that mean?"

"It has to be a one-off, Nathan."

CHAPTER 40

The timer on the microwave dings, and Emilio Flores almost burns his finger grabbing the hot bowl with his bare hand. "Damn it," he mutters to himself as he races the bowl over to the waiting plate on the counter. Using a tea towel, he flips the bowl over and taps out the scrambled eggs onto the buttered toast.

"Come down, Mateo," Emilio calls up the stairs to his son. "Now! Breakfast is ready. And we're going to be late."

"I don't want to eat, *Papá!*" the eight-year-old replies.

That's unusual, Emilio thinks as he stands at the sink and runs cold water over his throbbing finger. Not only is Mateo always hungry, but he's also the most compliant kid. Sometimes, Emilio worries that his son is too accommodating—always doing as he's told and never complaining. He would like to see more defiance from Mateo. *But not this morning.* "Too bad. *Papá cocinó esto,*" Emilio yells over his shoulder. "Now you're going to eat it."

His wife, Isabelle, is already at the church helping her sister with the last-minute preparations. *Isabelle will kill us if we're late.* After all, Mateo is the ring bearer for his aunt's wedding.

It takes another five minutes and two more shouts before Mateo finally appears in the doorway to the kitchen. The first thing Emilio notices is his son's white shirt. It's stained in several places with slick yellowish blotches that resemble grease.

"Mateo Flores!" Emilio barks. "*Mamá* just washed and ironed that shirt. What did you get all over it?"

"It's not my fault, *Papá*," Mateo says as he begins to unbutton his shirt.

Emilio suddenly notices how pale his son looks. He takes a step closer. "What's the matter, buddy?"

"My chest hurts. My back, too." Mateo slips off his shirt. "And I don't know what these are."

Emilio can only gape at his son's exposed chest. Fluid-filled sacks the size of golf balls—some even bigger—cover much of his skin. And Mateo's back is worse. A steady trickle of yellow fluid runs down and soaks the back of his pants.

CHAPTER 41

Amber answers the door with a phone to her ear. "Come in," she mouths to Lisa as she turns back toward the living room.

Lisa has only taken a few steps inside the house when her niece comes flying down the hallway toward her. Lisa crouches down and spreads her arms. Olivia jumps into the embrace.

"I'm not scared, Tee!" Olivia trumpets as Lisa straightens and spins her around.

"Scared of what?" Lisa asks, kissing her niece's forehead.

"The needle."

"Of course you aren't. You're way too brave for that. Bet you won't even flinch."

Olivia drops back to the ground. "What's 'flinch'?"

Lisa flings her arm back, leans away, and contorts her face into an expression of exaggerated fear.

Olivia giggles. "I definitely won't flinch."

Amber approaches holding out the phone to Lisa. "Can you talk?"

"Who is it?" Lisa asks, reaching for the phone.

"Dad."

Lisa's hand freezes where it is.

"Come on," Amber whispers. "He just wants to say hello."

Reluctantly, Lisa takes the phone. She walks down the hall and into the kitchen before she brings it to her ear. "Hi, Dad."

"Liberty!" Ian Dyer says. "I mean Lisa, of course. Old habits die slowly when you're this old."

She hasn't heard her father's voice in over two years, maybe three, but he sounds as robust and animated as ever. "How are you?"

"I'm fine, muffin. Good as ever. The upside of the farming life. All the fresh air and GMO-free food keeps even ancient bodies like mine going."

"Mom sounds good, too. I spoke to her a few days ago."

"You did, did you?" A familiar accusatory edge creeps into his tone, and Lisa realizes her mom must not have mentioned the call.

"Just a short chat. About nothing, really," she says, falling back into the old habit of trying to protect her mom from her dad's ire.

"Your mother never tells me anything," he says with a laugh. "Who can blame her?"

But she knows him too well to buy the self-deprecating routine. It is so typical of her father. He has to be in charge of every situation. The moment he perceives he has lost that control, he lashes out. While he was never physical with any of the family during Lisa's childhood, they all lived in fear of his emotional lability. When he threw one of his frequent tantrums, he would scream at the top of lungs, spewing words that could slice like a whip. Other times, he used silence as a weapon—refusing to speak to or even acknowledge Lisa for weeks on end after some perceived slight or other.

"It's good to hear that my two girls—well, three, when you count the little one—are all together now."

"Yeah, we get to see a lot of each other."

"That's wonderful. Must make up for you not ever getting to see your own parents."

Exhaling slowly, Lisa forces herself to do a quick five-senses exercise. *The cutting board. The hum of the fridge. The light pressure of her watchband. The scent of coffee. The salty taste of her own saliva.* "Olivia's shooting up like a weed these days," she says.

"I saw her last week," he says pointedly. "Such a funny little one. As spunky as you were at that age."

"You think?"

"Definitely. Just hope she won't turn out to be as defiant."

Multiple responses come to mind, but Lisa decides not to engage him.

"Listen, I wanted to talk you about this vaccine," he continues.

"What about it?"

"Amber tells me you're planning to give Olivia a shot."

"I am."

"And you think it's a good idea?"

"I do."

"I heard about the girl who almost died from it."

"So did I, Dad. In fact, I spoke to her myself."

"And you want to take the same kind of chance with my grand-daughter?"

"It's not Russian roulette. It's one reaction among thousands. This meningitis has already killed a lot of kids, including one of Olivia's classmates."

"You don't need to worry about that."

"And why's that, Dad?"

"Because we Dyers have good *natural* immune systems. I never let you or your sister anywhere near those toxic vaccines they tried to foist on you when you were babies. And neither of you ever came down with anything more than a head cold during your whole childhood."

"And we should take that as proof enough that Olivia is safe from the most dangerous bacteria this city might have ever seen?"

"It is for me." He huffs. "What do I know? I just raised you from nothing. But you're the one who went to medical school."

"That's right, I did."

"The most corrupted academic institution on the planet."

Lisa focuses on her breathing. "Let's not start—"

"Where the learning is bought and sold by corporate interests, who convince every last one of you that expensive chemicals and invasive surgeries are all somehow preferable to nature itself."

"Speaking of chemicals, are you taking your medications, Dad?"

"That's right. There it is again. The arrogance. The I-always-know-better attitude that makes you so damn special. So infallible."

"I've got to go, Dad."

"Don't take my granddaughter down with you!"

Lisa hangs up the phone. She rubs her eyes. *He will not get to me*, she reassures herself, gathering her composure as she heads back into living room.

"How did it go?" Amber asks as she accepts her phone back.

"Nothing changes," Lisa says.

Olivia tugs at her sleeve. "Are we doing this, Tee?"

"Yes, we are," Lisa says, more determined than ever. "How about over there on the couch?"

Olivia hurries over to it and sits down. "Which arm do I get it in, Tee?"

Lisa taps her own shoulder. "The left one. That way you'll still be able to draw right away."

Olivia yanks her collar down over her shoulder to expose the skin.

"You're too keen." Lisa laughs. "I still have to get the stuff ready."

Lisa reaches into her handbag and pulls out the supplies Fiona gave her, including the vial of Neissovax, a one-cc syringe with attached needle, and an alcohol swab.

Olivia's eyes go wide as Lisa pulls the cap off the syringe to reveal the needle underneath. "So big?" she asks.

"It's actually very small. Won't be any worse than a mosquito bite."

Olivia watches with mouth open as Lisa flicks the yellow cap off the vial, plunges the needle in, and sucks up the half cc of vaccine.

"You want to hold Mom's hand?" Lisa asks.

"Can I?"

Amber kneels beside Olivia's right side and takes her hand.

Lisa pulls Olivia's collar back and rubs the alcohol swab over the skin on her shoulder. "I'm going to count to backward from five. You ready?"

"Ready." Olivia squeezes her eyes shut.

Lisa raises the syringe. She looks over to Amber and, in that moment, sees persistent doubt in her sister's eyes.

"Five . . . four . . . three . . . two . . ." Lisa jabs the needle through Olivia's skin before reaching "one" and presses down on the plunger.

"Hey!" Olivia calls out in a mix of pain and amusement. "You tricked me."

"Yes, I did." Lisa withdraws the needle and recaps it. "So sue me."

"Not fair." Olivia laughs as she rubs her shoulder.

Lisa ruffles her hair. "You were super brave!"

"I was, wasn't I?"

As Lisa is applying a small bandage to the inoculation site, her phone rings. She extracts it from her purse and, seeing the call comes from her office, answers.

"There's been another one," are the first tense words out of Tyra's mouth.

"Another . . ." Lisa says, although she already knows. Her eyes dart instinctively over to her niece, who clutches her left shoulder with her other hand.

"Vaccine reaction. And it's bad, Lisa. Very bad."

CHAPTER 42

Lisa rides the elevator alone to the rooftop. Hard as she tries, she can't shake the mental image of Mateo Flores. And she can't stop thinking of her visit to see him, a few hours earlier, in the children's ICU.

Mateo wasn't on the ventilator when Lisa arrived, although he might be on one by now. Most of his body from the neck down was already covered in mummy-like circumferential bandaging. But as the nurse reapplied strips to his arm, Lisa got enough of a glimpse of the transparent, yellowish fluid-filled sack of skin over his shoulder to understand how extensive the blistering must have been. According to the attending doctor, the rash was spreading by the hour. And Mateo had lost so much fluid through the blisters that the ICU team was having troubling keeping his blood pressure from dropping critically low, despite all the intravenous fluids they were pouring into him.

Though he was sedated, Mateo was unbelievably stoic. He didn't cry once during the dressing change, and he even showed the nurse a shy smile. His parents, however, were inconsolable. His father, Emilio, wasn't angry like Mia's dad had been. He simply seemed helpless, begging Lisa for reassurances she couldn't offer. If she had to choose, she would have opted for anger and blame over his desperation.

The elevator opens, and Lisa steps out into the rooftop bar. Nathan sits at the same high-top table as before. He appears as rattled as Lisa feels. A beer bottle dangles between his fingers as he stares glumly out toward the dark waters of Puget Sound. It's the first time Lisa has seen him with strands of hair out of place and a shirt that's not perfectly pressed.

"Hey," she says as she slides into the chair across from him. "Where's Fiona?"

He shakes his head. "She wouldn't leave the warehouse once she heard about the latest kid to react. She's going through the supply. Testing each batch over again, herself."

"What does she hope to find?"

Nathan merely shrugs.

"Mia attended a vaccination clinic two days before Mateo did," Lisa says. "And the two clinics are eight miles apart. We checked the serial numbers. They didn't get their vaccines from the same batch."

He takes a long swig of his beer and then asks, "How's the boy doing?"

"Not great. Mateo's suffering from toxic epidermal necrolysis, a more extensive form of Stevens-Johnson syndrome, involving the whole body rather than just the mouth or face. It leads to severe blistering and fluid loss. Oftentimes multi-organ failure. Even death."

"Jesus," Nathan mutters. "But it's basically the same reaction as Mia's?"

"Another manifestation of the same disease, yeah. Both caused by a delayed immune response." She pauses. "To Neissovax."

"So Mia's reaction wasn't a one-off?"

Lisa shakes her head.

"When the board gets wind of this . . ."

"Two kids are fighting for their lives, Nathan."

"There are more important things at stake than money. I get it. But it's still going to devastate Delaware. The stock price will tumble. People are going to lose their jobs. Their careers."

Lisa can't help but wonder if he's thinking of himself. "This link between Neissovax and the severe skin eruption was bound to come out at some point," she says. "Maybe this isn't the worst way to find out."

"How could it be any worse, Lisa?"

"We've already shown that Neissovax is effective against one of the deadliest strains of meningococcus where nothing else works. It might be too essential not to use, despite the risks."

"Doubt that." He pushes the drinks menu toward her, but she waves it off. "You're going to suspend the vaccination campaign?"

"We'll decide at tomorrow morning's meeting, but we might have to. At least, until we figure out exactly what we're dealing with."

"Doesn't matter much, anyway."

"Why's that?"

"Once word gets out about the second reaction—"

"We have to announce this one. We can't afford to have another case leak out. We'd lose all credibility."

"Of course. The point is, even if you do keep the clinics open, who's going to show up now?"

"We know Neissovax works. And there have only been two reactions among six thousand doses given."

"One in a million is enough for the anti-vaxxers to jump all over this. But one in three thousand?" He lowers his beer. "Would you vaccinate someone you love with those kinds of odds?"

"I already did."

"Who?"

"My niece."

"Ah."

Lisa realizes the worry she feels is out of proportion to the actual risk, but she can't stop thinking about Olivia. She's already called Amber twice to check up on her niece, who's doing fine according to her sister.

Nathan leans forward. "How are you holding up?"

"Honestly?"

"Yeah."

"I've had better days. Better weeks. Better months, even."

He smiles, and his blue-gray eyes light with their now familiar charm. "Are you going to stop at years or are we going all the way up to decades?"

"Up to you." She can't help but smile back.

"Things OK on the home front?"

"Very quiet."

"That's good, right?"

"I'm getting the silent treatment."

"I remember that."

Something in his sympathetic gaze releases the emotions that have been stewing inside since her call with her father and her visit with Mateo. "I feel like such a fucking failure, Nathan!"

"This isn't on you, Lisa." He reaches out and touches the back of her hand.

"The vaccine is just the tip of it," she murmurs. "I'm forty-one years old and nothing in my life works right now. Professionally, I'm losing control over the worst infectious outbreak to hit this city. Personally, my marriage is crumbling. My mentor is dying, and I can't do anything to help her. I'm estranged from my parents. My own sister doubts me . . ."

Nathan squeezes her hand. "Can't really speak to your family or your marriage. Though everyone goes through that kind of turmoil at some point. But I can tell you that you are phenomenal at your job. Compassionate, innovative, and decisive. You've been dealt an absolute shit hand. As bad as this crisis is, it would be so much worse without you."

She stares back at him, wondering why Dominic never offers her such reassurances, and then gives him a small smile.

Nathan's fingers slip between hers. "Matter of fact, the only good thing to happen to me since I came to Seattle is meeting you."

Lisa looks down at their interlocking hands. She realizes she doesn't want the contact to end. Reluctantly, though, she wriggles her hand free. "Thank you, really," she says without looking at him. "I better go."

CHAPTER 43

The Outbreak Control Team meeting is well attended, but it feels to Lisa as if the air has been sucked out of the room. The members accept the bleak statistical update for day twelve of the meningococcal outbreak—three confirmed geographical clusters, twenty-three dead, two antibiotic prophylaxis failures, and forty-nine infected—with collective resignation.

Lisa suppresses a yawn. It was another near-sleepless night. Dominic was still petulant, but at least he was talking to her. He even asked about the outbreak. But after her roller coaster of a day, she didn't have the energy—or, if she was being honest, the patience—to discuss it with him. Besides, the encounter with Nathan at the bar left her too confused and conflicted to want to talk about much of anything with her husband.

Lisa moves to the next slide. "In terms of the vaccine reactions: Mia Meyer has been transferred out of the ICU and is expected to be discharged in the next few days. Mateo Flores is in critical condition and his prognosis is guarded as of this morning."

Benning holds her hand up. "Our offices are being inundated

with calls," she says, referring to city hall. "Mainly from families of kids who have already received the vaccine."

"Ours, too," Tyra says.

"And the national coverage is exploding," Kevin says. "Fox News did a whole segment on the dangers of new vaccines this morning."

"Fox, huh? What a shocker," Angela says. Her voice is subdued this morning. Beyond the ravages of her illness, she looks defeated to Lisa.

Lisa looks around the table. "The next vaccination clinic is scheduled to open in less than ninety minutes . . ."

"You're going to cancel it, right?" Benning asks.

"That's what this group needs to decide."

"There's not much choice, is there?" Angela asks. "Who's going to show up?"

"This vaccine works, though," Moyes pipes up unexpectedly. "You saw the statistics. This meningitis outbreak has reached a tipping point. And the antibiotic prophylaxis failure represents another major vulnerability. More children are going to die. Probably many, if we halt the vaccination campaign now."

"You might be right, Alistair," Lisa says. "But so is Angela. Between the news of the second reaction and those gruesome photos of Mia going viral, even if we do run clinics, people aren't going to come."

"It's odd, though, isn't it?" he says.

"What is?"

"That there was no hint of any kind of delayed immune responses in all the previous Neissovax trials. Why are we seeing them now for the first time?"

"It's still a pretty rare reaction," Lisa says. "Maybe we're only now hitting the critical mass of subjects required to see the signal. After all, we've inoculated over six thousand. Four times as many as were enrolled in the pooled trials."

Moyes shakes his head. "Is it possible Delaware hid something in their initial results?"

The question reminds Lisa of Max's insinuation about the coincidental timing of the outbreak and the new vaccine, which dripped with similar conspiratorialism, but she pushes that out of mind. "Why would they hide a complication like that in the trials? It's far worse for it to come out during the clinical rollout when it's too late for damage control."

"At this point, we should consider all possibilities," Moyes says. "Have we tested the vaccines involved in these two cases of skin eruptions?"

"Fiona Swanson, Delaware's director of product safety, has retested the batches they came from. There are no concerns."

"Not the batches, Lisa. I meant the individual vials."

"How would we do that? They've already been dispensed."

Angela sits up straighter. "There'd be residual vaccine left inside the vials."

Moyes nods. "Or inside the syringes themselves."

Before Lisa can answer, the door opens, and Ingrid leans her flushed face into the room. "So sorry to interrupt, Dr. Dyer," she says quietly.

Realizing that it must be important, Lisa hops to her feet and steps out into the hallway.

"There's a Dr. Sandhu looking for you," Ingrid says. "He says it's urgent."

The name means nothing to Lisa. "From where?"

"The medical examiner's office."

Lisa ducks back into the conference room to ask Tyra to finish chairing the meeting, before hurrying into her office. Ingrid patches the call through.

"I am sorry to interrupt, Dr. Dyer," Sandhu says in a British accent. "However, I felt this was rather urgent."

"What is, Dr. Sandhu?"

"I've just completed an autopsy on a twenty-year-old male who died three days ago."

"Died how?" Lisa asks with growing alarm.

"I've concluded the ultimate cause of death is Stevens-Johnson syndrome."

"What's his name?"

"Darius Washington."

She doesn't recognize it. "Did he die in hospital?"

"He never reached the hospital. The swelling in his throat caused an acute occlusion of his airway. He died at home. Of asphyxiation."

"Oh my God . . ."

"I've obviously followed the recent news. The reason I am calling, Dr. Dyer, is that I also discovered swelling over his left deltoid that is consistent with a recent inoculation."

Stunned, Lisa mumbles her thanks and hangs up. She immediately logs into the vaccination database on her computer. It takes only seconds to confirm that a Darius Washington received his Neissovax immunization at the first vaccination clinic on the campaign's opening day.

The same one where Mia got hers.

Lisa clicks open the website that catalogs all the vaccination reactions. She searches for the names *Darius* and *Washington* but doesn't find a match for either. Surely his friends or family would have known about his vaccination? *Why didn't anyone report him?*

With this third critical reaction, Lisa recognizes that any chance of the first two being coincidence has been shattered. Moyes was right. How could those rashes not have manifested during the clinical trials?

She picks up her phone and calls Fiona.

"There's been a third case," Lisa explains as soon as Fiona answers. "This one didn't make it."

Fiona is quiet for a long moment. When she speaks, her voice is as fragile as crystal. "I see."

"This latest victim, Darius Washington . . . he got his vaccination at the same clinic as Mia Meyer did. Our very first one. Which means two of the eight hundred inoculated there reacted this way. And we could still see more from it."

"I've checked that batch repeatedly," Fiona insists. "There were zero imperfections."

"What about the individual vials? Have you tested those for contaminants?"

There's another pause. "The spent vials?"

"Yes, there should be enough liquid left inside to test them."

"Even if that were true, the first clinic was five days ago. Those used vials are long gone."

"Gone where?"

"We collect them and ship them back to Littleton for sterilization and recycling."

"How about the clinic where Mateo got vaccinated? That was only three days ago."

"I'll double-check, but I'm sure the same is true."

"OK," Lisa says, feeling increasingly despondent. "Thanks."

"Lisa . . ."

"Yes?"

"You're sure this person died from a reaction to Neissovax?"

"Yes."

"I can't believe this is happening," Fiona says, her voice cracking. "There were so many scenarios I envisioned. Terrible ones, too. But this? I never expected anything like this."

"Why would you?" Lisa asks, as much of herself as Fiona. "But it's happened. And now we have to limit further damage."

After she hangs up, Lisa's mind keeps turning back to Darius. How could no one in his life have associated his death with the vaccine?

She rises and heads back to the conference room but finds it empty. She heads over to Tyra's office, where the program director sits typing at her computer.

Tyra looks up at her. "There wasn't much left to discuss after you left . . ." she begins, but stops. "What's wrong, Lisa?"

"There's been a third reaction. A death this time." Lisa goes on to update her about Darius.

Tyra's shoulders slump. "Now what?"

"For starters, we cancel all the vaccination clinics. Immediately and indefinitely."

"They've won. The anti-vaxxers."

"No one wins here."

Tyra nods blankly.

"I need to speak to Darius's family. Urgently. Can you help me track down his next of kin?"

"Will do."

"We have two people who reacted out of a single clinic. Statistically speaking, it just doesn't fit, Tyra. Not if Delaware's trial data is to be believed."

"None of this makes sense, Lisa."

"I already asked Fiona about the individual vials, but they've been recycled. What about the syringes themselves? What happens to those?"

Tyra straightens, and her jaw sets with determination. "We round them up in sharps containers. Eventually we pool those into giant bins before they're sent out for biomed waste disposal."

"How often do those go out?"

"I'm guessing weekly, but I can let you know."

"So they might not be gone?"

"I'll look into it."

As Lisa wanders away from Tyra's office, her thoughts drift to her niece. She feels a chill at the memory of Olivia's trusting smile after she buried the needle into her shoulder. She lifts her phone and tries her sister again, but it rings through to voice mail. "Hey, how's the little one feeling?" she says on the recording, trying not to sound as worried as she feels. "Call me, Amber, please."

CHAPTER 44

The cargo doors to the warehouse are wide open. Three workers transfer a pallet from the back of the truck onto the waiting forklift. Despite the industrial nature of the scene, to Nathan, the whole experience feels more like a funeral. The ambience is the perfect fit for his current mood.

As hard as the unanticipated skin reactions and cessation of the vaccine campaign have hit Nathan, Fiona appears to be taking all the developments even worse. With bloodshot eyes and taut lips, she has never looked more exhausted or dejected to him.

"Twenty-five thousand extra doses that no one will ever see," he remarks as he watches them unload the extra supplies that were shipped urgently only the day before from the plant in Littleton.

"What do we do with them?"

"Nothing. Store them with the others, for now."

"For destruction?"

"Possibly."

"How could this have happened?"

"Terrible luck? Or karma? Maybe it's some kind of cosmic lesson for tempting fate as much as we did."

Fiona motions to the stacks of boxes on the warehouse floor. "We used the exact same product here as in the trials. Same dose, same equipment, even the same packaging. Nothing was different."

"We used more of it this time, Fee."

"That could statistically explain one, maybe two, never-before-seen reactions. But three? And two from the very same clinic? If that's random, then it's cataclysmically bad luck. Like being struck by lightning in a light rain. Twice."

Nathan stares at her. "What are you suggesting, Fee?"

"Just that none of this makes sense."

"I agree. But that doesn't help us. And it certainly won't help Delaware's bottom line."

"Who cares about that right now?"

I still do. But he's too ashamed to admit it. They lapse into silence as Nathan watches the workers pile more pallets on the floor that he realizes will likely end up back at the warehouse where they started from or in some massive incinerator.

"What's next?" she asks.

"I'm going to go back to New York. Might as well face the board sooner than later."

"And me?"

"I was hoping you'd stay here. Supervise our supplies until we've decided on the next steps."

She nods to the nearest security guard. "You want to assign me a door and give me a gun, too?"

"You're not the only one hurting here, Fee."

Her eyes lower, and her cheeks color.

Nathan softens his tone. "We're all just on edge."

She nods minimally.

Nathan's phone vibrates, and he pulls it out of his pocket. When he sees Peter Moore's name on the screen, he answers on speakerphone.

"Is it true?" Peter barks. "About the third one? A fucking John Doe?"

"He's not a John Doe, Peter," Nathan says. "He just never made it to the hospital. The coroner was the one who made the connection."

"No one reported him before that?"

"Not according to Public Health."

"Jesus Christ!" Peter growls. "This was supposed to be a fucking one-off. As in, no more goddamn reports!"

Nathan takes him off speaker and brings the phone to his ear. "Did you hear what I said, Peter? The coroner reported him. And the hospitals reported the first two."

Fiona eyes him curiously, but Nathan waves away her concern.

"Doesn't matter," Peter snaps. "This was your launch. Which means it was your mess to clean. More specifically, your mess to prevent."

"I didn't make the vaccine."

"No, you just cleared it."

"That's not exactly how I remember it."

"Pretty sure your business card reads 'responsible for new product development.'" Before Nathan can reply, Peter adds, "I expect you in my office tomorrow morning." He hangs up without another word.

Fiona reaches out to Nathan, but her hand stops short of his arm. "Are you OK?"

Nathan laughs bitterly. "I have this mental image of Peter's office right now. The torn cardigan strewn on the floor. And his owl-shaped mug lying in pieces beside it. As shattered as that Zen-like persona he's been putting on since his stroke."

Fiona eyes him with concern. "Peter is going to try to make you take the fall for this, isn't he?"

"How does that old expression go? 'Success has many fathers, but failure is an orphan'?" He groans. "At this point, I might as well throw on a curly red wig and call myself 'Annie.'"

CHAPTER 45

"What's going on?" Amber asks as soon as Lisa answers the phone.

"How's Olivia?" Lisa demands, spinning her chair away from the computer screen.

"She's OK," Amber says warily. "But why do you keep checking in? What do you know?"

Lisa hesitates. "We suspended the vaccine program."

"Why?" Amber asks, her voice barely above a whisper.

Lisa tells her about the third vaccine reaction.

"Dad was right," Amber protests.

The words cut, but Lisa doesn't have the strength to argue. "I'm sorry, Amber. I didn't know. Look, it's still less than a one-in-a-thousand chance of—"

"How long?"

"For what?"

"How long after the injection could Olivia still react?"

"Days? I guess. Not more than a week."

"*A week*, Liberty?"

"It's all happening so quickly."

Lisa hears Amber's stilted breath in her ear. She can tell that her sister is on the verge of tears.

"We trusted you."

"It's going to be all right."

"I got to go," Amber snaps, and abruptly ends the call.

The guilt gnaws like a rotting tooth. Never before has Lisa doubted her path since leaving home and choosing science over the unfounded beliefs and paranoia that rule her father's world. But the realization that she might have exposed her niece to grave danger through her own stubbornness rocks her belief system to the core.

She's still obsessing about it as Tyra steps into her office.

"You all right?" she asks.

"Yeah, fine. Just thinking."

"If you say so," Tyra says with a click of her tongue. "I followed up on our conversation from this morning."

"And?"

"The bad news is that all used syringes from the first vaccine clinic have already been collected and destroyed, including, obviously, the ones given to Mia and Darius."

"And the good news?"

"The same isn't true of the clinic where Mateo got vaccinated."

"You found his syringe?"

"Not only his. All of them from that clinic. They're individually labeled, so it didn't take us long to find Mateo's. Even better, there was still a drop of liquid left in the hub of his syringe."

"You've sent it off to the state lab?"

Tyra nods. "They've promised to run a full screen. They know it's a top priority."

"Thank you."

"Oh, I also have the number for Darius's dad. That poor man. He's in town making arrangements to have his son's body flown home to Georgia."

"Can you text it to me?"

"Will do," Tyra says as she turns to leave.

As soon as Tyra forwards the number, Lisa calls it, and a man with a gravelly voice answers. "Hello."

"Mr. Washington, I'm Dr. Dyer with Seattle Public Health. Do you have a few minutes to talk?"

"Not at this moment, Dr. Dyer," he says in a Southern accent. "I'm tied up here at the morgue trying to sort out how to get my boy home."

"I'll meet you there," Lisa says without giving him a chance to refuse.

Lisa heads down to the garage and gets in her car. She turns on the ignition, and the voices on a radio talk show fill the interior. The host is interviewing an immunologist who specializes in vaccines, a soft-spoken man who's doing his best to downplay fears over Neissovax. But the host keeps provoking him with leading questions and unfounded insinuations.

Lisa changes the station, but the topic remains the same. "This is all about the insatiable greed of these drug companies," a phone-in caller bemoans. "I heard the company behind this untested vaccine is making billions off flooding Seattle with their deadly crap."

"Maybe not billions, but no doubt they're making a healthy profit," the host replies.

They're giving it to us for free! Lisa wants to yell at the radio.

"Not to mention the priceless advertising and free marketing opportunity they're receiving," the host continues. "At least, the opportunity they thought they were going to get before it all blew up in their faces."

The next caller is even more indignant, and she specifically calls out Lisa, although not by name. "Where is the leadership in Seattle Public Health?" the woman cries. "How could they have let this happen to our kids?"

Lisa can't help but keep listening, though she's relieved when she pulls into the parking lot of the Seattle medical examiner's office— to get out of the car and away from the radio's vitriol.

Inside the office, Lisa finds Darius's father, Isaac Washington, in the otherwise empty waiting room. Wearing a suit and tie, the man, who looks to be in his sixties, is stocky with square shoulders and a dignified presence. But his expression is crestfallen as he fills in a form, which Lisa presumes represents some kind of legal release of his son's body.

"I'm so sorry for your loss, Mr. Washington," Lisa says.

"Thank you," he says with a small nod.

"Your son was studying engineering at UW, right?"

"Civil engineering," Isaac says with obvious pride. "He was going to build bridges, tunnels, and roads back home. It's all he wanted to do since he was little. He would've built some fine ones, too."

"I'm sure he would have, Mr. Washington," she says. "When did you last hear from him?"

"Day or two before he died. He called home almost every day."

"Did Darius mention anything about a vaccination?"

"Nah. Nothing like that." He bites his lower lip. "His mother was worried about the meningitis scare, though. I know she gave him a good talking-to about it."

"Did Darius have any family here?"

"No."

"Friends?"

"Lots of those," Isaac says. "He lived with his best friend, Jayden Rogers."

"Do you have Jayden's number?"

Isaac digs into his pocket and brings out a small notebook. As he flips through the pages, looking for the phone number, he pauses to look up and ask, "So is it true? The vaccine killed Darius?"

She considers couching her answer in medical terms such as

unexpected complications and *hyper-immune reactions*, but in the end, she simply nods.

"How can that happen?" There's no accusation in his tone, only disbelief.

"We . . . We still don't know."

Isaac tears a blank page from the back of the book, copies down a number, and hands it over to her.

Lisa thanks him for his time and, with nothing more to say, hurries out of the oppressive building. As soon as she steps into the hot afternoon sun, she tries the number for Jayden, but his phone goes straight to voice mail. She leaves a message asking him to call her, adding that it's urgent.

As Lisa drives away from the morgue, the memory of the pain in Isaac's eyes lingers, compounding her guilt. She's glad now for the distraction of the radio and is about to change it to her favorite jazz station when a familiar voice sounds over the speakers.

"Frankly, I think it's a travesty," Max Balfour says.

"How so, Dr. Balfour?" the host asks.

"Public Health rolled the dice with the children of Seattle. And it came up snake eyes." Lisa can picture the smug smile on the face of the anti-vax naturopath.

"It's that simple?"

"Look, I am not doubting the good intentions behind this vaccination campaign," Max says, his tone simultaneously empathetic and condescending. "But I have seen it time and time again. There is so much money to be made in developing new vaccines. Billions and billions of dollars."

"What about all the risks they take on?" Lisa rhetorically asks of the radio, thinking of how it costs more than a billion dollars to bring a new vaccine to market, with no guarantees of recouping the investment.

"Big Pharma puts so much pressure on our health agencies,"

Max continues. "These corporations spend a fortune manufacturing studies that allegedly 'prove' the vaccines are safe. And they probably spend as much money suppressing the unbiased studies that usually show they're not."

"Like in this case, Dr. Balfour?" the host asks.

"Exactly. Big Pharma took advantage of the panic caused by this meningitis outbreak to push an unproven vaccine that should never have seen the light of day. Now the public is faced with these devastating vaccine injuries, and a poor family has lost a son for nothing. What's worse is they've vaccinated thousands of other people over the past few days. Who knows how many more will still react? And how permanent the damage will be?"

"Is there anything that can be done to prevent it?"

"Careful surveillance and awareness will help," Max says. "Obviously, they've suspended this program now that the dangers are so clear. But there's nothing unique about this vaccine or their approach."

"Can you elaborate?"

"Look what the government is still planning to do with the mandatory HPV vaccine campaign. So many of us in the vaccine hesitancy movement, including doctors like myself, have been arguing for a safer and more rational approach over the willy-nilly distribution of more and more vaccines. They treat our children like pincushions. And at such a cost."

"Are you referring to all vaccines?"

"Vaccines have historically had their place. But like any manufactured drug, they're poisons. Most of which are unnecessary." He pauses. "Maybe now others will finally realize that, too."

"A complete FUBAR," Lisa murmurs to herself. "What have we done?"

CHAPTER 46

Yolanda opens the door, and Max bounds inside her one-bedroom condo. He sweeps her into a hug, kisses her, and spins her around and around. Prone to motion sickness, Yolanda feels dizzy, but his affection makes it so worthwhile. She feels loved. Nothing is more important to her.

"What are we celebrating?" Yolanda giggles as she inhales a whiff of her favorite peppery cologne.

"We won!"

For a moment, Yolanda wonders if he entered them into some contest she wasn't aware of. "What did we win?"

"The battle." He kisses her again. "Along with a tidal wave of public support. Which is the key to winning the actual war."

She suddenly realizes that he's talking about the vaccination campaign and, reluctantly, breaks off the embrace. "This isn't a war, Max."

"It is for some of us."

"Everyone at my office is really upset."

Max strokes her cheek. "Wasn't your fault. You were only doing what you all thought was best. I get it."

Yolanda shifts away from him. She loves Max more than ever, but he's rejoicing over one of the biggest catastrophes to ever hit her office. "This isn't so easy for me, Max. I can't even count how many inoculations I've given over the past few days."

"No one's doubting your good intentions, beautiful."

"What if I gave the shot that made one of those poor kids so sick?"

"I'd never blame you."

"But, Max, this feels kind of . . . wrong."

The smile leaves his lips. "What does?"

"To celebrate a bunch of kids getting sick from a vaccine. Especially one that we hoped would stop this awful meningitis."

Max's eyes narrow, and his upper lip curls. "A few kids got sick," he snaps. "Big deal! Do you have any idea how much damage has been done by vaccines over the years?"

"I know how important this is to you." She moves toward him, but he recoils from her touch.

"You don't have a fucking clue, Yolanda!"

"Max!"

"You hand out those shots like candy. Without a second thought. You have no idea what it's like to have to live with the devastating consequences of them, day in and day out."

She has never seen him this ferocious. Her face feels as if it's on fire, and she can't fight back her sudden tears. "Max . . ."

"Do you know how much time I've invested? How much I've already lost? How long I've had to wait for a moment like this?"

Her words won't come, and she can only shake her head.

"You're damn right I'm going to celebrate this! I'm sorry for those kids, but I wouldn't change a thing." He holds her gaze with an intensity that frightens her. "You can't win a war without a few casualties."

CHAPTER 47

Lisa stares at her screen without digesting the contents of the spread-sheet splashed across it. It's after ten p.m., and she's exhausted. But she can't bring herself to go home and face the prospect of explaining to her husband how her professional life is unraveling in front of her eyes. It's not that he wouldn't understand; her weakest moments often bring out the best in Dominic. But the last thing she wants right now is his pity. So, when Nathan texts to tell her that he'll be leaving Seattle at the crack of dawn, she responds without thinking that she will come over to say good-bye in person.

The day, which Lisa thought couldn't get any worse after her visit to the morgue, kept finding inventive ways to do just that. Six new cases of meningitis were reported across the city with three more deaths. She had to run a gauntlet of reporters and camera-men outside of her building. And no sooner had she reached her office than she received a terse call from the governor, demanding to know what went wrong with the vaccination campaign.

Lisa walks into the lobby of Nathan's hotel, aware of how risky it is to come this late in the evening feeling as vulnerable as she does. With or without alcohol, her judgment is already impaired, which becomes even more apparent to her when she steps into the bathroom to fix her hair and reapply lipstick. But as she rides the elevator to his suite on the thirty-fourth floor, she also realizes that it's the first time in days she's looked forward to something. She has no idea how she might respond if Nathan touches her the way he did the night before. But she doubts she would be as quick to leave this time.

The elevator door opens, and a few butterflies wing inside her chest as she walks down the corridor toward his room. She hesitates at the door, her arms as frozen as her feet. Then her hand drifts toward the door, as if it has a mind of its own, and gently knocks.

Moments later, Nathan fills the doorway. He's unshaven and wears jeans with a black T-shirt—a look Lisa can't help but find appealing. He steps forward and wraps her in a hug that feels more intimate than it should. But she finds comfort in the firmness of his arms and the warmth of his cheek against hers, so she lingers in the embrace until he finally lets go.

He leads her inside the spacious suite, which boasts a view of the water to match the one from the rooftop bar. Beyond the couches and coffee table, the sliding door to the bedroom is partly open. The bed is made, and a half-packed suitcase rests on it.

Nathan walks over to the makeshift bar on the side table. "Can I get you something to drink?"

"What are you having?" she asks.

He lifts a crystal tumbler—which looks to be almost down to the ice except for a few drops of brownish liquid—and swirls it in his hand. "On a day like today there's not much choice, is there?"

"Bourbon?"

"Scotch."

"Can't do whiskey." She chuckles. "A misadventure in the eleventh grade that ended in the emergency room has led to a lifelong self-imposed ban."

"Wine, then?"

"Sure?"

"Bordeaux OK?"

"I guess." She laughs. "I'll slum it this once."

He uncorks a bottle of red and pours her a glass. Then he refills his own tumbler from a bottle that she assumes to be an expensive single malt.

Nathan hands her the nearly full wineglass. "To pipe dreams," he says, tapping his glass to hers.

"That's a morbid toast."

"What do you suggest?"

"To brave gambles," she says, clinking glasses again.

She sits down on the couch and, despite the other chairs in the room, he lowers himself beside her.

Lisa places her phone on the coffee table and then says, "I need to ask you something."

He motions with his glass. "Please."

"Those phase-three studies on Neissovax. Is it possible . . . ?"

"That the study investigators covered up bad skin reactions like the ones we've been seeing here?" he asks calmly.

"Yeah."

"Anything's possible, but why? Those studies were carried out by reputable and independent scientists who would have zero to gain by manipulating the data. And even if we had the world's sketchiest investigators in our back pocket, why would we hide something like this if we knew it was only going to come to light as soon as the vaccine went to market? We could've cut our losses and quietly pulled the plug in the trial phase. But now? This is an unparalleled disaster for Delaware."

"I suppose."

"Tomorrow I'm going to have face the music back in New York. And that music is going to sound a hell of a lot like gunshots from a firing squad."

She frowns. "How can they blame you?"

"Easy. I'm the one who was supposed to ensure none of this happened."

"Basically God, then?"

"Basically." He shrugs. "With more fiscal accountability."

"That's not right, Nathan. Especially since I'm the one who drew you into this." It's her turn to reach out and clutch his wrist. "I'm sorry."

"For what? You were trying to do your job. To protect the public."

"Maybe, but the irony is I ended up exposing the public to even more risk. And you know what's worse?"

"It gets worse?" He chuckles grimly.

"We struggle every day to convince people of the essential need for vaccination. And we depend on a near-global buy-in to establish herd immunity. There's already so much skepticism, ignorance, and bias out there. And now I've inadvertently played right into the hands of the anti-vaxxers."

"Lisa . . ."

"It's true. Earlier, I heard one on the radio who cited Neissovax as the ultimate cautionary tale for *all* vaccines. And he was damn persuasive, too."

"It's all raw right now. It just seems worse than it is."

"I'm being realistic, Nathan. Not since Andrew Wakefield published that damn fraudulent, debunked study that linked autism to the MMR vaccine has anyone breathed as much life into the anti-vax cause."

This time, Nathan reaches for her. "None of this is your fault."

She stares at him. "I wish you didn't have to leave tomorrow."

"It's not tomorrow yet."

Then her phone rings on the table, breaking the spell. She recognizes the number on the screen—which ends in four nines—as belonging to Darius's roommate. She gently pulls her hand free of Nathan's and grabs the phone. "I'm sorry, I need to get this," she says as she rises.

She points to the bedroom, and he nods, so she steps inside the room and answers the call. "Dr. Lisa Dyer."

"Hey, this is Jayden Rogers. You called?"

"Yes." Lisa hurriedly explains who she is and her role in the outbreak management. "Jayden, were you the one who found Darius?"

"Yeah." He goes quiet for a moment. "It was brutal."

Lisa waits for him to elaborate.

"Darius, he was in bed," Jayden says. "His face was just a mess. The sheets were soaked in this yellow gunk. And his eyes—they were like bulging out of his head." His voice falters. "I mean he's black and all, but his skin was like navy color."

"Can't imagine how traumatic that must have been."

"Brutal," he repeats.

"Did you know that Darius had been given the meningitis vaccine two days before?"

"Of course."

"How?"

"We went together."

"To the clinic? You were vaccinated, too?"

"Yup."

Lisa looks over to Nathan, who eyes her quizzically. "How are you feeling?" she asks.

"Fine," Jayden says.

"Why didn't you report what happened on our public-health website?"

"I did."

"After Darius died?"

"Yeah, like right away."

She feels as if the ground is shifting beneath her feet. "You sure the report went through?"

"Positive."

"You got an email confirmation?"

"I did," he says. "And then I got another email a couple hours later."

Lisa goes cold. "What did that one say?"

"Not much. Thanked me for the report. Said they looked into it and concluded that what happened to Darius wasn't related to the vaccine. Something about it being too far delayed and not a typical allergy."

Nathan's face creases with concern. "What is it?" he mouths.

She breaks off the eye contact. The implications of Jayden's words weigh in on her like a tunnel collapsing overhead. Someone must have hacked the website and deliberately suppressed the report of Darius's death. How many other reports have been buried, too? And by whom?

Her mind spins, and she shoots Nathan another quick look. *Was it you?*

CHAPTER 48

"Is it something I did?" Nathan had sent Lisa the text after she made her abrupt departure the previous night, mumbling an excuse about a work emergency. She hasn't responded to it or the three others he sent overnight—the last one, just after four a.m.

Who else, other than someone inside Delaware, would have such a vested interest in seeing adverse events wiped off the website? Lisa remembers how obsessed Nathan seemed with the site, and how often he asked about it. Was he in on it? Or Fiona? Or all of them at Delaware?

So, yes, Nathan. It might just be something you did.

Lisa checks her watch again. It's almost 7:30 a.m., and still no call from her web designer. She turns her attention back to her long list of emails and forces herself to craft coherent replies. At times, the letters blur into one, and she can't stop yawning.

Lisa barely remembers what a good sleep feels like. The previous night's was the worst one yet. The sight of Dominic, waiting at home for her with an open bottle of red and two glasses, precipitated another torrent of guilt. If Jayden hadn't called when he did, she probably would have ended up in Nathan's bed. Instead, she wound up having sex with her husband again. But she couldn't approach anything close to genuine arousal. Dominic picked up on her perfunctory effort. "I hope sex isn't becoming just another chore in our relationship," he griped as he turned off his bedside lamp, leaving Lisa in the dark to stew through a night of worries, doubts, and self-recrimination.

The phone vibrates on her desk. The long string of numbers without any dashes or intelligible area or country codes tells Lisa that it must be Austin, her webmaster, calling as usual on a voice-over-Internet-protocol line.

"Top of the morning to you, Dr. D," he chirps in his weird vernacular that's a hybrid of Gen-Z speak and something straight out of the fifties.

Austin is as close to a tech genius as Lisa has ever met, although technically she never has, since he lives in San Diego and they've only ever interacted via phone or electronically. She has no idea what he looks like, but she envisions him with a beard and a man-bun. This morning, she has no time for his chattiness. "What did you discover, Austin?"

"Some sophisticated prodding, Dr. D."

"Prodding?" Lisa asks.

"Yep, I was up until the wee hours tracing backward," Austin says. "Got to say, I admire the dude's work. We installed a tight firewall. The full Chuck Norris. But the dude kept prodding and finally weaseled his way up our backside using multiple VPNs to access the database."

Lisa understands enough of the description to appreciate the hacker hid his identity behind virtual private networks. "So you're not going to be able track down an IP address for him or her?"

"Not a hope, Dr. D. The dude was bouncing from VPN to VPN, going full chameleon. Last IP address I could trace him to was somewhere in Latvia. But who the heck knows? Dude might be my downstairs neighbor."

"Can you tell how many reports were removed from the database?"

"Nope. This wasn't some bored fourteen-year-old chilling on his mom's Mac. Hell, maybe it was. Either way, it was some NSA-level shit. No idea how often he was mucking about inside our guts. Or what exactly he did. I was lucky to even find a couple of partial fingerprints. He went to Herculean efforts to conceal them."

"How about the email?" Lisa forwarded Austin the bogus email reply from "Seattle Public Health"—which included the official logo—that Jayden had sent her. It was, as Jayden described, a concise letter discounting Darius's reaction as being unrelated to his vaccination. As brief as it was, clearly it had been written by someone with medical knowledge.

"Sorry, Dr. D. That email address is one ginormous doo-doo," he says. "Comes from a massively generic domain. You'd have better luck tracking down a specific grain of sand in the Sahara."

Lisa sighs. "Can we learn anything from the hack?"

"Yep. Whoever did this wasn't fucking around."

Frustrated, she thanks Austin for his efforts and disconnects.

Lisa appreciates that even if she does report the breach to law enforcement, the chances of them identifying the hacker are remote. But the level of sophistication involved only convinces her even more that someone from Delaware Pharmaceuticals, with its endless resources and bottomless pockets, had to be behind it.

"Who keeps these kind of idiotic hours?" Angela asks from the doorway of the office.

Lisa grins to hide her surprise at the sight of her old boss. More than the deepening hollows of Angela's cheeks, it's the cane in her right hand that concerns her. "You used to be here by seven every day when you occupied this seat."

"I also used to smoke when I was in college," Angela says. "Doesn't mean I was right to."

Lisa can't help but laugh. "Do you have a minute? I could use your advice."

"Got lots of minutes. Well, some anyway." She hobbles into the office and eases herself into the chair across from Lisa.

"It's just been one disaster after another, Angela," Lisa says, her voice thickening.

"The vaccine?"

"Everything. This outbreak is spiraling out of control. The only vaccine that can stop it is fatally flawed. The press and the anti-vaxxers are having a field day. And now we're dealing with fraud and, possibly, a corporate conspiracy."

Angela holds up both hands. "Whoa, whoa. Slow down. Start from the top."

Lisa summarizes the developments of the past few days. When she gets to the part about the website tampering and her conversation with Austin, Angela grumbles, "Those greedy sons of bitches! You think they knew the whole time about this potentially deadly reaction?"

"I don't know. But why would Delaware hide a side effect if they knew it was eventually going to come out in an even more public way, like it did here?"

"Maybe they were hoping they could get enough of a toehold in the community to make their vaccine invaluable before its downside was discovered."

Lisa rubs her forehead. "The chances of them pulling that off seem remote."

"What else, then?"

"I have no idea."

Angela snaps her fingers. "What about corporate sabotage?"

"Sabotage *themselves*?"

"Sure. Say someone planned to make money selling the stock short. Keep the vaccine's flaw a secret and prop up the share price until it has a spectacular fall?"

"That sounds a bit farfetched."

"It does, doesn't it? Maybe I saw it in a movie?" Angela shrugs. "So what are you going to do now?"

Lisa leans on the desk, her chin in her hands. "I have no idea."

"You have to take it to the authorities. This is a crime. Potentially, a federal one."

"The FBI?"

"That'd be my guess."

Lisa knew she'd have to do this sooner or later. "First I want to confront Nathan and Fiona. I want to hear it from them."

"What if you just end up tipping them off?"

"My tech guy is a boy genius. He couldn't find any link back to Delaware. I don't think anyone else will. They'd be far too sophisticated to leave a trail."

Angela considers it for a moment. "Lisa, this is a lot to take on. Your ship is leaking from every angle right now. But you got to keep your eye on the prize."

"Meaning?"

"This outbreak. It's nearing a point of critical mass. Without the vaccine, you have to intensify all your other containment strategies."

"We're pursuing our contact tracing religiously."

"Yeah, but between the antibiotic prophylaxis failures and the noncompliance with treatment, it's not going to be enough."

Lisa throws up her hands. "What else can we do?"

"Kids are going to be heading back to school in a couple weeks . . ."

Lisa sees her point. The risk of accelerated spread will soar once the potential carriers of the pathogen mix in among the school population. "You're thinking we should close the schools?"

"They did in Iceland."

Lisa's head spins, considering the implications, especially in the wake of the long school closures during the COVID pandemic. "Yeah. Maybe."

"And what about quarantines?"

"It might even come to that."

Angela stares at her for a long hard moment. And then she breaks into a small laugh. "I'm still waiting for my thank-you card for handing you this plum job!"

CHAPTER 49

Nathan feels more confused than ever. After Lisa bolted from his room, she didn't answer any of his texts, leaving him worried and rather embarrassed. He thought they'd had a connection. Then she suddenly contacted him, demanding an urgent meeting and forcing him to postpone his flight home.

He enters the coffee shop across from Pioneer Square and is surprised to spot Fiona sitting beside Lisa. With her hair up and glasses on, Lisa looks as attractive as ever in a pale taupe suit. But her smile is cold, and her eyes are all business.

Nathan looks over to Fiona, whose perplexed expression reflects his own state of mind. He turns back to Lisa. "You didn't mention a group meeting."

"Sorry," Lisa says, without sounding at all apologetic. "More efficient this way."

"What's going on, Lisa?" Fiona asks.

"I was hoping to ask the same of you two."

Fiona's forehead creases. "What are you talking about?"

"Our reporting website. It's been hacked."

"Hacked?"

Lisa nods gravely. "Someone breached it. Got into the database and erased at least one critical report."

"Which one?"

"The death of Darius Washington."

Fiona's jaw drops. "What?"

"You're sure?" Nathan asks.

"Someone not only deleted the report on Darius, but they also sent a bogus reply to his roommate, who submitted it."

"Why?"

"The only plausible explanation I can think of is that he or she"—Lisa glances from Nathan to Fiona—"wanted to protect the interests of Delaware Pharmaceuticals."

"Wait a minute . . ."

"There are only a few people who would have the motive and the access to pull it off."

"That's crazy!" Fiona's voice cracks with indignation.

"To protect Delaware how?" Nathan asks, although his mind is already turning over. "To wait for even more complications? And even bigger lawsuits?"

Lisa hesitates. "There's no other explanation."

"And you think we're the ones responsible?"

Lisa stares back at him. "You've got to be the prime suspects at this point."

"Come on," Fiona mumbles, her face reddening.

"Again, Lisa," Nathan insists. "Why we would do this?"

"Maybe to stall for time until Neissovax was so entrenched in the battle against this outbreak that we would have to overlook the one little worrisome side effect?"

He scoffs. "That's weak."

"OK." Lisa jabs a finger at him. "Tell me who else would have any possible reason to do it. Or even the opportunity."

"This is a catch-twenty-two. How can we justify what we don't know?"

They lapse into a distressed silence.

"I'm reporting this to the FBI," Lisa finally says.

Nathan can't formulate a reasonable response, but Fiona leans forward and asks, "What will they do?"

"Investigate," Lisa snaps. "I understand they do that from time to time with unsolved crimes. Especially cybercrimes and interstate corporate conspiracies."

Fiona's throat bobs, and she looks away.

"I don't mean to sound so harsh. But look at it from my perspective. I have no idea who to trust."

"You can trust us," Nathan says.

"No." Lisa's eyes meet his. "I can't. Not unless you can convince me someone else is behind this cover-up."

"We just found out about it," Fiona says.

Lisa gets up from the table. "I have to go."

Nathan resists the urge to grab her wrist as she walks past him. "You want us to take a polygraph test?" he asks.

"Better you explain it to the FBI," Lisa says without slowing.

Fiona and Nathan watch her stride away.

"A couple days ago we were celebrating the successful launch of a lifesaving vaccine," Nathan mutters, more to himself than Fiona. "Now? The drug is dead on arrival, and we're being accused of a criminal conspiracy."

Fiona locks eyes with him. Never has she looked sadder, and yet there's also a serene calm in her gaze. "Walt was an atheist. Not even the least superstitious. But right before they put him on the ventilator, he smiled and whispered to me, 'Everything happens for a reason.'"

CHAPTER 50

Lisa looks down and sees her fingers trembling where they rest on top of the steering wheel. The confrontation with Nathan and Fiona has left her feeling rawer and more conflicted, without confirming anything. They both seemed so indignant and convincing, each in their own way, between Fiona's quiet outrage and Nathan's visible hurt.

But what if it was just an act? Angela was right. She should never have tipped her hand. They could be furiously destroying the evidence of their complicity at this very moment. But what difference would it really make? Exposing the cover-up doesn't help Lisa control the outbreak. Kids are still dying of the infection and, now, the potential prevention, too. Putting Nathan, Fiona, or anyone else who might be involved behind bars won't stop the spread of the lethal meningitis.

Still, Lisa realizes it's time to involve the professionals. "Call Ingrid," she tells her car's voice recognition system. A moment later, her assistant answers. "Hey, it's me," Lisa says. "I need you to track down the number of whatever federal agency is responsible for cybercrimes. I'm assuming it's the FBI, but I don't really know."

"Cybercrimes?" Ingrid echoes.

"Long story," Lisa says. "It's urgent."

"OK, sure," Ingrid says. "Speaking of urgent, Dr. Merkley called twice this morning looking for you."

"Who's Dr. Merkley?"

"Says he's from the toxicology lab."

A cool rush runs from Lisa's scalp to her toes. "Text me his number!"

As she impatiently waits for her phone to chime with Ingrid's text, Lisa realizes she's only a few blocks from the state toxicology lab on South Walker Street. She heads straight over and pulls into the parking lot, just as the text from Ingrid arrives.

Instead of phoning, Lisa walks through the main entrance and up to the reception desk and identifies herself to the bored-looking middle-aged woman behind it, who doesn't stop chewing on the end of her pen. After a quick call, the woman motions to the elevator behind her and says, "Third floor. Jimmy's office is down the end of the hallway."

Lisa rides the elevator to the third floor and hurries past a series of doors, until she reaches one with a plaque that reads: "Dr. James Merkley, Director."

Before she can knock, the door swings open to reveal a bearded man in jeans and a frayed, short-sleeve polo shirt, who looks to be in his mid to late thirties. "You must be Lisa," the toxicologist chirps, and then taps his chest. "I'm Jimmy."

"Thanks for seeing me, Jimmy," she says, surprised by his age and relative informality.

"No. Thank you for the fascinating challenge."

"Challenge?"

"Of extracting all those toxins from a single drop of residual fluid inside the syringe."

She does a double take. *"All those toxins?"*

"Come. Let me show you."

Before she can ask anything more, Jimmy marches past her and back down the hallway toward the staircase. Lisa's heart is pounding as she follows him down one flight of stairs and into an open lab space.

White-coated technicians work at stations separated by freestanding machinery of various shapes and sizes crowding the floor. Some have built-in screens, while others have enclosed hoods or tubes snaking in and out of them. The only consistent feature is that all the equipment is as white as the walls. For the all the gadgetry surrounding them, Lisa is surprised by how quiet the lab is aside from a steady low-grade hum and intermittent beeps and chirps. They walk past a gloved and goggled technician who sits at her bench, carefully pipetting drops of a bluish liquid out of a test tube and onto a test strip.

Jimmy stops beside a series of tall machines that are the size of closets and together resemble appliances in an ultramodern, high-end kitchen. He pats the side of the nearest one affectionately, as if it were an old pal he hadn't seen in a while. "This puppy is the most sensitive mass spectrometer on the market, bar none. We ran your sample through the LC-MS, and lo and behold—"

"LC-MS?"

"Liquid chromatography mass spectrometry," Jimmy says. "It's all the rage in toxicology these days. Basically, it's totally replaced gas chromatography, because with GC, you need your compounds to be volatile or at least heat stable for them to—"

Lisa cuts him off again with a raised hand. "I struggled in chemistry, Jimmy. It almost kept me out of med school. I totally believe you. I just want to hear what you found."

Flashing a gap-toothed grin, Jimmy reaches into the basket beside the machine, pulls out a few printed sheets, and holds them up for Lisa to see. The first page shows a densely colored graph with various spikes and waves of reds, greens, purples, and blues.

Lisa squints at it. "What am I looking at?"

"A histogram of all the various components we found in your sample." Jimmy flips through the next few pages, which show more bar charts, line graphs, and pie charts that mean nothing to Lisa, until he finally reaches a page with a list of medications that she does recognize.

Her heart is already in her throat when Jimmy says, "So, aside from the active vaccine protein itself, we also found—ranked highest to lowest in terms of their relative concentrates—sulfonamides, lamotrigine, allopurinol, fluconazole, carbamezapine, and traces of oseltamivir."

"That can't be right," Lisa says as she gawks at the hodgepodge of medications listed on the printout. "You found all of those meds in the one syringe?"

"Yup." He shrugs. "This wasn't a vaccine so much as a drugstore sampler of some of the more common antibiotics and antiseizure drugs."

"In other words, it was poisoned."

"Well, technically, none of these are toxins. They're all pharmaceuticals. But it's about the most contaminated sample I've seen in a hell of a long time."

The realization hits her with the shock of a hammer to her thumb. "There's zero chance all these medications ended up in this syringe by accident."

"Nada. There's not a pharmaceutical company in the world that would release such a dirty vaccine from their plant. They're legally mandated to test every single batch for quality control. And this sample would've set off a five-star alarm in testing."

"So someone added these toxins to this particular syringe?"

"Or tampered with the vial of vaccine itself, yeah." Jimmy scratches his beard. "But why? All of these medications are relatively benign."

"Benign, maybe," Lisa says as her stomach flips. "But each one of them is also strongly associated with Stevens-Johnson syndrome."

CHAPTER 51

Lisa's whole body feels numb as she drives away from the lab. She still can't wrap her head around the implications of what the toxicologists found in a single drop of leftover vaccine.

Poisoned?

Before she left, Jimmy agreed to run urgent toxicological screens on as many of the hundreds of other used syringes from Mateo's clinic as the lab could perform. He pointed out that they were lucky to be able to extract enough of a sample from Mateo's syringe, and it would be hit-and-miss with each of the others. Moreover, if several of the other syringes were also poisoned, they would only need to randomly sample to estimate how many of the total were tainted. "Unless all of them were," he added ominously. He also informed her that the process would be quicker now that they knew what toxins to look for.

The news should have been reassuring to Lisa. Unless the entire supply was poisoned—which she knows from Fiona's exhaustive screening not to be the case—the revelation means that the vaccine itself is not dangerous. Potentially, it could even be reinstated on the front lines to prevent the spread of the lethal meningococcus.

But that glimmer of hope is totally overshadowed by the dark intent behind what she just learned.

First, the cover-up to hide the complication. And now an even more malicious conspiracy to poison the vaccine itself. *What kind of person or people would do this?*

The triple buzz of her phone draws her attention. She glances over to the screen, where it's mounted on a holder in the air vent.

"Olivia has a rash," the text from her sister reads. "Taking her to Bellevue Hospital."

Lisa's stomach plummets. "Call Amber!" she screams at her car's voice recognition system. But the line rings straight to voice mail.

"Oh no. Please, no," Lisa mutters repeatedly as she tries her sister three more times without reaching her.

Lisa swerves into the right lane, to the angry honk of a truck she cuts off. Her pulse pounds in her temples as she zigzags through freeway traffic, driving more aggressively than Tyra at her most impatient, as she races toward the hospital.

She peels into the ER's parking lot and abandons her car out front in an area clearly marked as ambulance parking. She runs into the ER and up to the triage desk, where she steps in front of an elderly woman who's sitting in a wheelchair with oxygen tubing running up to her nostrils.

"Where is Olivia Dyer-Tegan?" Lisa demands of the triage nurse.

"How rude!" the elderly woman gripes.

The seemingly unflappable triage nurse smiles politely. "Ma'am, you will have to wait your—"

"I'm Dr. Dyer, the chief public-health officer." Lisa plasters her ID tag against the Plexiglas that separates her from the nurse. "And this is a public-health emergency."

The nurse consults her computer screen. "Bed fourteen." She points to the set of metal doors to her right. "I'll buzz you in."

Lisa flies through electronically opening doors. She scans the numbers posted above the stretchers, which are separated by curtains, until she sees "14," dashes over to it, and yanks back the curtain, terrified of what it will reveal.

Amber sits in a chair at the bedside while Olivia is propped up in the bed, wearing a hospital gown.

"Tee!" Olivia says with a huge smile.

A sense of relief overwhelms Lisa. Her tears flow at the sight of her niece, whose color appears normal, and whose face is unmarred by blisters or rash.

Olivia frowns. "Why so sad, Tee?"

"Not sad at all." Lisa's voice quivers, and she wipes her eyes with the back of her forearm.

Amber reaches out and gives her elbow a quick squeeze. "Turns out it's just a localized reaction. They're seeing lots of them, apparently."

"Let me see your arm, Liv," Lisa says, stepping toward the bed.

Olivia slides the oversize gown off her shoulder to show the saucer-sized raised red welt at the site of the injection. Lisa immediately recognizes it for the harmless reaction that almost any vaccine can induce. "Thank God," she murmurs.

"I didn't want to overreact," Amber says. "But after all your concerned calls . . ."

"I get it." Lisa steadies her breathing. "But why didn't you pick up your phone? You scared the hell out of me with that message."

"Sorry, they asked me to turn it off."

"I'm OK, Tee," Olivia reassures her.

She strokes her niece's cheek. "I know, hon."

Lisa stays a few minutes longer to confer with Olivia's attending physician, but she has to head back to her car once the page comes on the overhead speaker demanding, "Whoever is parked in the ambulance bay, please move your vehicle immediately!"

Lisa drives back to her office. On her way in, she stops at her assistant's desk. "Did you find the number I asked you to track down?"

"I did," Ingrid says. "It's the FBI. They have a field office here in Seattle."

"Can you put in a call in for me? I need to speak to the agent in charge. Tell him or her it's urgent."

Lisa heads straight into her office and is closing the door behind her when Tyra puts her hand out to stop it. "Where have you been?" the program director asks.

"Come in," Lisa says, and shuts the door as soon as Tyra is inside.

"What in the name of Jesus H is going on, Lisa? Angela told me about the website. I feel so violated. As in personally."

"Oh, Ty, it gets a lot worse than that."

"How could that be possible?"

Tyra's eyes go wider as Lisa explains the toxicology results on Mateo's syringe. "Who?" Tyra whispers.

"No idea. But it had to be someone with access to the vaccine."

"And you're sure the vaccine was tampered with after the vial left the manufacturing plant?"

"Almost certain," Lisa says. "We'll round up a bunch of vials from Delaware for testing. But it makes no sense that they were tainted at the plant. You've seen how anal Fiona is. It would have been picked up on the quality-control testing."

"Unless the quality-control folks were in on it . . ."

"There are too many barriers," Lisa says. "Besides, the lab is going to test all of the syringes from that clinic. The vials were packed together in boxes of two hundred and fifty. If the whole batch was tainted, the toxins will turn up in every one of those syringes."

"Not if someone at the factory was only randomly poisoning individual vials."

"True." Lisa tilts her head and studies her friend. "Ty, it sounds as if you want the toxins to have come from the plant."

"I do," she says gravely. "I really do."

"Why?"

"Think it about, Lisa. If the vaccine wasn't tampered with in the factory, then it means the vials were poisoned here in Seattle."

"And?"

"How many people around here would have access to those vials?"

Lisa sees what she's getting at. "Very few outside of our own staff."

"Maybe a couple of the folks from Delaware," Tyra says. "But even then, they didn't handle the individual vials after they were opened. Our nurses were the only ones who did."

Their eyes lock. "Tyra, we'll need to go through a list of the nurses who worked the clinic where Mateo got his shot. And cross-reference them with all the nurses who worked that first clinic where Mia and Darius got sick, too."

CHAPTER 52

Lisa has walked, jogged, cycled, and driven past the nondescript building on the corner of Third and University in the heart of downtown multiple times without ever realizing that it housed the Seattle field office for the Federal Bureau of Investigation.

She heads to the seventh floor and opens a glass door that's emblazoned with the distinctive FBI seal. Even though she has never been inside an FBI office, it's exactly as she envisioned, down to the large framed side-by-side photographs of the president and the FBI director hanging on the near wall.

"Can I help you?" asks the young man behind the reception desk.

"I'm Dr. Dyer from Seattle Public Health. I have an appointment to see Special Agent-in-Charge Douglas."

"I'll let the SAC know you're here," he says as he lifts the phone.

Moments later, two people emerge from the corridor, both wearing dark suits. The man is handsome, midfortyish, and African American. The woman walking beside him looks to be in her thirties, and she is as tall as he is, at least six feet, with a fair complexion and curly red hair.

They both offer Lisa somber smiles. "Good to meet you, Dr.

Dyer," the man says. "I am Chris Douglas. And this is our ASAC—assistant special agent-in-charge—Eileen Kennedy." He motions back down the corridor. "Please. Join us in my office."

Lisa follows them down to his office, which is no bigger than Lisa's but boasts a better view, looking down the hill and out onto Elliott Bay. Lisa and Eileen sit down across the desk from Douglas. "I hope you don't mind getting us both for this meeting, Dr. Dyer," Douglas says.

"Lisa, please," she says. "And at this point, I'll take all the help I can get."

"I saw your press conference on the vaccine, Lisa," Eileen says. "I have to say, I thought you handled it with a lot of poise."

"Thank you. In fact, it's the vaccine that brings me here today."

"So we gathered." Douglas's forehead creases as he opens a wire-bound notebook on his desk while Eileen lifts the screen on her laptop. "Do you mind elaborating?"

"In the past day, I've stumbled across what I think are two major crimes involving the vaccine. And I don't know if or how they're related." Lisa goes on to tell them in detail about the website breach and the tampering with the vaccine itself.

Douglas jots notes while Eileen types on her computer. Each interrupts to ask for the occasional clarification, but for the most part they simply listen. Neither of them comments at all as Lisa describes how she confronted Nathan and Fiona over the reporting database.

"Wild," Eileen says when Lisa finishes.

"Yes, thank you so much for bringing this to us." Douglas's frown lines deepen. "On the surface, these two crimes appear to serve opposite ends."

"It's true," Eileen says. "It would be logical to assume the cover-up was perpetrated in response to—*not* in addition to—the poisoning of the vaccine."

Lisa nods. "Especially if someone inside Delaware Pharmaceuticals was desperate to hide what they thought—as we did—was an unexpected side effect of the vaccine itself."

Eileen narrows her gaze. "You have another theory, though?"

"It's also possible someone might have wanted to induce enough severe immune reactions to ensure the vaccine appeared unequivocally responsible, before the vaccination campaign was halted."

"I don't quite follow," Douglas says.

"With brand-new vaccines like Neissovax the surveillance is very tight. We could have stopped the campaign after the first serious reaction to investigate. In fact, we probably would have if we'd heard about Darius Washington's death."

"What would be the issue with that?"

"Well, reactions like Stevens-Johnson syndrome or toxic epidermal necrolysis are rare and sporadic. But they do happen with many different drugs. Even spontaneously, sometimes. If we'd stopped the campaign after one reaction, we couldn't know for sure that the vaccine was to blame. In fact, it took three victims before we were certain."

Eileen sucks air in between her lips. "You're saying someone might've wanted to cover up the reactions until there were enough bodies to guarantee this vaccine would be labeled a serial killer?"

Lisa shrugs. "It's just another hypothesis."

"Could it be an act of domestic terrorism?" Douglas postulates.

"I'm an epidemiologist. I'm way out of my league here. But it seems to me the point of this sabotage wasn't about the victims or the terror, but about fatally damaging the reputation of the vaccine itself."

"And who would have the motive to do that?" Douglas asks.

"Anti-vaxxers?" Eileen offers. "Or maybe a pharmaceutical competitor? Or even someone inside Delaware itself. Out of spite or for personal gain."

Lisa doesn't comment, but she can't help but think again of Nathan and Fiona. She feels connected to each of them in different ways, and she's still bothered by their last accusatory encounter. She could imagine one of them being desperate enough to attempt to cover up the complications attributed to Neissovax. *But to poison the vaccine?* That's almost beyond thinkable.

Douglas folds his hands on the table. "Basically, we're looking at all the usual suspects in a case of corporate sabotage."

"Absolutely," Eileen says, sounding almost enthusiastic about the challenge.

The two agents ask Lisa a few more specific questions, including details about the toxicology results and accessing the website. Then Douglas rises from his seat. "Thank you again for bringing this to our attention," he says. "Obviously, I'll need to elevate this to Washington. There are potentially national issues involved. But we'll immediately launch an investigation and put the full resources of our field office behind it." He turns to Eileen. "ASAC Kennedy will be the lead investigator."

Eileen turns to Lisa. "I'm going to need your help, Lisa, if that's OK? For a road map to the world of vaccines. And to the other side, too. The anti-vaxxers."

"Whatever you need."

Eileen smiles warmly. "Until we understand the playing field better, I suggest you keep all of this strictly confidential."

"Of course."

Lisa heads back to her car, feeling simultaneously reassured and distressed by her meeting with the federal agents. Reporting the conspiracy has made the criminality of it sink in. Someone was actively trying to undermine their attempts to tame the most lethal outbreak Seattle had seen in years. And Lisa wasn't sure who to trust.

On her way back to the office, Lisa passes a few blocks from Delaware's warehouse and spontaneously decides to drop in on it. There are fewer staff inside than on her last visit, and a palpable pall hangs in the air.

Lisa finds Fiona in her office, motionless in her seat while staring at her screen. Once she notices Lisa, she speaks without making eye contact. "I wasn't expecting to see you so soon."

"Understandable," Lisa says. "Where's Nathan?"

"In New York, while I'm grounded here. And my poor mom is alone and beside herself."

"What's the matter with your mother?"

"She's in a care home back east. She gets anxious. It's nothing." Fiona finally looks up warily. "How did it go with the FBI?"

Lisa ignores the question. "I'm going to need samples of Neissovax, Fiona. At least one vial from every separate production batch."

"Why?"

"We need to do some independent analyses."

"You don't trust our testing?"

"At this point, we need to do our own."

"I am a clinical pharmacologist, Lisa. I'm good at what I do. Whether or not you believe me about the website is one thing. But to question my ability to oversee decent quality control?"

Lisa recognizes the hurt burning in the other woman's eyes and has to resist the urge to explain to Fiona that it has nothing to do with her competence as a scientist. "This isn't personal, Fiona. We've had three major reactions and one death related to the vaccine."

Fiona stares at her for a long moment, and then nods. "I'll send you the vials."

"I'd just as soon take them with me now."

"Of course you would." Fiona scoffs. "We don't have vials left from all of the batches."

"As many as you can provide."

Fiona gets up. "I'll be back in a few minutes."

Lisa leans against the desk while waiting for Fiona to return. The steady ticking of the art deco clock draws her attention. Eventually, she lifts it, surprised by its substantial weight. On the bottom, she notices a carved inscription that reads: *To G, With all my love. W.*

Lisa assumes the *G* must stands for some pet name, and she feels a pang of sympathy for Fiona. To have lost her otherwise healthy husband to complications of the flu—or possibly even the flu shot— strikes her as particularly cruel. She wonders if that's what motivates Fiona to do the work she does.

Fiona returns cradling a box. At the sight of the clock in Lisa's hand, she scowls slightly, and Lisa carefully replaces the timepiece where it was.

Fiona lowers the box onto the desk and opens the top flaps. She pulls out one of the presealed packages holding fifty vials of vaccine. "We still have vaccine from six separate batches." She motions to the tag on top of the seal. "These numbers indicate the date of the original production runs in the plant at Littleton."

"OK, thank you."

Fiona carefully replaces the package in the box, closes the flaps, and then passes it to Lisa.

"Oh, Fiona, one other thing."

"There's more?"

"Yes, please don't ship any of the supply back to Massachusetts yet."

"Why not?"

"We might not be done with it."

Fiona grimaces. "You're still planning on using it?"

"All I can tell you is that we might not be done with it."

CHAPTER 53

Nathan focuses on the simple blue, rectangular shape of the UN's Secretariat Tower, which is framed in the center of the CEO office's window. But today it doesn't provide the usual calming effect.

"You were saying?" Peter asks in the same chilly tone he has been using since Nathan first sat down across from him.

"I have no idea how this could've happened, Peter. There was no signal noise whatsoever in all the trials. This complication came out of nowhere."

"To fuck this company into near financial ruin, apparently," Peter snarls as he slams his hand on the desk. "Did you see the share price today?"

The value of Delaware's stock price has fallen by almost 30 percent since the announcement of the vaccine trial's suspension. "Wait until the market gets word of the criminal cover-up they're trying to pin on us," Nathan says.

Peter's fingertips blanch as he presses them against the wood. "That cannot happen, Nathan."

"How do we stop it?"

"What evidence do they have?"

Nathan shrugs.

"Exactly. They've got nothing."

Nathan eyes the CEO for a long moment. "Those 'spies' you mentioned last time we spoke. What do they know about the website?"

"They only watch, Nathan." Peter's lips break into a sly smile. "But there's little they don't see."

Nathan's stomach churns at the veiled threat. "I should probably go back to Seattle," he says.

"What for?"

"Not fair to leave Fiona there alone to deal with all of this," Nathan says, but mainly he wants to get as far away from the office—and Peter—as possible. "She tells me that Public Health has confiscated a bunch of samples of Neissovax to analyze themselves."

"What will they find in them, Nathan?"

"The same thing we did. The vaccine is pure."

"Hmm."

"They've also asked us to keep the entire supply in the warehouse there."

"More evidence?"

"No idea. Lisa is leaving us in the dark now."

"Then what's the point of you going back?"

Nathan wonders the same. He cannot believe how much has changed in a single day. Yesterday, he thought Lisa was destined to become his lover. Now she threatens to be his undoing. And yet he still wants to see her again. "Maybe Lisa will confide in me. Maybe I can convince her in person."

"And maybe she won't, and maybe you can't."

"Something tells me we haven't seen the end of this yet."

"What more could there be?"

Nathan shakes his head. "Not sure."

Peter studies his fingers for a long moment. "Fine. Go to Seattle. See what you can sort out."

Nathan rises to his feet.

"I've always liked you," Peter says. "You know that, right?"

Nathan nods once.

"I suppose I've always seen a bit of my younger self in you."

There was a time when Nathan might have taken that as a compliment. Not today.

"But, Nathan, this company comes before anything or anyone." Peter's tone is frigid. "I hope you understand that."

Only too well.

CHAPTER 54

Lisa struggles to get through the morning's Outbreak Control Team meeting on day fourteen of the epidemic. Not only because of poor sleep. Her thoughts drift and dart in multiple directions, and she feels guilty for withholding the news of the poisoned vaccine from the rest of the committee. But the FBI agents were adamant about the need for secrecy, and with good reason.

Had Angela shown up, Lisa knows she wouldn't have been able to keep that bombshell to herself. But Angela's chair remains empty throughout the meeting. Lisa tries not to assume the worst about her friend, but it's difficult, particularly in light of all the depressing developments about the worsening spread of meningitis. In total, thirty-one people have already died—thirty-two, including Darius—the oldest of whom was only thirty-six years old. With the infection raging in four distinct geographical clusters across the city, Seattle's death toll is poised to eclipse Iceland's. Even more frustrating, two of the recently hospitalized victims had chosen not to take the prophylactic antibiotics that they were given, despite the warnings.

We won't be able to control this without restarting the

Neissovax campaign! Lisa wants to scream, but she says little during the meeting.

She is just sitting down back at her desk when her phone rings. She answers and a familiar voice says, "Lisa, hello, it's Edwin Davis from Harborview ICU."

"Oh, hi, Edwin."

"I get it," he says with a sad chuckle. "At this point, I wouldn't want to hear from me, either."

"You've got new patients from the outbreak?"

"Indirectly, I suppose."

"How so?"

"I admitted another patient with a severe vaccine reaction. Thought you'd want to hear."

"I do." Lisa's heart sinks. "Stevens-Johnson?"

"More like toxic epidermal necrolysis. The poor girl is covered from head to toe in blisters."

"Who is she?"

"Her name is Brooke Hogarth. Nineteen years old."

Lisa jots the name on the notepad by her phone. "Do we know when Brooke got her vaccine? And at which clinic?"

"Two or three days ago, but I'll have to get back to you about the where."

"Never mind. I'll be able to figure it out on my end." She takes a slow breath. "Is Brooke going to make it?"

"Her blood pressure is very soft, and she swelled up like the Michelin Man." He clicks his tongue. "But yeah, my gut tells me she'll pull through."

"That's something," Lisa says with relief. "I hear Mateo is slowly recovering, as well."

"He is. Very slowly." Edwin exhales. "Lisa, these are two of the worst rashes I've ever seen."

"You don't have to convince me."

"But they're still not half as bad as the meningitis cases we've been wrestling with."

"No doubt." The new reports of critically ill kids don't affect Lisa as much as they did only the week before. Part of her worries she might be running out of capacity for more pity. "OK, Edwin, please keep me posted."

"Will do."

Lisa is about to hang up when she's hit by an afterthought. "Can you save a sample of Brooke's urine?"

"Her urine?"

"I'll explain later."

"All right."

Lisa thanks him. As soon as she disconnects, she searches the vaccine database for the clinic where Brooke was inoculated. Her hope that it was one of the two clinics the other three victims attended are soon dashed. Brooke was vaccinated two days after Mateo.

Lisa calls the toxicology lab and tracks down Jimmy. "Perfect timing, Lisa," the toxicologist chirps. "I was just about to call you."

"There's been another critical reaction," she says.

"Oh? Do tell."

"The patient's in the ICU. If I can get you a sample of her urine, can you test it for the same medications you found in the syringe?"

"Definitely," he says enthusiastically. "Nothing better for concentrating toxins than the old kidneys. If she got the tainted vaccine, we should be able to isolate most of the same contaminants in her urine that we found in the other syringes."

"*Syringes?*" Lisa gasps. "As in plural?"

"That's what I wanted to tell you," Jimmy says. "So far, we've run through about eighty of those used syringes. We were only able to extract enough of a sample to test about half. But among those, two more syringes have tested positive for the same six toxins we found in the first one."

Lisa goes cold. "One in twenty, then?"

"Roughly, yeah."

She thinks aloud. "So the toxins weren't in the entire batch of vaccine."

"Which fits with the rest of the picture. We've run screens on vials from every one of the unopened batches of vaccine you sent over. None of them are contaminated."

"Whoever's been poisoning them was doing it one vial at a time."

"That, or one syringe at a time," Jimmy cautions.

"And either the poisoner was tainting the doses at the clinic, *or* he or she was sneaking in tainted vials and substituting them for legitimate ones."

"The logistics of smuggling them in seems way easier than tampering with them on-site."

"I agree," Lisa says. "There'd be too many eyes on him or her inside the clinic."

"Probably."

Lisa considers the situation for another moment. "There were four hundred people inoculated, give or take, at Mateo's clinic. And so far, Mateo is the only one who's had a major reaction." She makes the calculation in her head. "If one in twenty doses were tampered with, that would mean that about twenty of the vaccines were poisoned at the clinic."

"Does that math add up?" Jimmy asks.

"I think it does. No matter how many different medications you contaminated a vaccine with, only a fraction of those inoculated are going to go on to develop a life-threatening immune-mediated skin reaction."

"Yeah, yeah," Jimmy concurs. "That's logical."

"We now have four confirmed skin eruptions out of six thousand people vaccinated."

"And if we're assuming that one in twenty of the doses were poisoned . . ."

"Up to three hundred people might have been poisoned," she says with a chill.

"How long after exposure might these people still react?"

"A week or two, probably," she says. "But they would be at highest risk in the first few days after inoculation."

"Holy! So a bunch more kids could still get sick?"

"Yeah," Lisa says just as Tyra walks into her office and closes the door. "Thanks, Jimmy, for everything. I'll make sure we send over that urine sample today."

She hangs up the phone and immediately says to Tyra, "We have another vaccine reaction. And more poisoned doses. Potentially lots of them." She walks Tyra through the estimates, and then asks, "Do you know how many nurses worked at the clinic Mateo attended?"

"Ten," Tyra says. "But they worked in pairs. Each giving half the shots."

"Four hundred patients divided among ten nurses, means each one of them gave forty shots, give or take," Lisa thinks aloud.

Tyra's eyes narrow. "So, theoretically, one nurse could easily have administered all twenty poisoned vaccines at each clinic."

"One of our own? I can't wrap my head around that."

Tyra eyes her steadily. "I cross-referenced the two clinics involved. I emailed you the list."

"How many nurses worked both clinics?"

"Eight in total. All of whom have been with us for at least a year. Three of them more than ten."

"We can narrow it down even further, once we throw in the clinic the latest victim attended."

"That might not be necessary," Tyra says, wiggling a finger at Lisa's computer screen. "I emailed you an article."

"An article?"

"Yeah. It was written by one of the boyfriends of the eight nurses in question. Open it."

Lisa clicks on Tyra's most recent email and opens the attached hyperlink. Her screen fills with a blog post titled "Light Finally Shone on Vaccine Genocide."

Just as Lisa opens her mouth to ask which nurse, the author's name catches her eye: "Dr. Max Balfour, ND."

CHAPTER 55

"**D**o you mind closing the door?" Lisa asks Yolanda as she steps into her office.

Yolanda is as nervous as she is excited. She's always liked Lisa's easygoing and informal style, but she's never been called into her office before. And Tyra's presence reinforces how important the meeting must be.

"Please, sit," Lisa says with a welcoming smile.

Yolanda lowers herself into the chair beside Tyra, flattening the hem of her dress to ensure it doesn't ride up or lie funny.

"Thanks for coming, Yolanda," Tyra says.

Their smiles are almost too bright for this early in the morning. Yolanda's discomfort rises. She doesn't know what to say, so she just nods.

"You've been putting in a lot of long hours at the vaccination clinics," Lisa says. "Thank you for your dedication."

"No more than anyone else on the team," Yolanda mumbles. "And now that we've suspended the program . . ."

"It's been a moving target for all of us," Lisa says sympathetically.

"We're considering relaunching the campaign, Yolanda," Tyra says.

"With Neissovax? After all that's happened? With the rashes and all?"

Nothing is decided," Lisa says. "But since you've worked so many of those clinics, we wanted to get your impression."

"My impression?"

"Yeah, like a debrief," Tyra says. "How'd you find them compared to any of the other vaccine clinics you've run in the past."

Relaxing slightly, Yolanda considers the question. "They're different."

"How so?"

"You know, with those very detailed consent forms. All the questions from the families. And the staff from the drug company . . . observing over your shoulder. To be honest, it's kind of intimidating."

"Like you're being watched all the time?"

"Exactly." Yolanda giggles. "Like being in a fishbowl."

"But it's only our own staff who handle the vials, right?" Lisa says. "I mean once they're open."

Yolanda eyes her swiftly, alarmed again. Lisa should know all of this. "Yeah, just the nurses. We crack the vials, draw up the doses, and give the shots."

"So they'd never be out of your sight between opening the vials and disposing the syringes into the sharps container?"

"Never."

Tyra gives Yolanda's arm a reassuring squeeze. "After what's happened, we're just covering all our bases, Yolanda. You understand? We'll be debriefing everyone on the team."

Lisa smiles again. "Before we even consider relaunching the campaign."

"So aside from the fishbowl thing," Tyra says. "You never saw anything else that concerned you about the clinics?"

"Honestly, no," Yolanda says. "After a couple of days, we were really getting the hang of them. The flow was good. I thought we were really efficient."

"We did, too," Lisa says.

Tyra nods. "Proud of you all."

"Thanks for this feedback," Lisa says. "And if anything else occurs to you, please let us know."

"Will do," Yolanda says, confused but also relieved that the interview is ending.

As Yolanda begins to stand up, Tyra asks, "You're still with Max, aren't you?"

"Yes."

"Things good? Haven't heard you mention him in a while."

"Absolutely," Yolanda says, although she hasn't spoken to Max in almost two days. Not since their heated discussion at her condo. He didn't reply to her phone calls or respond to the multiple texts that she can't stop herself from continuing to send.

Tyra seems to pick up on her doubt. "Can't always be easy, huh?"

"Are relationships ever easy?" Yolanda asks with a nervous laugh.

"True enough." Tyra laughs, too. "Although, after twenty years, I finally got my husband trained. Almost, anyway."

Uncertain how to respond, Yolanda only nods.

"We hear that Max has some pretty strong views on vaccines," Lisa says.

Yolanda freezes. She's always been embarrassed to discuss his anti-vax position at work and has only ever mentioned it to her closest friends on the team, Katerina and Stacy. "Yeah. At first, we argued a lot over that. Tried to persuade each other. Nowadays, we mainly agree to disagree."

"I bet," Lisa says. "I see Max has become a bit of a spokesperson for the anti-vax movement. He publishes a lot online. I've even heard him on the radio."

I knew this would get back to me! "I'm not proud of his views or anything. And it doesn't affect my work at all. Not at all."

"It's your own business." Lisa extends a hand in her direction. "One hundred percent!"

"But Max has taken an interest in Neissovax, hasn't he?" Tyra says.

"He's obsessed with all vaccines," Yolanda blurts.

"I got that feeling when I ran into him at one of our clinics," Lisa says.

Yolanda gawks at her. "Ran into him?"

"He told me he was considering getting his son vaccinated. Said he wanted to check the clinic out for himself."

"Does that sound like something he'd do?" Tyra asks.

Not in a million years! "It would kind of surprise me," Yolanda says.

"Why do you think Max went, then?"

"I . . . I don't know."

"It's not possible he was spying on the clinics, is it?"

"*Spying?* No, he wouldn't."

"But Max wanted to know all about Neissovax, didn't he?"

"I guess. He's so focused on his cause and all."

Lisa nods, her expression understanding. "What sort of questions did he ask?"

"I don't know," Yolanda says, trying to tamp down her rising panic. "Like about the clinics and how well attended they are."

"And how you run them?"

"Maybe. He just seemed super curious about everything."

"Did Max ever ask you to bring vials home for him?" Tyra asks.

Yolanda feels her jaw drop. "I . . . I'd never!"

"What is it, Yolanda?" Lisa asks, sensing Tyra's hit on something.

"He kept pestering me to show him what the vaccine looked like."

"You mean the vials?"

Yolanda can't make eye contact with either of them. Chin down, she nods slightly.

"And did you?" Lisa asks.

"I . . . I took a few photos on my phone," she mumbles. "And I sent him those."

CHAPTER 56

Nathan finds Fiona in front of her computer in her cubicle in the warehouse, her face as blank as the screen, her gaze miles away.

"I came directly from the airport," he says, pulling her out of her trance. "What's going on?"

"Not here." Fiona motions to the gaping space above the temporary walls. "Let's take a walk."

"OK."

She calls a car on her ride-share app, and they head out to meet it. As they pass the bank of refrigerators lining the near wall, Nathan asks, "Still full?"

"Sixty thousand doses."

He shakes his head. "To think, only a few days ago we were worried about running out."

"Things change."

Their ride pulls up out front of the warehouse, and they climb in the back of the nondescript sedan. Fiona doesn't stop fidgeting during the whole ride. She never mentions where they're heading, and he doesn't bother to ask or attempt any small talk.

The driver drops them off at Alki Beach Park, one of Seattle's westernmost points, where the isthmus juts out into Elliott Bay. It's a warm late-summer day, but a canopy of unpredictable gray clouds hovers overhead and keeps the stunning waterfront trail clear of most other visitors.

It's not until they step onto the path that Fiona speaks again. "An FBI agent came to interview me," she says. "Not just any agent, either. She's assistant head of the Seattle field office."

"About the database?"

She nods.

"What did she ask you?"

"Questions about my level of access and admin rights. That kind of stuff. She also wanted to know how often I logged on. And from where."

"All information she could easily find out for herself."

"She was also very curious about my level of technical expertise."

"In what sense?"

"Whether I had any web design or programming experience." She looks over to him. "Which I don't."

"How did she seem to you?"

"Hard to tell. Friendly enough, but she has a good poker face." Fiona pauses. "She must assume we're the ones who doctored the website."

"Why do you think so?"

She walks a few feet farther before she answers. "Because I would, if I were her."

Nathan slows, as does Fiona, but she doesn't look at him. "You didn't, though, did you, Fee?"

She shakes her head.

"You think I did?"

Fiona kicks at a pebble. "I think someone on our side would've been very motivated to cover up the connection between Darius Washington and Neissovax."

"And you think it was me?"

She finally looks up at him. "Was it?"

He grimaces. "How long have you known me?"

"Five years."

"And you think I'm capable?"

"Not really. But people surprise you, Nathan. Sometimes in the most terrible ways. Do things you couldn't even imagine them capable of." She begins to move again, and he follows in step. "I can't think of anyone outside of the company with a reason to have done it. Can you?"

Nathan sighs. "Neither can Lisa, apparently."

Fiona stares off to the horizon for a while before she says, "You like her, don't you?"

"She's married."

"My sense is that's not going to last."

"Even if that were true, what would be the point? She lives three thousand miles from me and is convinced I'm a conspirator."

"And yet you still like her."

He snorts. "I'm a sucker for hopeless predicaments."

"No, you're not, Nathan. You just need something substantial. And Lisa is definitely that."

"A substantial pipe dream."

"Not so sure about that."

They tread along the trail in silence for a while, passing benches, gardens, and even a small replica of the Statue of Liberty. On most days, Nathan would have found peace and comfort in the stroll along the practically deserted trail, with the soft sound of waves lapping at the beach and the cries of the gulls gliding overhead. Not today. The volatile clouds have begun to darken and sputter, reflecting his internal uneasiness. And like the weather, he expects his own situation only to worsen.

"I don't think it's just about the website breach," Fiona says apropos of nothing.

"What do you mean?"

"Special Agent Kennedy. I think there might be more to her investigation."

"What makes you say that?"

"She demanded samples of Neissovax." Fiona's pace begins to increase as she speaks. "Why would an FBI agent be interested in testing our vaccine?"

"It's probably standard procedure."

"Yeah, but Lisa already confiscated samples. Why does the FBI need them, as well? What do they have to do with a potential cybercrime?"

"I don't have the faintest clue."

"Have you heard anything else about this?" she asks. "Do they have concerns about the vials themselves?"

"I haven't met this agent, Fee." He holds up a hand. "I'm as much in the dark as you are."

"I mean, I could understand why Lisa wouldn't trust my—our— quality-control measures. But the FBI? What could they possibly be looking for?"

Fiona doesn't appear indignant as she has in the past when her performance has been questioned. Rather, she seems worried.

"It's going to be OK, Fee."

She turns to him with a foreign look that's somewhere between hurt and anger. "Just don't tell me everything happens for a reason. I've heard that lie before."

CHAPTER 57

"Thanks for coming so quickly," Lisa says to Eileen, when she arrives at her office within thirty minutes of receiving her text.

"It sounded important."

"It is," Lisa says, lowering her voice and glancing over to the closed door. "We found a person of interest."

Eileen chuckles. "You're stealing our terminology now?"

Lisa's smile is fleeting. "There's this vehement anti-vaxxer. He's medical—a naturopath. And his girlfriend is one of our public-health nurses."

Eileen's neck and shoulders straighten. "Who administered some of the shots?"

"Yes." Lisa goes on to explain what they've discovered about Max, including Tyra's recent revelation that one of the other public-health nurses, Katerina, spotted him at a different vaccine clinic from the one Lisa had seen him at.

"A person of extreme interest, I'd say," Eileen says. "Would he have had access to the vaccine through his girlfriend?"

"Yolanda swears not. She says she only sent him a photo of the vial."

"And why would he want that?"

"Can't think of a legitimate reason."

"As a naturopath, would Dr. Balfour be able to prescribe the medications that were found in those tainted syringes?"

"Not the antibiotics or antiseizure drugs, no. They'd be considered outside his scope of practice."

"How would he get his hands on them?"

"Same as anyone else. He could have taken them from a friend or a loved one's bottle. Also, he could have gotten them prescribed to himself through his own doctor. Or, more likely, at a walk-in clinic or an urgent care."

Eileen nods. "He could've just told them he ran out, right?"

"Exactly. None of these meds are narcotics or potential drugs of abuse. And they're generally considered fairly safe. So most MDs would be far less reluctant to prescribe them to a stranger."

"OK, let's say he did get prescriptions for himself. Could we track them down?"

"Yes! Like most states, Washington has mandatory e-prescribing now. In other words, there'd be an electronic trail of any of his prescriptions that should be accessible. Although I don't know the legality of accessing them."

"Let me worry about legalities."

"So what's next?"

"This is a really strong lead, but he's not our only suspect," Eileen says. "And I still have to interview Yolanda and the other nurses who worked the vaccine clinics in question."

"Understood," Lisa says, feeling a bit deflated at the prospect of exposing her staff to potential interrogation.

"I've already begun to interview the employees at Delaware."

"Including Nathan and Fiona?"

"Only Fiona so far. Nathan was in New York when I went to their warehouse."

"What did you make of her?"

Eileen leans back in her chair, considering it for a moment. "She was relatively forthcoming, but she seemed . . . worried."

"As if she were hiding something?"

"Not necessarily. Just concerned about the situation. Particularly the allegations you leveled against Nathan and her."

Lisa sighs. "I should never have gone to see them."

"What's done is done. Besides, Fiona doesn't seem to know about the tainted vaccines yet. She was upset when I told her that we were seizing the entire vaccine supply."

"I already had the tox lab test the unopened vials, and none of them were contaminated."

"We'll have to retest them in our own forensics lab for legal chain-of-evidence purposes."

"Makes sense," Lisa says, feeling sheepish for overstepping her bounds.

"I also checked to see if any of the gyms where the clinics were held had any kind of video surveillance systems. But sadly none of them did."

"I bet they do at the warehouse where Delaware stores the supply."

"They do. But getting those files will require a court order, which will take a bit longer."

"Damn."

"We haven't had much luck on the website tampering. Our cyber-crime experts have reached the same dead-end trail as your guy did."

"Which confirms it had to have been a pretty sophisticated hack, right?" Lisa asks. "Unlikely a naturopath could have pulled that off. At least, not without help."

"Even if he could have, I still think the hack of the website happened because of the tainted vaccine. Which would mean the two parties were acting independently."

"I think so, too. If Max did poison those vaccines, it's almost certain he wasn't behind the cover-up."

"Agreed." Eileen hops to her feet. "Let's go find out if it was him."

CHAPTER 58

Max breaks into a smile as he steps into his private office and recognizes the first of the two visitors waiting for him. Based on what his spooked assistant told him, he assumed both women must be from the FBI. But he's somewhat relieved to see Lisa standing beside the statuesque federal agent.

"Good to see you again, Dr. Dyer," Max says, and Lisa nods a curt greeting in return. He turns to the other woman with an extended hand. "And you must be the special agent in charge."

"Agent Kennedy." Eileen shows him a professional smile. "Thanks for taking the time to meet us, Dr. Balfour."

"My pleasure." Max walks around his desk and lowers himself into the chair behind it, motioning for the women to sit down across from him. "This must be important to bring such high-ranking officials to my humble office."

"Not necessarily, Dr. Balfour," Eileen says. "The FBI has been asked to look into certain irregularities regarding the recent vaccination program. Since Dr. Dyer managed the campaign, I've asked her to join us for perspective. I hope that's all right?"

"Absolutely. I always enjoy my chats with Dr. Dyer." Max crosses one leg over the other knee, trying to appear as casual as possible. "You mentioned irregularities. Can you be more specific?"

Lisa opens her mouth, but Eileen answers before she has a chance to speak. "To be clear, we haven't confirmed there is substance to these concerns."

"Sure. I get it. But what kind of concerns?"

"Let's start with the website," Eileen says.

"Start with? My website?" Max uncrosses his leg, and then puts it back again.

"No, the Seattle Public Health's website. The app that was created for reporting adverse reactions to the new meningitis vaccine."

Max leans back slightly. "And how can I help with that?"

"We believe somebody tampered with the records on its database."

He frowns. "As in altered the data?"

"Potentially, yes."

"And you think it might have been me?"

"We're exploring all possibilities."

He looks directly at Lisa and asks, "Why would I hack your database?"

"You do hold some strong views on the subject of vaccines," Eileen says.

"You mean the dangers of vaccines, don't you?"

"Is it fair to say that you're a prominent anti-vax activist?"

"We prefer the term 'vaccine hesitancy.' But yes, I'm committed to raising awareness about the issue. Still, even if I were the most ardent vaccine opponent alive, how would hacking the database help me advance our cause?"

"Our investigation is in the early stages. But we've come here because many consider you to be a leader of the local anti-vaxxers."

"Leader? We're a loosely affiliated community, not a military organization." He laughs. "Besides, no matter how motivated I was, I couldn't hack my way into my own website. And I have the admin password for it. I think tampering with a government website would be a bit beyond my skill set."

Lisa views Max impassively, but Eileen accepts the explanation with a simple nod. "On another note," she says, "I read a few of your most recent blog posts. Sounds as if you viewed the complications from the vaccine as a big victory for the cause."

"Victory?" Max purses his lips. "It would be morbid to gloat over something like that. Kids got very sick. At least one of them died. As a parent of a child who suffers from a severe vaccine injury, I'm very sensitive to that. I feel awful for those families."

"Maybe, but the posts read like you were celebrating what happened."

"Not the complications from the vaccine. Only that they were uncovered early. *This* time. And that our cautionary voices were finally heard. It's way overdue." He glances again at Lisa, whose expression is still blank. "Our cause has been marginalized forever. It's kind of rewarding to be finally validated."

"But last time we met . . ." Lisa speaks up for the first time. "You told me you were seriously considering getting your son vaccinated."

"I was concerned about this meningitis scare. I still am." Max shrugs. "Then, after seeing the clinic for myself, I decided against it."

"You mean *clinics*," Lisa says.

"Sure. Whatever. I decided it wasn't worth the risk to expose my son to another vaccination." He grins. "I think you'd have to concede that it wasn't such a bad decision in retrospect."

"What I meant is that you attended multiple clinics."

The smile involuntarily slips off his face. "Who told you that?"

"Your girlfriend works for Public Health, doesn't she?" Eileen asks.

"And that's relevant how?"

Ignoring the question, Eileen says, "We understand you hounded her for the specific details about those clinics."

Max feels his neck tightening. He tries to summon an indifferent tone, but he realizes he can't. The words topple out of his mouth. "Of course I was interested in this new vaccine! As you keep pointing out, this cause is my passion." His eyes dart to Lisa. "And Seattle Public Health has tried to force not one but *two* toxic vaccines down our throats in the past month alone." He forces himself to take a deep breath. "Since when did activism become a crime?"

"Activism isn't a crime," Eileen says. "Not even spying on the clinics would constitute one."

He waits for her to continue, but she leaves the argument half-finished. "Where is the crime, then?" he asks.

"Can you tell us why you wanted vials of the vaccine so badly?" Lisa asks.

"Yolanda never gave me a single vial!"

"Not from your lack of trying."

Max only scoffs in response.

"What were you planning to do with those vials, Dr. Balfour?" Eileen demands.

He plants his hands on the desktop and pushes himself upright. "What's this really about?"

"We're looking into the possibility that the vaccine was sabotaged."

"Sabotaged?"

"As in someone poisoned the vials, Dr. Balfour," Lisa says. "And that's why those kids reacted as badly as they did."

"And you're accusing me?" His voice rises with each word.

"We are just asking," Eileen says. "At least, for right now."

His rage explodes as if a detonator had been tripped. "Isn't this just fucking typical? Big Pharma is worried about their precious bottom line. They need a fall guy. And so they sic the feds on me. Make up some absolute bullshit about poisoned vials. How the hell do you poison a poison, anyway?"

"Dr. Balfour, you should—"

Max shakes a finger at them both. "Kill two birds with one stone, huh? Big Pharma gets to save their huge profits and frame the anti-vaxxer. How fucking convenient!"

"You need to calm down, Dr. Balfour," Eileen says in an even but stern tone.

"You really want to know what I was doing at those clinics?" Max yanks his desk drawer open. Out of the corner of his eye, he sees Eileen's hand dart inside her blazer. He throws his hands up, realizing she's reaching for her gun. "No. No. It's OK. I just want to show you something. In the drawer."

The agent keeps her hand where it is.

"To explain what I was doing at those clinics," he says, forcing the civility back into his tone.

"Slowly," Eileen says, relaxing her arm.

Max carefully extracts what looks like a pen from the drawer. He holds it out to them.

The two women share a confused glimpse.

"A pen?" Lisa asks.

"It's certainly supposed to look like one," Max says.

"What is it?"

"A spy cam." He holds it up as if filming them with it. "I was using a hidden camera to secretly record the clinics."

Lisa grimaces. "What for?"

"To make an exposé."

"Of what?"

"Anything that would paint those clinics and the vaccine in a bad light." Max stares at her defiantly. "I got footage of a girl passing out right after she got her shot. Another time, I got a clip of nurse who didn't change her gloves between injections. And then I got this video of one dad who barely spoke English being basically bullied into signing the consent form." He moves the pen back and forth between the women. "I spliced the clips together in a video we were going to post. We were planning to use the empty vials as visual aids. Maybe even dramatize them a bit with some crusted blood or whatever. But things turned out just fine even without the vials."

"Who's *we*?" Eileen asks.

"Some friends in the community. The plan was to make the clip go viral."

"You were doing this to discourage people from getting their kids vaccinated?"

Max lowers himself back into his seat, feeling calm descend back over him. "We never did post it. It wasn't necessary." He can't help but look over to Lisa. "Not after the vaccine revealed itself for the threat it always was."

CHAPTER 59

"**D**o you believe him?" Lisa asks Eileen from the passenger seat as the agent drives them away from Max's office.

"Some of what he said. Not all," Eileen says. "But there's no denying his video is real."

Before they left, Max played them his "exposé" on his laptop. The video did capture the incidents he cited—a kid fainting, a nurse not changing her gloves, and another staff member appearing to rush a Hispanic man through signing the consent form—along with a few other clips where Lisa couldn't even discern what the supposed infraction was.

"Could you imagine anyone being talked out of getting vaccinated by that piece of crap?" Lisa asks.

"You're not exactly his target audience," Eileen points out.

"His whole story could still be bullshit. Max would have had every reason for spying on those clinics if he were behind the poisonings. Maybe he threw the video together as a cover story in case he did fall under suspicion."

"He's by no means ruled himself out as suspect, Lisa. I'm still going to look into his e-prescription records to see if we can trace those contaminants back to him."

"But?"

"We have to consider others, too."

"Who?"

"Anyone with motive plus opportunity."

"No end of people with motive. Anti-vaxxers, antipharma activists, disgruntled employees, terrorists, or any other whack job you can imagine. But Max is the only one I can think of with both an obvious motive and a clear opportunity."

"Which is why we have to focus on anyone else with opportunity. It's a much shorter list." Eileen taps her steering wheel. "Starting with your nurses who worked all three clinics where recipients ended up developing bad skin reactions."

"Only eight nurses worked both of the first two clinics in question. And Tyra is narrowing down the list to include those who also attended the latest victim's clinic. Probably no more than four in total."

"We've also got to look into people on the Delaware side."

"Fiona should be able to provide you a list of her staff who worked those same clinics," Lisa says.

Eileen glances over at her. It's only when her eyes return to the road that she says, "Nathan and Fiona would've also had the opportunity."

Lisa can't imagine any of her staff being involved in poisoning the vaccine, let alone Nathan or Fiona. Given the alternatives, she still hopes Max is responsible, but she left his office far less convinced of his guilt than when she arrived. "It's probably worth tracking down the e-prescription records on those nurses in question. As well as for Nathan and Fiona, huh?"

"I intend to. And as you pointed out, the perpetrator could be stealing pills from a loved one. So I'm going to look into close relatives as well."

"Makes sense," Lisa says, feeling even more dejected. "Max has a special-needs son. And Fiona mentioned a debilitated mother in a care home. All I know about Nathan's family is that he has two teenage sons."

"We'll cast the net fairly wide."

A silence falls over the car. Eileen is too professional to show it, but Lisa senses the agent shares in her disappointment over the setback with Max.

Eileen drops Lisa off at the Public Health building just after five p.m. Even more trucks and vans tattooed with media logos line the street out front, establishing how ravenous the press must be for details on the latest Neissovax reaction. Whether Max was involved in tipping the scales or not, the anti-vax movement continued to reap huge gains in the public opinion war from the continued fallout. Lisa shudders at the thought of how the public will respond to the news of the poisoned vaccine. *A total FUBAR.*

She can't bear the thought of facing the media right now, not with some of her own staff under investigation, so instead she heads directly to her car and, on a whim, drives over to Bellevue, to her sister's place.

Olivia answers the front door. She wraps Lisa's midsection in a hug.

"Was the hospital sick of you?" Lisa asks when Olivia breaks off the embrace and then drags her inside by the hand.

"They said it was nothing, Tee," Olivia says. "That Mommy over-acted."

"Over*reacted*," Amber corrects with a laugh as she joins them in the living room.

"Show me your arm," Lisa instructs.

Olivia slides up her sleeve to reveal that the patch of redness has faded, and the welt is almost unnoticeable.

"Better." Lisa nods approvingly. "Is Daddy home?"

"Meetings," Olivia says with an exaggerated attempt at an eye roll that makes Lisa chuckle.

Lisa grabs Amber's arm. "Mommy and I are going to chat in the kitchen for a bit."

"Can I watch my show, Mommy?" Olivia asks.

"You get thirty minutes on the iPad." Amber checks her watch. "Starting . . . now."

Olivia turns and races down corridor toward one of the bedrooms.

"Should I open a bottle?" Amber asks Lisa when they reach the kitchen, which smells of sautéed onions and unidentified herbs.

"Not for me, thanks."

Amber wiggles four fingers in a beckoning gesture. "Tell me."

Lisa notices a pot simmering on the front element. "How much time do you have?"

"Work- or home-related?"

"Both, I suppose," Lisa says. "But the crisis at work is even more acute than the one at home."

"Worse than it's been the last few days?"

Lisa considers it for a moment. "Different."

"How so?"

Lisa glances around out of instinct, and lowers her voice. "There's nothing wrong with the actual vaccine."

Amber frowns. "What about those life-threatening rashes? The news said there was a fourth one reported today."

"Poison."

"What?"

Lisa explains about the sabotaged vaccine.

"What a fucking nightmare."

"You're telling me. The worst part is, I have no idea who I can even trust anymore."

Amber raises an eyebrow. "Nathan?" Even though Lisa has never told her sister much about the pharmaceutical-company executive, Lisa knows her sister intuits her attraction to him. "You think he could be involved?"

"Maybe," Lisa says. "I can't see him poisoning a vaccine. But the cover-up? Yeah, sure, I could see that."

"Hey! It's not your responsibility to figure this out." Amber pats her wrist. "That's why you brought in the FBI."

"It *is* my job to control this meningitis outbreak. And we're going to need Neissovax to do it. But we can't use the vaccine until we find out who's contaminating it and how."

"Crap, that's a real conundrum."

"Even if and when we do ensure the vaccine supply is pure, how will we ever win back the public's trust?"

"One step at a time." Amber flashes a cheeky grin. "Besides, you're relentless. You'll wear them down. Just like you did me."

Lisa snorts a small laugh. "Amber . . ."

"Yeah?"

"Dad wasn't right, after all. This vaccine would've been totally safe if someone hadn't tried to sabotage it."

"I know." Amber clears her throat. "I'm sorry, Lisa."

"For?"

"Doubting you. It's just that when those kids got sick after the vaccine and then Liv—"

"Don't even." Lisa cuts her sister off by wrapping her in a hug. "I began to doubt myself. You had every right to."

Amber clings tightly to her for a moment. "Stay for dinner?" she asks as she slips out of Lisa's arms. "I made Olivia's favorite, lentil stew."

"Smells great, but I better go deal with the home front. Whichever general said it first got it right. Never fight a two-front war." She says a quick good-bye to Olivia and then heads out to her car and drives home. Lisa finds Dominic in the kitchen, where he's grilling salmon on the stove. There's only one plate on the countertop beside a single wineglass.

"I just assumed I'd be eating alone again," he says when she walks in.

"That's OK, I'm not really hungry."

He puts down the spatula and turns toward her. "We're running out of things to do separately, Lees."

"I'm under a bit of stress at work right now."

"You're not the only who's under stress."

"What are you saying?"

"We had our struggles before this outbreak, sure. But I thought with the counseling, we were making real progress. Then you have your little crisis at work—"

"My little crisis?"

"OK. Public-health emergency. Whatever you want to call it." He folds his arms across his chest. "Suddenly our marriage is on the back burner. You stop communicating with me. I'm walking on eggshells all the time. And all the gains we made in counseling are wiped out."

"This 'little crisis' is a lot a bigger than you or me. Kids are dying."

He tilts his head. "All I know for sure is that your job is tearing us apart."

My job? There's so much she could say. About his petty resentments and lack of concern about her feelings that have done most of the damage. But all she says is, "I'm sorry you think so, Dom."

"What do you think?"

Her gaze falls to the ground. She's overcome by an emotion she doesn't fully recognize. She can't tell if it's clarity or surrender. But she suddenly realizes what has to be done. "I think we need some time apart."

"Don't know how much more of that we could possibly find," he mutters. "But maybe you're right. Maybe I should sleep in the spare room for a while."

"No, you stay in our room," she says. "I'll move to the guest room. For now."

"For now?"

"I'm going to start looking for another place."

"Lees . . ."

"It's for the best, Dom," she says, turning away from him. "You know it is, too."

Dominic doesn't follow her as she heads into the bedroom and gathers a small bag with toiletries and a few changes of clothes. Part of her still wishes he would, but mostly she's relieved and unsurprised he doesn't.

They've fought before. And each of them has slept nights, sometimes a few in a row, in the guest bedroom. But as Lisa unpacks her toiletries in the en suite bathroom, she experiences an unfamiliar sense of finality. As sad as she feels, though, there are no tears.

She heads back into the guest bedroom and puts her bag on the bed. The old wooden clock on the far wall catches her eye. Although the design isn't art deco, it still reminds her of the one on Fiona's desk. Lisa remembers Walt's romantic words that Fiona quoted from the anniversary card and the loving inscription carved on the bottom of the clock. She feels another pang of envy over the kind of relationship Fiona and her husband must have shared.

Lisa considers Walt's tragic death again. She remembers Fiona's description of how it happened. Then, somewhere in the recesses of her brain, a connection begins to form.

CHAPTER 60

Nathan checks his watch, which reads a few minutes after eight p.m. His stomach growls, and he realizes it's after eleven in New York. Not that his internal time zone had time to reset during his thirty-hour round-trip home.

On his only day back in New York in over a week, Nathan took his sons to a Mets game. Baseball was a compromise. Ethan had begged Nathan to take him out to practice driving while Marcus lobbied for them to go to the latest Marvel movie. No one was fully satisfied with the ball game, especially after the Mets got shut out. While Nathan always appreciated being with his sons, he was too distracted by the Neissovax catastrophe to focus on them or the game. His mind never really left Seattle.

Ever since his flight touched back down at Sea-Tac, earlier in the afternoon, Nathan has been texting and calling Lisa in the hope of convincing her to meet. But she hasn't responded at all. He's just about to give up for the day and head down to the restaurant when a text from her appears on the screen. "Where are you?"

"Back at the hotel," he replies.

"Be there in fifteen."

Nathan stares at the screen. He didn't expect that. He considers taking a shower but realizes there's no point. If their last interaction is anything to go by, he will be lucky if he can keep the conversation civil. He wonders why Lisa wants to meet so urgently. A stone forms in the pit of his stomach. *What else has she found out*?

The wait is short. In less than a quarter of an hour, there's a knock at the door. Nathan opens it to find Lisa standing there in gray sweatpants and a blue workout shirt. Her face is unsmiling, and there are fresh bags beneath her eyes. There are no hugs as she walks into his suite, and he doesn't even consider offering her a drink.

"What's up?" he asks.

Her eyes lock on to his. "Were you involved in the cover-up of Darius Washington's death?"

He shakes his head.

She stares at him for a long time, neither accepting nor challenging his denial. "I need to ask you about Fiona," she finally says.

"Fiona?"

"More specifically, her husband. Walt."

"I never met him."

"She told me Walt died of Guillain-Barré syndrome."

"He did."

"Do you know if he developed it after getting the flu or after the flu shot?"

He considers her question for a moment. "After the shot."

"You're certain?"

"Yeah, it came up once when we were discussing vaccine complications and Guillain-Barré syndrome. But she acknowledged he would've been even more likely to have gotten it from the flu itself." He shrugs. "Why is that relevant?"

Lisa closes her eyes and exhales. "Delaware is one of the main suppliers of the flu vaccine in the US, isn't it?"

"Generally speaking. But vaccine supply is regional. And it varies from year to year."

"The Northeast is one of Delaware's main territories, though. Particularly, New York State."

"I suppose. I don't handle flu vaccines at Delaware." Nathan frowns. "What's going on, Lisa?"

"The flu shot that Walt got must have come from your own company."

"So?"

"Neissovax," she says softly. "It's been poisoned."

"*Poisoned?*" For a moment, he assumes he misunderstood her. But the look in her eyes is unmistakable. "What the hell?"

She drops down onto the couch. "We screened the used syringes, Nathan. From the clinics where those kids reacted. We found traces of multiple different contaminants in the vaccine. Six different medications, each of which could cause Stevens-Johnson syndrome. None of them were there by accident."

The realization hits him with the impact of a rockfall. "And you think . . . Fiona did it?"

"I don't want to. And I'm still not totally convinced. But consider it, Nathan. How many people would've had access to the vials of vaccine?"

"Not many," he mutters, his mind still reeling from her disclosure. "But Fiona? I've worked with her for more than five years. She's my friend. One of the gentlest people I've ever met."

Lisa digs her phone out of her purse and shows it to him. "Do you remember this?" Filling the screen is an online article with a headline that reads: "This Year's Flu Shot Has High Rate of Complications."

He reads it and shrugs again.

"From six years ago. The year Walt died." She lowers the phone. "Apparently, the rate of Guillain-Barré syndrome was almost double the norm that year. There was a lawsuit. Does any of that ring a bell?"

"There are lawsuits every year in our business," he says, rubbing his forehead. "Particularly related to the flu shot. I vaguely remember it being a bit more of a concern five or six years ago. But Peter made it go away." He slumps onto the couch. "He's very good at that."

CHAPTER 61

The moment Lisa reaches the hotel lobby, she calls Eileen. "Fiona's husband died of complications from the flu vaccine!" she says before the agent has a chance to speak. "A vaccine manufactured by Delaware Pharmaceuticals."

"That's a hell of a coincidence," Eileen says.

"How could it be just a coincidence? Even Nathan couldn't explain it once he learned about the poisoning."

"You told him?"

"I had to, Eileen." Lisa brushes away the concern in the agent's tone. "As a pharmacist, Fiona would have the know-how to sabotage a vaccine. No one had more access to the vials than her. And now we've established motive, too."

"Yeah."

"Have you heard anything on the e-prescription records yet?"

"I've had some trouble getting around the red tape in Washington State. So I haven't got access to Max's records yet. But I did get the ones from New York."

Lisa stiffens. "And?"

"Nathan's had no prescriptions whatsoever in the last two years.

Fiona only gets two regular prescriptions: venlafaxine and mir-
tazapine."

"California rocket fuel."

"What's that?"

"The nickname for the popular combination of those two anti-
depressant medications. But neither was found in the contaminated
vaccines. No other prescriptions, huh?"

"None."

Disappointed, Lisa thanks Eileen for the information and agrees
to meet her in the morning.

She has barely stepped out of the hotel when a text from Fiona
pops up on her screen. "Do you have time to talk?" it reads.

"Sure," Lisa texts back, wondering if Nathan tipped her off. "In
person? I'm near your hotel."

"Meet at the bar?"

Lisa texts the thumbs-up emoji and then adds, "Twenty minutes," to make it seem like she's not already there.

She paces out in front of the hotel in the warm dusk as time
crawls by. When she sees twenty minutes have finally passed, she
hurries back inside and rides the elevator to the top floor.

Lisa steps into the rooftop bar and spots Fiona sitting at their
usual table at the window, across from the door to the rooftop deck.
Aside from the muscular bartender who's sorting glasses and a
young couple who are already standing to leave, the bar is empty.

Lisa takes a slow breath and summons a calm expression as she
heads over to the table and sits down across from Fiona.

Fiona offers a somber nod. "Drink?"

"Water's all I need tonight," Lisa says, motioning to the two
glasses already on the table.

Fiona sweeps back a few strands of loose hair from her forehead. "I feel terrible about the situation, Lisa."

"Which situation?" Lisa asks, wondering again if Nathan mentioned the poisoning to her.

"Pretty much everything that's happened since we launched this lousy campaign. But specifically, the website hack. The one you think Nathan and I were behind."

"You weren't?"

"No." Fiona hesitates. "But I know who was."

"Who?"

Fiona leans closer. "Peter Moore," she says in a hush.

"Your own CEO? What makes you think so?"

"It's like him."

"How so?"

"The man's a sociopath," Fiona says. "As dirty as they come. Around Delaware, people call him 'The Fixer' for all the problems he makes disappear."

"What sort of problems?"

"Lawsuits, fiscal irregularities, unethical research, sketchy development practices . . . you name it."

"And Moore had access to our reporting website?"

"Yes."

"How do you know?"

"Because I gave it to him," she says in a small voice. "My username and password."

"And he hacked the website?"

"Not personally, but I bet you one of his people must have deleted the report about the boy who died." Fiona shrugs. "What's one more body to Peter Moore?"

"Then why give him your password, Fiona?"

"He bullied me, like he always does," she murmurs. "The same way he bullied Nathan and me into agreeing to go along with this vaccine trial when we both knew it was premature."

"We pushed from our side, too, if you remember."

Fiona gives her a swift glance. "Yeah, but Peter needed the launch to happen."

"Why?"

"To make Neissovax invaluable to you—and the rest of the world—before anyone else learned about its deadly little side effect."

"Hold on! You knew about the skin reactions even before you got to Seattle?" Lisa asks, though the story makes no sense in light of the tainted vials.

"I'd heard rumors."

"What kind of rumors?"

"At one of the European study sites for the first big trial, there was an unusual skin reaction. Serious, too. The rash didn't show up for a few days, so the investigator didn't include it in the results. Who knows? Maybe Peter got to him. Anyway, it was never reported. I only found out secondhand, through a French colleague."

Lisa's head spins. "And you're sure Moore knew all this?"

"Yes."

"How?"

"From me. But I never put in writing. So no doubt he'll deny it."

Lisa is still digesting the latest revelation when her phone rings. She looks down to see Eileen's number. "Sorry, but I have to take this." She rises and walks away from the table to answer.

"I found some more e-prescription records," Eileen says as soon as Lisa picks up.

"On Max?" Lisa asks.

"No. From New York. On a Jennifer Swanson."

Lisa turns her back to the table. "Swanson? Is she Fiona's mother?" she whispers.

"Yes. And it's a long list. Multiple medications for heart disease, blood pressure, and diabetes." She pauses, and Lisa hears pages shuffling in the background. "But over the past six months, Mrs. Swanson has also been prescribed lamotrigine, co-trimoxazole, allopurinol, fluconazole, carbamazepine, and, most recently, oseltamivir."

The phone freezes in Lisa's hand. "All six of the contaminants in Neissovax."

"Yes."

"I'm with Fiona now."

"Where?"

"Her hotel. The rooftop bar."

"Stall her! I'm on my way," Eileen says, and then is gone.

Before turning back to the table, Lisa takes a slow breath and wills the emotion out of her expression. With each step back, she's aware of Fiona's eyes on her and feels as self-conscious as someone trying to look natural while aware that she's being filmed.

"Everything OK?" Fiona asks Lisa once she reaches the table.

"Just my husband." Lisa clears her throat as she reclaims her seat. "All good."

"The call came up as just a number on your screen." Fiona points out. "You don't store your husband's contact on your phone?"

Lisa shifts on her the chair. "He was calling from the hospital."

"At this time?"

"He had an emergency add-on case in the cath lab." Nerves get the better of her, and Lisa can't help but expand on the lie. "A young guy with bad coronaries. He would've had a heart attack any day without intervention."

Despite Fiona's placid expression, Lisa sees the skepticism in her gaze. "What was the call really about, Lisa?" she asks quietly.

"Your mother," Lisa replies, recognizing the futility of obfuscating.

"My mom?"

"More specifically, the record of her recent prescriptions."

The surprise vacates Fiona's expression, replaced by something akin to admiration. Her shoulders relax, and she suddenly looks at ease. Peaceful, even. "How did you figure it out?"

The question is posed so casually that Lisa almost misses its significance. "We tested the used syringes."

"The used syringes," Fiona echoes. "I was so careful to get rid of the spent vials. But nothing I could do about those syringes. I offered to take care of the sharps containers, but your team wouldn't allow it. And I couldn't push too much."

"I guess not."

For a long moment, Fiona is as silent as she is immobile. "I didn't mean for anyone to die," she finally says.

"I believe you," Lisa says, wanting to keep her talking.

"He bullied me back then, too."

It takes Lisa a moment to gain her bearings. "Peter Moore?"

She nods. "After Walt died. Peter bullied us all. There was a class-action suit."

"Over the flu vaccine?"

"Yes," Fiona says. "Something was wrong with Delaware's supply. There were twice as many cases of Guillain-Barré syndrome as usual. A bunch of other people died, too. A law firm in DC launched a class-action suit on our behalves. But they were no match for Peter's legal army. He forced a settlement on us through the National Vaccine Injury Compensation Program."

Lisa says nothing, sensing that her best approach is to let Fiona vent.

"You know how much I got for Walt's death?"

Lisa shakes her head.

"After legal expenses? Eighty-three thousand dollars." Fiona chuckles grimly. "Eighty-three thousand. That's what Delaware Pharmaceuticals and Peter Moore valued the slow, painful murder of my husband at."

Lisa wants to keep her talking. "You decided to get even?" she prompts.

"No." Fiona's gaze drifts to the window and her voice goes even quieter. "Not at first. Initially, I just wanted an explanation. To understand how it worked inside the belly of the beast. I was worried they might recognize me from the class-action suit, so I switched from my first name, Gayle, to my middle name, Fiona, and reverted to my maiden name, Swanson. Then I took a job at Delaware. No one there made the connection."

"You said 'not at first.' What changed?"

"I saw how little they cared about the damage they were doing. Profit. Share prices. Bonuses. Those were their only measures of success. Lives lost didn't really matter at Delaware." Fiona's eyes redden. "And then I met other victims' families. And the more I heard about the suffering Delaware's shoddy vaccines had caused, the more I realized something had to be done."

"And then Neissovax came along?"

"Fate, right? How could it not have been?" Fiona closes her eyes and exhales. "The poetic irony . . . After what their flu shot had done to Walt, I was being gifted the opportunity to make amends through their latest vaccine. To take Delaware down and reveal the dangers of wanton vaccination in one swoop."

"Not as easy as it sounds, is it, though?"

"The razor's edge," Fiona admits. "So many variables, so much to balance. The vaccine had already passed phase-three trials without issue. If there were too many reactions, too quickly, I knew you would've smelled a rat and halted the program from the outset."

"It had to be subtle."

"Very. The reactions had to be severe enough to make the vaccine unsalvageable, but uncommon enough that they still might not have shown up in the early clinical trials."

"Like what happened with the rotavirus vaccine?"

"Exactly! And delayed hypersensitivity reactions like Stevens-Johnson syndrome were the ideal answer. But even with multiple toxins, they can be elusive. Hard to elicit."

"You had to poison multiple vaccines to get a single significant reaction."

"About thirty for every one, as it turns out. But it's luck of the draw, isn't it? I wasn't expecting to get two reactions out of the first clinic alone."

"I guess not."

Fiona's chin falls to her chest, and her head begins to bob. When she looks up again, tears stream down her cheeks. "I didn't mean to kill the boy, Lisa. Or anyone."

"You poisoned them, Fiona."

"They needed to be sick, yes. But I expected the reactions to be treatable. I thought . . ." She clears her throat and wipes her eyes. "I thought they would recover."

Lisa's phone dings with another notification, and she looks down to see a text from Eileen that reads, "In the lobby."

Before she even looks back up, Lisa catches a blur of motion out of the periphery of her vision. Cold water splashes her face as ice cubes smack painfully off her cheek and forehead. By the time Lisa is able to wipe the water from her eyes, Fiona is up and sprinting for the patio door.

Lisa jumps up, but her foot slides on a stray ice cube. She grabs the table to steady herself and pushes off just as Fiona yanks open the patio door and darts through it.

Heart in her throat, Lisa squeezes through the closing door.

Fiona still has three good strides on her. She doesn't slow as she hurls herself at the patio's raised glass railing.

"No!" Lisa cries, diving toward Fiona, who's more than halfway over the top.

Landing hard on her right knee, Lisa catches Fiona by the calf of her dangling leg.

"Let me go!" Fiona kicks wildly at her with her other leg, slamming Lisa in the chest and almost slipping free.

Despite Fiona's kicks and the throb of her knee, Lisa clings on to the woman's ankle. Pulling as hard as she can, she rolls away from the railing.

Fiona resists for several seconds but then her grip slips, and she topples down hard on top of Lisa.

Lisa blindly throws her arms out around Fiona's chest and holds on with all her might.

Fiona's hot breath fills her face and her spittle lands on her nose as she cries, "Let me go," repeatedly while struggling with the frenzy of a deer tangled in fencing.

"Stop!" a man yells, and Lisa suddenly feels Fiona being pulled out of her grip.

She rolls over and pops up to a sitting position to see the bartender on top of Fiona, pinning her to the ground.

"Calm down!" he tells the still-struggling Fiona. "Everything's going be OK."

But the way Lisa sees it, nothing really will be.

CHAPTER 62

The grounds are lovely. Walking paths, ponds, and little gardens with benches are scattered throughout the sprawling wooded property. Inside, it smells of fresh coffee and baking. If Lisa didn't know better, she would've assumed the converted old mansion was a high-end bed-and-breakfast instead of a hospice for the dying.

The room is west facing with a peekaboo view of the ocean through the trees. Angela sits propped up in the bed. Her cheeks are skeletal and her eyes deeply sunken, but her smile is amused and still vibrant. "This whole place looks like the backdrop for a photo shoot in some Lands' End catalog," she says. "But I like it here. Cliché that it is, it's kind of peaceful."

"And the family?"

"They like it, too." Angela motions to the pullout couch across the room. "Howard can sleep over. When he's not being overly emotional. That lovable old wuss."

Lisa leans forward in her chair and takes her friend's bony hand in hers. "He's a keeper."

Angela meets her gaze. "I should've probably told you sooner that my chemo was a bust. But I was worried you'd kick me out of the office if you knew I was on my last legs."

"Are you kidding? You kept me sane through the worst of it."

"Being back on the job during the outbreak . . ." Angela clears her throat weakly. "It gave me a sense of purpose. Kept me out of this place for an extra week or two. Thank you."

"I'm the one who's thankful. Honestly, Angela. No idea what I would've done without you."

"Enough! My ass doesn't have room for any more smoke blown up it." Angela chuckles. "So where are we at?"

"A mixed bag," Lisa admits. "We're officially three weeks into the outbreak as of today, and the latest count is forty-nine dead among a hundred twenty-two infected. But the good news is that in the last three days, there have only been four new cases and one death."

"Strange times in Public Health when we consider one death as good news," Angela says. "How's the Neissovax campaign going?"

"It's picking up steam. Yesterday was the fourth day of the re-opened clinics, and we had over four hundred people through."

"So they're coming back?"

"Yes, but there's still so much distrust out there. To reach true herd immunity against this meningococcus, we need to vaccinate eighty percent of Seattle's youth. But we're miles away from that target."

"It's going to take time, Lisa. Fiona did a lot of damage."

"Yes, she did," Lisa says.

A week has passed since Fiona's arrest and the authorities went public with the news of the tainted vaccines. There was only one more case of Stevens-Johnson syndrome reported in that time—an eleven-year-old girl, who was already recovering. Only one of Fiona's victims, Darius Washington, died directly from the poisoning, but no one knows how many families were scared out of vaccinating their children because of her. Some might have died as a direct result of not being vaccinated, while others might still suffer from how much Fiona's sabotage impeded efforts to immunize the rest of the community.

"It's not only Neissovax. Or Seattle." Angela sighs. "Imagine how many people might be reconsidering all types of other vital vaccines because of her fraud."

"The irony is it wasn't even over her anti-vax beliefs," Lisa says. "Not primarily. In the end, she just wanted to make Delaware pay for the death of her husband. Simple vengeance."

"People are so fucked," Angela mutters, and then looks at Lisa with a penetrating gaze. "Speaking of husbands, how's it going with yours?"

Lisa hesitates. "I found a condo. I'll be moving out at the end of the week." She hasn't told anyone else yet, not even Dominic or Amber.

"About damn time."

"You think so?"

"You haven't been happy in years, Lisa. Not really."

"I guess not, no."

"And you kept making more excuses. Fertility issues, blah, blah, blah." Angela nods to the couch. "One thing I've learned through all of this is how much it matters to be with the right person." Her voice cracks. "Especially at the end."

Lisa doesn't have words to respond, so she keeps quiet and continues to cling to her friend's hand.

Angela finally breaks the silence. "I was never willing to consider you my protégée before. Too worried you'd disappoint me." She winks. "But you made me proud."

Lisa fills with paradoxical emotions. Angela's approval means the world to her, but it only emphasizes how important her friend is. Lisa has no idea if Angela has days or weeks left, but it devastates her to think how much she's going to miss her. She can barely croak out the words, "Thank you."

"You're going to land on your feet, Lisa." Angela chuckles. "Take it from someone's who isn't."

CHAPTER 63

Nathan knocks at the door to Lisa's office. She looks up from her desk in surprise. "Your assistant said it would be all right if I dropped in," he says.

"Sure. Come in." Her tone isn't warm, but at least she doesn't sound as suspicious as she did during their last few encounters.

Nathan steps inside, closes the door, and sits down across from her. "I just came to say good-bye."

"You're heading back to New York?" she asks, tugging at her ear.

He can't help but notice that the wedding band is missing from her ring finger. "Yeah, for good this time. One of our other VPs, Sonya Silverstein, will be taking my place here."

"Here? So you're not leaving Delaware?"

"Nowhere else to go." He would love to explain it to her, but he can't. "I just won't be overseeing the day-to-day operations on Neissovax anymore. I'll connect you and Sonya via email this afternoon."

"Thank you," she says. "All things considered, the relaunch of the campaign has gone smoothly, wouldn't you say?"

"Better than I expected, for sure. Obviously, we're still fighting a headwind on the publicity front, but back at Delaware they're pretty pleased."

She eyes him knowingly. "Its share price has rebounded well in the past week, hasn't it?"

"For now. Let's see what happens after the class-action suits are launched for the damage Fiona inflicted."

"Have you had any contact with her?"

"No," he says nonchalantly, hiding his conflicted feelings. He hates Fiona for what she did, but he can't help missing his friend and confidante. And a small part of him empathizes with her desire to make Delaware pay. "I talked to her attorney. Apparently, Fiona hasn't spoken to anyone while in custody, not even him."

Lisa nods. "The night we caught her, she swore Peter Moore was behind the hack of the website and the cover-up of Darius's death."

"Did she have proof?"

"No. And in almost the same breath that she accused him of masterminding the hack, she also made up a story about some doctored European study to frame Peter for the adverse reactions."

"Hard to know what to believe, huh?"

"Or whom." Lisa stares hard at him. "It doesn't make any sense for Fiona to have been involved in the cover-up. She wanted those reactions to come to light."

"You still think it was me?"

"The FBI is investigating. But I get the feeling the tracks are too well covered. Not sure we'll ever find out who was behind it."

He's silent for a long moment before he stands. "With all the terrible stuff that happened after the launch, you were the one bright spot in all this. I really respect you. I enjoyed working with you, Lisa. And the time we spent together." He meets her eyes. "I'm sorry it had to end like it did."

She shows him a hurt smile. "I wish it had been different, too, Nathan."

He lingers in her gaze a brief moment, before he finally turns to go.

A tinge of melancholy accompanies him as he trudges down the hallway and out of the Public Health office.

It could have been all so different. Especially with Lisa.

But Nathan is glad to be heading home to his boys. Not to the office, though. He's dreading what punitive reassignment Peter will have in store for him. Leaving Delaware isn't an option. Peter has him over a barrel, as he hasn't been hesitant to remind him.

Nathan would give anything to go back and do it over again. It was such a pivotal time. Everything hung in the balance. He was convinced Darius's death was a tragic coincidence and not caused by the vaccine—and time had proven him right, technically—but he also understood that word of it would destroy the campaign. So Nathan had his dark web IT consultant purge the report on Darius, which he would've never done if he had any inkling of the other serious reactions that were to follow.

Maybe, from a criminal perspective, he got away with it. *Maybe.* But what's done is done.

In the process, he sacrificed a piece of himself and his soul.

And for what? It changed nothing. And cost so much.

CHAPTER 64

The thirtieth-floor, northwest-facing condo is a quarter of the size of the home Lisa left behind, but she doesn't mind. The house always felt too big for just Dominic and her. She's happy to have traded all the unused space for the view from her new place. Last night, she got butterflies standing on the balcony and watching the sun set behind the Space Needle and the Olympic Mountains beyond Elliott Bay, against a fuchsia sky.

The condo is finally furnished, but the unopened boxes scattered on the living room floor and piled against the far wall represent a problem that the bedrooms and bathrooms also share.

"What are you going for here?" Amber gently kicks at the box by her foot. "Warehouse chic?"

"Yeah, Tee," Olivia chimes in. "When are you going to unpack?"

Lisa sweeps Olivia up in her arms. "Why do you think I invited you over, brat?" She plants kisses over her niece's forehead.

Giggling, Oliva wriggles free of her grip. "I don't know how to," she says as she lands on the ground.

"You don't want to decorate your room, then?" Lisa asks, referring to the condo's second bedroom.

"I do! I do!"

"Then you better get drawing. We'll need a lot more pictures for your walls."

"I'm on it, Tee!" Olivia spins and scurries off for the bedroom, where she left her markers and paper.

Amber motions to the pile. "It's been three weeks since you moved in, hasn't it?"

"Not sure if you've noticed, but I've been kind of busy," Lisa says.

"That's the only reason?"

"I'm happy here, Amber. Honestly. Happier than I've been in long time. I'm not going anywhere."

"Then let's make it look a bit more permanent."

"That's the plan." Lisa sits down on the rug, reaches for a box, and uses the blade of her scissors to slice through the packing tape.

Amber kneels down beside her and helps remove wrapped objects from inside the open box. She stands a pair of candles up on the coffee table, but her hand freezes when she pulls the paper off a framed photo.

Without looking over, Lisa realizes it must be the photo from the holiday office party, the Christmas before last. In it, Lisa stands at a microphone, shoulder to shoulder with a flushed and beaming Angela, both of them looking more than a little tipsy in their elf hats. The staff gave Angela and Lisa framed copies at last year's party and insisted on a repeat performance of their doctored version of the holiday classic "Baby, It's Cold (and Flu Season) Outside."

Amber stands the frame in the center of the coffee table, glancing over to Lisa, who nods her approval.

"Hey, I read that piece in the *Seattle Times* about you," Amber says. "How you single-handedly beat the outbreak and the anti-vaxxers, despite the criminal conspiracy."

"Not too much sensationalism there," Lisa groans. "A load of crap, anyway."

"Why's that?"

"We haven't beaten anything. Definitely not this outbreak."

"It's not over, then?"

"It's contained. That's all."

"What's the difference?"

"We haven't had a new case of meningitis in almost two weeks. That's good news. No question. But fifty-one dead, Amber? Mainly kids. In less than two months . . ." Lisa exhales, experiencing a familiar gnawing in the pit of her stomach at the thought. "It can spring back up again, anytime. You can't declare an outbreak like this over until at least a year has elapsed without a case."

"What if everyone gets vaccinated?"

"Will never happen. Right now we're at about sixty percent of the target population. We'd need another twenty-five percent before we reach a level of herd immunity that would protect the public."

"As long as some people think like that naturopath, you'll never get everyone on board."

"Some of them will never be convinced, despite all the science in the world." Lisa sighs. The thought of Max depresses her. The man isn't wanting for intelligence, understanding, or even empathy. But he has glommed on to an explanation—flawed as it is—for the unexplainable thing that happened to his son. It wasn't much different in Fiona's case. For them, as for others, "vaccine injury" represents the bogeyman they can blame for the random and cruel twists fate foisted on them and their loved ones.

"How about you?" Lisa asks.

"You really need me to say it again?" Amber sighs. "Fine. You were right."

"No. Not that. Has your overall opinion of vaccines changed?"

Amber thinks for a moment. "Maybe. A little. I still have my concerns, but . . ."

"Yes?"

"Allen and I are considering getting Olivia the measles shot."

Lisa can't fight off her smile. There's something so validating in her sister's concession.

"I only said we're *considering* it . . ." Amber emphasizes. "By the way, Mom and Dad read the article, too."

"They read the *Times*?"

"No. I emailed it to Mom."

"And?"

"Mom's very proud of you."

"Not Dad, of course."

"He still thinks you're dead wrong about the whole vaccine thing." Amber chuckles. "But he did say that you can count on a Dyer to get the job done."

Lisa's grin only grows. She can't remember the last time she impressed her father, if ever.

"What about you, Lisa?"

"I'm still pretty sold on vaccines," she says, even though she knows that's not what her sister is getting at.

"You're not missing Dom?"

"Sometimes," Lisa admits. It has been strange to wake up every morning alone in bed. There are times she even misses the low growl of Dominic's snoring. But the one thing she hasn't experienced is regret.

"I'm more excited about the next phase of my life." Lisa laughs self-consciously. "Whatever the hell *that* is going to bring."

AUTHOR'S NOTE

Among the Himalayas of medical controversies, perhaps none looms as large as the debate over the benefits versus the risks of vaccination. In writing *Lost Immunity*, I realized I was wading into contentious waters. But my aim as a writer has always been to educate while entertaining, to help humanize health crises, and to guide an understanding of the complexities that surround specific disease processes.

Through this novel, I was determined to impart vital information about vaccines, and those who are skeptical of them, from a place of both expertise and compassion. Like most medical doctors, I view vaccination to be among the greatest achievements of modern medicine. I won't delve into the extensive research on the topic, but science is not on the side of the vaccine hesitancy (or anti-vax) movement. The evidence in favor of vaccines is incontrovertible.

However, traditional science is not what drives anti-vaxxers. There are numerous intelligent, informed, well-meaning people who have a deep aversion to vaccination, especially when it comes to their own children. They're aware of the rare side effects caused by vaccines. And they tend to rely on association or anecdotal evidence rather than traditional science to support their beliefs. Oftentimes, they connect their own personal tragedies—such as a loved one with autism—back to a vaccination event. Moreover, vaccine hesitancy is a broad umbrella that encompasses a spectrum of heterogenous beliefs, from those who will accept many but not all vaccines to those who vehemently oppose any form of vaccination.

But the fundamental concern to the vast pro-vaccine majority is that, while everyone is entitled to their own beliefs, those who refuse to buy into traditional vaccination programs impact more than just themselves or their loved ones. For a vaccine to be effective, it depends on the concept of herd immunity. Generally speaking, we need at least seventy percent of a community to develop immunity to an infectious threat in order to thwart its natural spread.

Never has this subject been more relevant than today. With the race on to achieve herd immunity against the COVID-19 pandemic through vaccination, global acceptance of a vaccine will be essential to stop this horrific disease.

Aside from entertaining and, hopefully, thrilling readers, I wrote this novel as an allegory for the debate over vaccines. That can be a delicate balancing act when it comes to an issue as emotionally fraught as vaccinations, and I hope I present both sides in a fair and compassionate light. No vaccine is entirely perfect. Any medication carries some risks. But at the end of the day, I wholly believe there is only one right answer in this crucial debate.

ACKNOWLEDGMENTS

Many people consider writing to be a solitary pursuit, but for me that has never been true. From the first inkling of an idea to the final draft, I work collaboratively with friends, colleagues, editors, and loved ones, bouncing ideas off them and inundating them with pages. This novel is no exception. It's impossible to acknowledge all those who helped me along the way, but there are several I do have to credit.

While this is a work of fiction, the issues at the heart of it—public health, epidemics, and vaccination—are very real. And I was fortunate to be able to lean on two world-class experts, Drs. Patricia Daly and Victor Leung, to ensure I got those details right.

I am blessed to have such an insightful, creative, and like-minded editor in Laurie Grassi, who works tirelessly to bring out the best in my writing. Two other talented editors—Jasmine Elliott in Toronto and Anne Perry in London—also helped to hone this story.

I'm thrilled to further my collaboration with the caring folks at Simon & Schuster, including Jillian Levick, Nita Pronovost, Gregory Tilney, David Millar, Felicia Quon, and Kevin Hanson. And

I'm grateful for the guidance of my agents, Henry Morrison and Danny Baror.

As always, I want to thank you, the readers, who inspire me to continue writing. I hope this novel will shed some light on a vital public health issue and help to separate some of the myths from the facts.

ABOUT THE AUTHOR

©Michael Bednar Photography

DANIEL KALLA is the international bestselling author of novels including *The Last High* and *We All Fall Down*. His previous book *The Last High* was an instant bestseller. Kalla practices emergency medicine in Vancouver, British Columbia. Visit him at danielkalla.com or follow him on Twitter @DanielKalla.

"Kalla has long had his stethoscope on the heartbeat of his times."

Toronto Star

Also by Daniel Kalla

The Globe and Mail and *Toronto Star* bestsellers

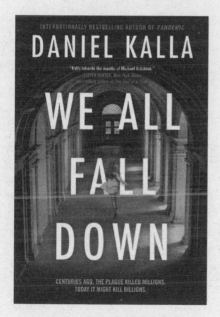

"A fast-paced thriller with an historical overlay and a dash of romantic tension."

Vancouver Sun

"A thrilling, frontline drama about the opioid crisis."

KATHY REICHS

SIMON & SCHUSTER